MAJORSKI'S GHOST

MAJORSKI'S GHOST

A Marty Fenton Novel

by

Bob Cohen

North Country Books, Inc.
Utica, New York

MAJORSKI'S GHOST

ISBN 978-0-925168-39-9

Library of Congress Cataloging-in-Publication Data

Cohen, Robert, 1941-
    Majorski's ghost : a Marty Fenton novel / Robert Cohen.
      p. cm.
     ISBN 0-925168-39-4
     I. Title.
PS3553.04272M34   1995
813'.54—dc20   95-12322
                                            CIP

NORTH COUNTRY BOOKS, INC.
PUBLISHER-DISTRIBUTOR
311 Turner Street
Utica, New York 13501

For

Nick, Tim, Jessye and Nanc

The ghost of forgotten actions
came floating before my sight,
And things that I thought were dead things
were alive with a terrible might.

Charles William Stubbs
1876

PROLOGUE

The two men sat at the kitchen table reviewing their plan. They had received their assignment the previous day, giving them ample time to work out the details. The instructions were clear and both men were professionals.

It would not be a difficult job.

They were big men, accustomed to quick action and split second timing. Having worked together for many years, each was able to anticipate the other's reaction to a situation, then respond appropriately. They were a very effective team.

The larger of the two men wore olive green denim pants tucked into brown fur lined leather boots, and a heavy red plaid flannel shirt over a black turtleneck sweater. He was a big boned Irishman in his mid-forties who still wore his hair in a flat top. He looked like an Irish cop, which was not surprising since his father, grandfather, and great grandfather had all been police officers.

The other man was about the same age as his partner, but slightly smaller. He had an athletic body and a well proportioned face with a ruddy complexion that came from frequent exposure to the elements rather than the contents of a liquor bottle.

He was a very neat man. Not a single strand of his red wavy hair was out of place. He wore a heavily starched white pin-point button down shirt under a tan cashmere sweater. His chocolate brown flannel slacks had a sharp crease and his ankle-high leather boots were polished to a high gloss.

The two men sipped coffee from delicate porcelain cups. Steam from the hot coffee rose toward the ceiling, vaporous dancers, twirling in the

1

gray light of dawn. The men spoke softly, using few gestures. The redhead did most of the talking, with the Irishman occasionally asking a question.

After a while they stopped talking altogether. They just sat, looking down at their hands...waiting.

When the telephone rang, the redhead jumped up and lifted the handset from the wallphone before it rang a second time. Since he knew who was on the other end of the line, he simply said, "Yes," and tucked the phone between his ear and shoulder. He pulled a pen and pad from his shirt pocket and took notes as he listened. After a moment he returned the handset to its cradle. Picking up the pad, he nodded to the other man at the table and started for the door.

The Irishman took the coffee cups and placed them in the sink. Then he opened a drawer under the counter and removed a .38 police special. He lifted the tail of his plaid flannel shirt and tucked the pistol into a holster at the small of his back.

The man with red hair put on a long green loden coat and a matching Kangol cap. His partner donned a bulky blue parka and a black wool watch cap.

Both men put on black leather driving gloves.

Then they opened the front door and walked into a stiff winter wind.

1

I've met research subjects in some unusual places, but I'd never conducted an interview in a railroad yard. Not until I arranged to meet Fred Majorski behind the Amtrak Station in East Syracuse.

I was trying to finish my master's thesis study and was having trouble finding participants. My research compared the social perceptions of older adults born in the United States with those born in Eastern Europe. I was interested in the relationship between the degree of political freedom a person experienced in childhood and the extent to which that person views strangers as friendly or hostile. Of course, anyone with a grain of common sense would predict that those who grew up in a politically open environment would be more likely to view strangers as having good intentions. But graduate degrees in psychology are not awarded on the basis of common sense. If I was going to become a bona fide psychologist, I would need to take into account other variables that contributed to the relationship between childhood political environment and stranger perception. Psychologists are very big on complexity.

For my thesis research, I wanted to find out how birth order interacts with political climate to influence one's reaction to strangers. According to Alfred Adler, the guru of birth order, personality and temperament were shaped, in part, by one's chronological place in the family. Dr. Adler believed that first-born children tend to be aggressive and achievement oriented while later-born offspring are more likely to be sociable. Being the second of two children in my family, I liked the idea that later-born children were supposed to be more sociable and decided

3

to test whether birth order, along with childhood political climate affected the way an adult reacted to strangers.

Finding American-born subjects was easy. Finding people fifty-five years and older who had been born in Eastern Europe was another matter. Fortunately, my advisor, Professor Singleton, had some good contacts in the ethnic social organizations of Central New York and was able to obtain some lists of people who met the criteria for my study.

I obtained Mr. Majorski's phone number from Club Polski. When I called him he seemed reluctant to participate. Although he spoke slowly, in a monotone with a slight Polish accent, there was an undertone of discomfort, even agitation, in his voice. I made a mental note that Mr. Majorski must be a first-born.

Feeling somewhat desperate —I had only managed to recruit fourteen of the fifty European-born subjects I needed for my study—I used my later-born charm to convince Mr. Majorski that his participation was vital to science and the future well-being of the human race. I don't know whether it was my persuasive power, the twenty dollar incentive fee my university research grant allowed me to pay participants, or Majorski's considered judgment that it was the only way he would get me to stop pestering him, but he finally agreed to become part of my study.

He explained that he worked the night shift as an engineer on the Conrail freight line and that the only time he could speak with me was at the tail end of his shift. We agreed to meet on Thursday morning of the following week at the railroad yard. I sent him a confirmation letter, asking him to call me if he could not keep our appointment. Majorski did not call, so I arose early on Thursday morning, and got ready for my trip to the railroad yard.

As a child I had sometimes imagined myself sitting high up in the cab of a steam engine, instructing husky stokers to pour on more coal as I skillfully guided the Twentieth Century Limited across the United States. Lathering my face with shaving cream, I wondered if I would get a chance to sit in the engineers cab.

After I shaved, I took a quick shower, grateful that my neighbors had not completely depleted the apartment building's meager supply of hot water. Looking out the window, I saw that it was still snowing. I put on a dark brown turtleneck sweater, a heavy plaid flannel shirt and a down vest. I pulled on a pair of loose fitting olive corduroy slacks, laced up my calf-length work boots, and grabbed my Land's End forest green canvas briefcase on the way to the door. I considered taking the elevator, but knowing its dismal track record, I decided to spare myself the frustration of discovering, once again, that it was out-of-order. Instead, I took the stairs, two steps at a time, and reached the ground floor just in time to see two elderly women emerge from the elevator. I turned left and walked through the narrow corridor leading to the front entrance of the building. Bracing myself for cold air and blowing snow, I opened the door and stepped outside.

My car was buried under an avalanche of snow thanks to the friendly neighborhood snow plow. Cursing the Department of Public Works I grabbed the snow shovel I kept in the trunk of my nineteen-seventy-nine Honda and began to dig.

Having removed the last mound of snow blocking the front wheel, I climbed into the car, cranked the motor for thirty seconds before it started and, exhaling a frosty sigh of relief, moved out onto the snow-packed street. Accelerating gently, I reached into the glove compartment for the scraper to clear the icy residue of my breath from the windshield. I skidded slightly as I came to a stop sign and turned right onto James Street, grateful to be off the slippery side streets.

James Street is a five-mile montage of Syracuse history. Moving east from downtown, I passed through a row of once-elegant brownstones gone to seed and a section of small stores that were never elegant. This was followed by a cluster of chrome and glass office buildings and a few high-rise, high-income apartment houses. What would it be like living in that world? If I had followed my original career plan to become a lawyer, I might be closing the door to my decorator-designed apartment on the way to my comfortable position as a junior partner in one of Syracuse's prestigious law firms instead of driving out to interview a reluctant railroad engineer for my master's thesis.

Actually, I was enjoying my belated stint in graduate school. At age thirty-eight, I had considerably more life experience than my fellow graduate students. Taking three courses a week, working ten hours a week, as a graduate assistant, and trying to conduct research for a thesis did not seem exceptionally stressful to me. Compared to some of my previous professions, the pace was fairly casual. Since graduating from college I had worked as an air traffic controller, a child welfare worker, and served for a brief time as an investigator in a large private investigation agency among other jobs. It was the lack of constant pressure along with my conviction that it was time to decide what I was going to do when I grew up that had attracted me to graduate study in social psychology.

It didn't help that the stipend from my graduate assistantship did not even cover the rent. Fortunately my advisor, Professor Singleton, was intrigued by my former career as a private investigator. Being concerned with his graduate students' welfare and intensely curious about the similarity between psychological research and investigative encore, Singleton had become a walking advertisement for my prowess as a private detective. The occasional job he steered my way helped to pay the rent, put *Stouffer's* dinners in my freezer compartment ——when they were on sale; otherwise, I settled for *Swanson*——and even allowed me to put more than my customary five gallons of gas into my car.

The high point of James Street was a long row of beautiful old mansions, another reminder of how time takes it toll, even for the wealthy. These grand structures, which once housed the elite of Syracuse, had been converted to offices and charitable headquarters as a result of increasing property taxes that priced them out of the market as private residences.

Moving toward the outskirts of the city, I felt as if I had gone back in time. Eastwood still looked like a 1950s neighborhood, completely intact, with wood frame houses and a compound of mom-and-pop stores that had successfully resisted the great chainstore encroachment. If things worked out for Ollie and me, it might be nice to live in one of those little frame houses with a glider on the front porch and a postage-stamp back yard. After last night however, that prospect seemed unlikely. Finally, James Street passed through an industrial complex before deserting civilization, winding along the edge of the railroad yards until it reaches the town of East Syracuse.

The yard was just like the movies. The three workers huddled around the fire in the large steel drum interrupted their handrubbing long enough to direct me toward the large diesel engine at the far end of the yard. As I trudged through the snow, I reconsidered my home visit policy——at least during the winter months. My small office in Huntington Hall looked very good to me at this moment.

My faith was restored, however, when Mr. Majorski motioned me to join him in the cab of the locomotive. Fulfilling a childhood fantasy, I eagerly climbed up into the cab and sat next to him. The interior of the locomotive was just as I imagined, dark and metallic, with lots of levers and a front panel filled with intricate gauges.

Majorski was a large man, roughly six feet, two inches and at least two hundred-thirty pounds. Although he was only three inches taller than me, I felt very small sitting next to the trainman. He was big-boned and carried his weight very well for a man who must have been approaching sixty-five.He made no unnecessary movements, no gestures at all and spoke with very little expression. He appeared to be a man who believed in conserving energy. Either that, or he was very depressed.

"Thank you for agreeing to meet with me, Mr. Majorski," I responded. "This won't be very hard. I'm just going to ask you a few questions. Try to relax. You can call me Marty if you want."

Majorski stared out at the tracks ahead of him. After about a half-minute, he turned his head slowly toward me. "Mr. Fenton, I'm not a man who gets bothered easily." He stopped, looked down at his large

6

hands, which were folded in his lap. I could not think of an appropriate response. Finally, the engineer spoke again. His speech was slow and flat. "I remember being bothered during the war, the big one," recalled Majorski. "And once, when I was a kid, I remember being bothered when my papa got drunk and busted up the house." He stared straight ahead as the huge engine moved slowly through the yard. "The other time I was bothered," continued the engineer, "was when my wife became sick. She had the big C. She was having these pains in her back, real strong pains. She went to the doctor. He put her in the hospital and two weeks later she was gone."

Majorski resumed his staring as the engine moved past a work crew. I wondered if he was aware that the train was moving. I tried to remember whether my graduate course on interviewing had offered any suggestions on how to handle a situation like this.

"Mr. Majorski, are you all right?"

The engineer seemed to consider the question briefly, then returned to his recounting of traumatic experiences. "Those are the only times I was really bothered...except for now. This one has really gotten to me."

An old pick-up truck drove up alongside the engine. A tall, thin man with a weathered face leaned out of the window and called up to the engineer.

"Hey, Majorski, there's a phone call for you back at the office. The guy says it's important."

Majorski applied the brakes, the metal wheels screeched and the train stopped. "I'll be right back Mr. Fenton. Don't run away with the engine," he said as he climbed down from the train and got into the truck.

After a few minutes I began to fantasize. Sitting in the cab, looking down on the tracks, I felt an urge to grab the controls, start the big engine and guide the train out of the yard. There was no doubt in my mind. I would head west, not stopping until I reached Colorado.

Unfortunately, I was too rooted in reality. Although I had avoided becoming a slave to the time clock or the nine-to-five ritual, I *was* conscious of time. And when my Casio indicated the engineer had been gone for a half-hour, I abandoned my fantasy and climbed down from the train.

I couldn't find Majorski. He was not at the old shack they called the office, and neither of the two men standing over the old metal coffee pot could remember seeing him. Finally, I located the gaunt trainman who had given Majorski the message. The thin worker, who was repairing a switch light, turned his wrinkled face toward me.

"I don't know where he is," the railroad worker said. "He took the phone call, listened for a minute, then went to his car. He moved real fast. Not at all like Majorski. He usually takes his time."

7

"Did he say where he was going?" I asked.

"Nope," he replied. "He just got in his car and headed north on Thompson Road. He sure was in a hurry."

The trainman returned to his repair work. Knowing that I would not get any more information from the thin man, I thanked him and walked to my car.

My Casio said it was eleven-thirty. I was concerned about Majorski, but I was also hungry and at that moment, even more concerned about my love life. If I hurried I might catch Ollie before she went to lunch.

2

I decided to take the bypass. The temperature had risen a few degrees, helping the salt to melt the snow on the road. My only problem was the dirty slush sprayed on my windshield by passing cars and trucks. If my Honda had been capable of going faster than forty miles an hour it wouldn't have been much of a problem.

As I struggled to keep my windshield clear I thought of Ollie and wondered if our relationship would survive this latest round of disagreement. I desperately hoped it would, but was not very confident.

The night before, Ollie had invited me to her apartment for a cup of coffee. What started out as a friendly, casual get-together of two people who liked each other but had slightly different perspectives on the nature of their commitment to each other, turned into another depressing heart-to-heart discussion about our "relationship."

As usual, I was the one who had steered the conversation in the wrong direction. And, as usual, our talk led us nowhere. After an hour and a half of mutual frustration, I threw up my hands and left, my head spinning and my adrenalin pumping.

Ollie was so different from the other women I had known. My feelings for her scared me. I felt more like a fifteen year old kid with an acute case of puppy love than a thirty-eight year old man who had dated dozens of women, had extended relationships with at least ten and even lived with a few without ever coming close to seriously considering marriage.

But Ollie was different.

I first met Ollie, whose full name is Olivia Tolliver, during the intermission of the play, *Equus*. My friend, Dan Bernstein, who taught anthropology at the University, had badgered me into giving up a night at the hockey game in order to go to the Civic Center Theatre. While I could not understand how a play about a boy who pokes out horses' eyes could compare with the excitement of a minor league hockey game, I finally succumbed to my friend's pressure.

Ollie was with an ex-lover of Dan Bernstein. While the two former sweethearts debated about the symbolic significance of the play, Ollie and I silently appraised each other.

She had long, reddish brown hair, pulled back into a single braid that came half way down her back. Her light blue eyes were set between a prominent forehead and high, full cheeks. She was of average height and while her loose fitting sweater and long, full skirt made it difficult to judge with any precision her shape and weight, my gambling instinct told me that a wager in favor of shapeliness would be well-placed.

I was to find out later that my instinct would have paid off handsomely.

Having completed my initial assessment, I—big spender that I am—offered to buy Ollie the house special: a half-pint of orange juice. She accepted and, while we sipped our drinks, I found out she was a sculptor who had graduated from Smith College and made a living by working at the gift shop at the Everson Museum.

She did not seem impressed by the knowledge that I was a graduate student in psychology. On the other hand, she did not giggle or make any wisecracks. Based on this relatively positive response, I asked her to have dinner with me.

To my surprise, she accepted.

While our courtship could not be characterized as whirlwind, we enjoyed being with each other. At first, we went out once a week, always on Saturday night. After a while we began having dinner together on Wednesday evenings, sometimes taking in a late movie. While I had never been noted for my reticence, I felt uncertain when I was with Ollie and was reluctant to approach her physically. It took me several months before I worked up the courage to kiss her. Our first embrace surprised me—in several ways.

We were sitting in my living room, sipping twenty-five year old Martel Cognac, a gift from my status conscious sister that had been collecting dust for several years in my kitchen cabinet. As Ollie stood to refill her glass, my ambivalence dissolved in a rush of arousal. I reached up to kiss her and found myself lifted off my feet, locked in a vise-like grip. Just as my face was turning from pink to red, I was swung around and dropped backward onto the couch. Literally breathless, I looked up to see Ollie standing over me, grinning. After telling me she didn't like surprises, she leaned down and kissed me on the forehead. Then, with the slightest effort, she gently lifted me to my feet.

That evening, I found out what was beneath Ollie's loose-fitting clothing. I also learned of another of her favorite pastimes. After a vigorous and totally satisfying evening of making love, I lay in bed next to her, running my hand along the firm, well defined muscles of her back and shoulders. Anticipating my question, she turned toward me and quietly told me that she had been seriously involved in body building for the past six years. She worked out with weights four days a week, occasionally participated in a body building competition —though never in upstate New York. She also told me she did not like to discuss this part of her life.

From that day on we never discussed her physique or her unique pattern of exercise. But, when we made love, I never failed to admire her powerful, well-proportioned body: graceful and athletic, with a slim waist, flat hard stomach and well-toned muscles, not big and square with huge bulging muscles, like some of the female bodybuilders.

It was not just Ollie's body I admired. She was a very bright young woman who knew more about art and art history than anyone I had ever met. Of course, I don't exactly travel in the elite circles of the art world. But my suspicions about her brilliance had been confirmed by some of her co-workers at the museum who told me if it weren't for the poor economy and the presence of two elderly staff members who refused to retire, Ollie certainly would have been promoted to the position of assistant curator.

Not only did Ollie know a lot about art, she was also a first-rate sculptor who had won awards in several regional juried exhibitions.

On top of all that, she was a quiet, sensitive person with a great dry sense of humor. She had the rare gift of being a good listener. She didn't judge or analyze what I said, but I always felt like she was interested in what I was saying. Even more important, she seemed to *care* about what I said.

Ollie was a very capable and independent person.

And that's where my problem began.

For the first time in my life I was ready to make a commitment to a relationship, to settle down with someone I really cared about.

Unfortunately we hadn't coordinated our game plans. Ollie kept telling me she liked me very much and was happy with the relationship we had. But she had absolutely no interest in giving up her autonomy or even planning for the future.

That was what was driving me crazy.

I got off the highway at the Townsend Street exit and drove to

Harrison Street where I turned right. I pulled my car into a No Parking zone and ran up the path to the Everson Museum. As I was about to open the door, Ollie stepped out, flanked by the two septuagenarian assistant curators, a rail-thin silver haired man who couldn't have been much taller than five feet and a very large woman with a fleshy face, whose thick brown hair had been coiled into a bun on top of her head.

"Hi, Marty," Ollie said, looking surprised. "What are you doing at the museum?"

It was a simple question, but I didn't have a simple answer. I suddenly felt very uncomfortable. The portly woman was glowering at me with her dark brown eyes. The frail man avoided looking at me as if he identified with my discomfort.

"I...I heard there was a good exhibit of...you know, those pictures you make with metal plates..."

"Do you mean etchings?" she asked, giving me a sly grin. "I'm afraid they're customarily exhibited on the walls of your bedroom. Besides, I didn't know you were an aficionado of fine prints?"

She had me back-pedaling and she knew it. Even worse, she was reveling in my discomfort. "Actually, I just heard this incredible recipe for Moroccan Couscous and I couldn't wait to share it with you," I said, trying to extract myself from my awkward position.

The large woman's glowering look now had an added edge of disdain, as if my mere presence tarnished the cultural integrity of the museum. Even the old man shook his head slightly at my lame attempt at humor, having turned his feeling for me from pity to disgust.

Ollie cocked her head to the right, crinkled her nose and squinted her left eye. Looking up at me, she asked, "Are you okay, Marty? Is something wrong?" She had this way of looking at me that said, 'even though you're acting like a total jerk, I am concerned about you and pray that you come to your senses——soon!'

"I'm fine," I lied. "I have some things I want to discuss with you. But they can wait."

"That's good," Ollie said, her face relaxing. "We're on our way to the Proctor Museum in Utica. They have some new pre-Columbian pieces we may be able to borrow next year. You remember Dr. Heinerman and Mr. Wonderby, don't you?" The fierce looking woman blinked, which I took as a sure sign of recognition. Mr. Wonderby bowed deeply at the waist. I held my breath, hoping he would not fall over.

I had a strong urge to apologize for my behavior, but held back, realizing I would probably just provoke more scorn from the assistant curators.

"Ollie, can I speak to you for a moment...privately."

She hesitated briefly, then stepped off the path and walked over to a large abstract metal sculpture in the middle of the lawn. I followed her,

feeling Dr. Heinerman's glare searing the back of my down vest.
"What's up?" Ollie said casually, "I thought you were okay, that we could wait 'til later to talk."

"I'm not okay," I said. "As a matter of fact, I'm pretty upset. I don't like what's happening with us. I know you don't want to make any long-term commitment. In my head I can appreciate your position, even respect it. God knows I've avoided commitments like the plague for my entire life. But none of that seems to matter. No matter how much I try to convince myself with logic, my gut tells me bold and clear that I want to be with you on more than a casual basis."

"Our relationship is anything but casual," Ollie said impatiently. "We've been over this several dozen times. We didn't talk about anything last night that hadn't been said before. So why are you so upset now?"

I started to tell her I wasn't upset but checked myself. It was no use trying to discuss the situation. "I'm upset because I already feel like a fool, screwing up what could have been a nice, quiet evening with you by bugging you about our relationship. Then I come down here, not exactly feeling self-assured, hoping to straighten things out between us, and within ten seconds I feel like an even bigger fool."

Ollie wrinkled her brow and looked at me intently. This made me feel even more uncomfortable. I had an urge to put my arms around her and bury my face in her silky auburn hair, but hesitated, remembering what happened the first time I surprised her with a spontaneous display of affection. The last thing I needed was to be flipped on my backside in front of the Everson's dynamic duo.

After what seemed like ten minutes, but was probably closer to ten seconds, Ollie unfurrowed her brow and held out her arms. Any fear of embarrassment I had gave way to my need to be with Ollie. I leaned forward and pressed my body against her's. She put her arms around me and held me tightly. Even through the layers of winter clothing I felt the warmth of her firm body. I took a deep breath and felt myself begin to relax.

After a moment, Ollie loosened her grip, reached behind her and gently took my hands in hers. She stepped back, still holding my hands, "I'm sorry, Marty," she said quietly, looking directly into my eyes. "I didn't mean to make you feel bad. It's just that...I don't know what to do when you start pushing me like that. We've gone over this so many times and you know..."

"I don't mean to push you," I said. "It's just that..."

Ollie shook her head. "No," she said, "let me finish what I was saying, okay?" I didn't really want to hear what I thought she was going to say, but didn't feel I had much choice. I nodded and she continued. "I want you to understand that my reluctance to make a commitment has very little if anything to do with you. You're a warm and caring man, Marty. I find you very attractive and I don't think I've ever met anyone else I like to be with more than you."

"So, what's the problem. I feel the same way about you."

Ollie gently tugged on my hands. "This is hard for me. I don't like to show my weaknesses. It makes me feel very vulnerable."

"Well, you sure do a good job of hiding them. I haven't seen any yet."

"That's because I don't let you see them. I've got more than my fair share of problems."

"Welcome to the human race."

"Stop it. This is difficult enough without your wisecracks." She let go of my hands and folded her arms across her chest. "What I'm trying to saying is I become uncomfortable when people get too close to me, especially people I care about. I know it doesn't make sense, but I can't help it. I try to talk myself out of it, to convince myself that these people aren't going to hurt me, that *you're* not going to hurt me...but it doesn't matter. Once the feeling takes hold of me I start to shut down."

Ollie was right. It didn't make sense to me. She was saying she cared about me and she obviously knew how I felt about her. So why couldn't she accept that I wanted us to be together; that we should be together, not just for a night or two, but...permanently. After all, I'm a pretty cautious guy. It had taken me thirty-eight years to be ready to make a commitment. If I could do it, what could possibly be making her back away from me?

I was about to pose that question to Ollie when our conversation was interrupted by a rumbling sound that resembled a rock slide. We both turned toward Dr. Heinerman, who was clearing her throat and impatiently pointing to her watch.

Ollie nodded at the stern-looking woman, then turned to me. I had never seen her look so uncertain. Her lips were pursed, her brow furrowed. Her eyes moved back and forth, unable to focus. Finally her eyes locked onto mine. "I really want to talk to you about this," she said apologetically, "but we're already late. Dr. Heinerman is a real stickler for punctuality. I'm sorry, Marty. We can talk about this when I get home tonight."

I started to tell her what Dr. Heinerman could do with her punctuality, but Ollie was too quick. She reached up, took my head in her hands and kissed me firmly on the lips. Before I could respond, she turned and trotted toward the odd couple.

"I'll call you when get home," she shouted over her shoulder. "Okay?"

I wanted to tell her it was not okay, but didn't think that would help my cause.

14

As I watched the three of them walk toward the parking deck I felt envious of Heinerman and Wonderby, getting to spend the entire afternoon with Ollie. It didn't make me feel any better to realize I was standing in several inches of icy slush that had seeped through my supposedly waterproof boots.

My only consolation was I had learned to carry an extra pair of shoes and socks to cope with Syracuse's weather.

Safe inside my old Honda, my feet dry once again, I thought about my options. Having discarded the idea of driving to Utica, throwing myself at Ollie's feet in front of the Proctor Museum, and asking her to marry me immediately, I settled for my second choice. Fortunately, I had brought my thesis materials. The day would not be a total loss. I would go to the university library and act like a scholar.

Four hours later, with three more note cards filled, and the first paragraph of the literature review chapter written, I returned to my apartment, brain weary and famished. In my haste to distance myself from the museum incident I had forgotten to eat lunch.

I popped a frozen package of macaroni and cheese into the microwave and opened a bottle of Clearly Canadian peach flavored sparkling water——one of my few indulgences. While I waited for the microwave to nuke the processed cheese I checked to see if anyone had called.

As a matter of principle, I refuse to buy a telephone answering machine. They are just too mechanical, too impersonal. I remember vividly the first time I found myself speaking to a machine. I was calling an attractive young woman I had met at a friend's party to ask her out. I was so intent on rehearsing my friendly, though not overly eager opening gambit, that I actually started to go into my speech when the voice at the other end of the line informed me she was sorry that no one was at home to receive my call. I didn't even wait for the beep to hang up. While trying to regain my composure, I vowed never to subject anyone to that mortifying experience.

So, yielding to my principles, I willingly paid thirty-two dollars and fifty cents per month to retain the We-Care Answering Service.

I wondered, as I collected the day's messages from Mrs. D. with the perpetual hacking cough, whether answering services were staffed by cast-offs from Ma Bell. I had not yet encountered an operator who could have passed the entrance exam for charm school. Then again, they probably didn't have much reason to feel happy, always finding themselves in the position of being the wrong person for the disappointed caller.

"Mr. Fenton," gasped Mrs. D. between coughs, "you had three calls. Lieutenant DeSantis, a Ms. Janet Pafko, and your mother, Mrs. Fenton." Mrs. D. is both considerate and professional, always making sure that I know my mother's name.

After quickly weighing the alternatives of business versus pleasure, I decided in favor of business and began to dial my mother's number. DeSantis probably wanted to go to the Blazer's hockey game. Since I didn't know in which category Janet Pafko fit, but doubted that it was pleasure, I placed her at the end of the list.

"Hello dear, is that you?" Ma asked as she yanked the kitchen phone off the hook before the first ring had stopped. I wondered if my mother hovered over the telephone all day, waiting to pounce on it at the first bell.

"Ma, you shouldn't answer the phone that way. How many times do I have to tell you, if it's me, I'll tell you, if not..."

"I know, they'll think I'm some kind of kookie old lady, which I happen to be. So what's the difference?"

"Okay, Ma. What do you want?"

"Just a second, Martin, dear. I have to find my list." My mother was very well organized. In fact, her penchant for lists was so intense that one of her friends, who considered herself a bit of an amateur psychiatrist, had diagnosed her list-making behavior as a fetish.

"Ah yes," Ma continued, "here it is! First,..."

"Have you written to your sister Grace?" I inserted, completing my mother's question.

"Martin!"

"Yes, mother, I know you don't like when I do that. But you always start with the same question."

"Martin, when you get to be my age perhaps you'll have developed a little more appreciation for how a mother worries about her children. After all, it's one of the few things I'm able to do by myself these days!"

Defeated, once again.

"Okay Ma, I won't interrupt."

"Thank you. I'm grateful."

Ten minutes later, saturated with admonitions and instructions, feeling alternatively guilty and angry, and resigned to the fact that my mother would always prevail, I agreed to call her more often and hung up the telephone. I wondered if I would ever be able to speak to my mother without becoming upset. As a child I had marvelled at the amount of energy she poured into charitable and social activities. Whether it was raising money for a new organ at the church or mobilizing a membership drive for the women's club, she always seemed to be in charge. While Ma gained considerable respect and admiration from the citizens of Teaneck, New Jersey, for her dynamic leadership, our family, which was subject to the same efficient style of organization at home, quietly resented her constant crusade for self improvement.

My older sister, Grace, coped by becoming involved in every

extracurricular activity she could join. She spent her afternoons, evenings, and weekends with the Girl Scouts, cheerleaders, Spanish Club, or any other group that happened to be meeting. For my mother, Grace's involvement was an affirmation of her own belief in growth through engagement. Daughter was a smaller version of Mother. For Grace, these organized activities represented an opportunity to escape from the continuous chiding of our mother.

When she was eighteen, Grace married the captain of the high school football team and followed him to Columbus, Ohio where he had an athletic scholarship at Ohio State University.

I chose a different style of coping. I was a fairly bright child with a sense of curiosity, but I did not find much satisfaction at school. Instead I invested all of my intellectual energy into puzzles. Crosswords, anagrams, jigsaw puzzles, mathematical problems--it didn't matter. I was fascinated by any mental exercise that required me to use ingenuity to solve a perplexing problem. I would spend hours patiently putting together the pieces of a complex puzzle. Cloistered in my bedroom, I was only a few feet from my mother, but miles away from her domineering influence.

Only my father seemed to be unaffected by my mother's aggressive drive for self improvement.

Dad was a striking contrast to Ma. He was a quiet man with simple desires. He owned a small automobile repair shop several blocks from our three bedroom flat in a two family wood frame house. He enjoyed fixing people's cars and liked owning his own business. Occasionally he felt bad that he could not provide more for his family, but for the most part he was satisfied with his life. He was content to sit in the livingroom, reading the evening newspaper while his wife skillfully used the telephone to organize a large-scale philanthropic event. Having dropped out of school in the tenth grade, he was proud of his daughter's social achievements and marvelled at my ability to solve even the most intricate puzzle.

If only Dad's ability to be content with what he had would have rubbed off onto me. Unfortunately I had never learned the secret of how he tuned out Ma's intrusive quest for making us better people. She still knew how to push my buttons.

The call to Lieutenant DeSantis was much easier.

I first met Lou DeSantis at University College, Syracuse University's evening division. Lou was taking a psychology course, one of many courses he had taken thanks to the encouragement of his wife, Angie. I was the instructor, and the two of us quickly formed a bond of mutual criticism, each of us selecting the other's avocation as an easy target. Once Lou found out I had worked as a private investigator, he chided me relentlessly, comparing me to Inspector Clouseau and other notable sleuths. Likewise, I picked up on Lou's penchant for using multi-syllable words, and delighted in poking fun at his intellectual pretensions.

The sparring relationship soon evolved into one of mutual respect. After the course was over, we continued to see each other, taking in a basketball or hockey game, or meeting for a beer after Lou's shift. While we still chided each other, Lou and I had become very good friends.

"DeSantis, here."

"Hello Lou, it's Marty."

"Hey guy, how've you been? Long time since we've interfaced with each other. My essential being has experienced a void as a result of the absence of spiritual engagement and dialogue between us."

Angie must have enrolled him in another philosophy course. "What's up, Lou?"

"Nothing much. Just thought you might want to share the heightened awareness resulting from vicariously experiencing the strategic encounter between the Blazers and the Red Wings."

"Tonight?"

"No, tomorrow."

"Sure."

"Good. I'll pick you up at seven-thirty and, Marty..."

"Yeah?"

"Try to work on your interpersonal skills. You're not a very stimulating conversationalist."

"Go to hell."

"That's a start."

Two down and one to go.

As soon as I heard the tense voice on the other end of the line, coming across as little more than a whisper, I knew that my hunch about Janet Pafko was correct. This was definitely going to be business.

"Hello, this is Marty Fenton. I'm returning Janet Pafko's call."

"Oh, Mr. Fenton, thank you for calling. I've been waiting by the phone, hoping you would call."

"Are you Janet Pafko?" I asked, finding myself mesmerized by the contrast of softness and intensity in her voice.

"Oh yes, I'm sorry. How stupid of me. Yes, I'm Janet Pafko. My father is Fred Majorski. I believe he spoke to you."

"Yes, he did. In fact, I met him this morning at the railroad yard."

"Oh, then you know where he went." Her voice was stronger, but still strained.

"No. He was called away during our conversation and didn't return."

Silence.

"Ms. Pafko, are you all right?"

18

"Not really. I'm very worried about my father. He was supposed to be home from work at noon and he hasn't returned yet. I haven't even heard from him. This is not at all like him. He's a creature of habit: home at noon, dinner at five, in bed by seven-thirty. He calls to tell me when he's going to be ten minutes late. I'm really concerned about him, Mr. Fenton."

"Have you tried calling anyone he works with? Friends? Any place he might stop in for a beer?"

"My father doesn't drink," she responded, more proud than indignant. "I called the railroad yard. They hadn't seen him. I tried the grocery store, the barber shop, even the service station he uses. No one has seen him."

"How about his friends, guys he hangs around with or..."

"My father doesn't have any close friends...he's kind of a solitary man. And his only relatives are Billy and me."

I felt like I had asked the twenty-first question in a game of twenty questions. "Ms. Pafko...is it Ms?" I asked.

"Ms, Miss, Janet, it really doesn't matter."

"Okay. I was wondering why you called me."

"I don't know," she said, her voice filled with despair. "I didn't know what to do. I don't have any close friends and the ones I have don't have a whole lot of common sense. I saw your name and phone number on a note pad in the kitchen and thought maybe you knew where he had gone."

I thought I heard her begin to sniffle. "I'm very sorry to have bothered you," she said. She was definitely sniffling.

"What is it you would like me to do?" As soon as the words left my mouth I regretted I had asked. The last thing I needed was to become involved with a weeping woman whose father hadn't come home from work on time.

"I don't know," she said, trying to regain control. "I just thought you might be able to help me...do you have any ideas?"

I was about to suggest she call the police if he didn't come home soon, when I thought, what if Ollie were in a similar predicament? What if her father didn't come home one night, leaving her sitting by the phone waiting to hear from him, worried sick?

I tried to push the idea out of my mind. It was ridiculous. Ollie was too damned independent to place herself in such a helpless position. She might organize a search party, or go out to look for him by herself, but she would never put herself at the mercy of a stranger she had never met.

How could I ever make such an association? It *was* ridiculous. And I was supposed to be a man of reason, a behavioral scientist.

19

"Ms. Pafko, do you think...would you like...I'dbe glad to sit down with you, to try to help you figure out where your father might be."

So much for being a man of reason.

"Oh, Mr. Fenton, I would really appreciate that. I just don't know where else to turn."

"Where would you like me to meet you?" I asked.

"Could you come to my house...now?"

At least there's a spark of assertiveness, I thought as I reviewed my social calendar. The Blazers' game was tomorrow night. Ollie wouldn't be back from Utica until later. I looked at the plastic container of macaroni and cheese congealing in front of me. Not very appetizing.

I took the directions to her house, told her I would be there within a half-hour and put on my down vest and work boots. Hurrying down the stairs I had more second thoughts about my decision to meet with Janet Pafko.

Still immersed in ambivalence, I stepped out of the building in time to watch a huge, slow-moving snow plow encase the street side of my car in a large mound of wet snow and slush.

3

Janet Pafko lived in a small, two-story frame house in the Eastwood section of the city. The house, painted yellow with white trim, was centered on a compact lot, no more than fifty feet wide and a hundred feet deep. Two snow covered spruce trees stood like sentries on either side of the front entrance. It was a modest but obviously well-cared-for house.

I trudged up the shoveled but still icy steps and rang the front door bell. Within seconds the door was opened by a short woman in her late twenties or early thirties. She had straight, shoulder-length brown hair. Her large bone structure would, under the best of conditions, make it difficult for her to appear slender. In spite of being slightly stocky, Ms. Pafko was well proportioned and had incredibly beautiful deep green eyes.

Those emerald eyes and her tightly drawn lips expressed barely controlled tension and fear as she greeted me. Guiding me to a small living room crowded with overstuffed chairs and a sofa, Ms. Pafko gestured me to sit in the large chair before seating herself on the edge of the sofa. There was something familiar about her, but I couldn't put my finger on it.

"Thank you for coming so quickly, Mr. Fenton. I'm very grateful."

"No problem. You sounded very worried on the phone."

The young woman shifted her position, looked down at her feet and, taking a deep breath, looked up at me. She released her breath through drawn lips. "I'm sorry," she said, shaking her head. "But I think my father is in serious trouble."

21

I leaned forward, waiting to hear more. She didn't say anything.

"Ms. Pafko, as I told you on the phone I saw your father this morning as part of my thesis research. As we began to talk he was called away for a phone call. That's the last I saw him."

"Oh my God," cried Janet Pafko. She began to tremble. "I know something has happened to him."

I started to rise, wanting to comfort the young woman. But, feeling unsure of how to be supportive, I sank back into the chair's thick cushions.

She did not seem to notice my awkward gesture.

"My father is not a very talkative man. He could go for days without saying anything more than 'pass the cream'——except to Billy."

"Billy?"

"My son. He's four. Billy and Dad are real close. We've lived with Dad since my ex-husband, Stanley, left us when Billy was one." She paused, then returned to the point she wanted to make. "Anyway, about a month ago Dad started acting real jumpy and nervous. He didn't sleep well; he seemed real distracted. He even snapped at Billy a few times.

"One night I asked him what was bothering him. He told me he was fine, but I kept after him. I told him he couldn't fool me. I knew there was something troubling him and it was beginning to get to all of us——even Billy. Finally, he broke down and started to cry. I've only seen him cry once before——when my mother died. He said he was real worried, that he knew something terrible, something he wished he didn't know. I asked him what it was but he wouldn't say anything else. He just went into his room and closed the door. He didn't come out for an hour. Then he went for a walk."

"Do you have any ideas about what your father might know?"

"No, not really. It doesn't make any sense. Dad doesn't drink or gamble, he never got into trouble. Once or twice a year he goes to see the trotters at Vernon Downs and occasionally he sees a movie when an old Bogart film is playing. Otherwise all he does is work and come home."

I concentrated, trying to think of something that would help me understand the old man's disappearance; a word or phrase Majorski had used, a question that might jog the daughter's memory. But nothing came. No clues, no questions, nothing but a churning stomach and a rush of nervous energy that made me want to get up and run. It was a feeling I had experienced before.

Once, when I was in high school, I had studied most of the night for a geometry exam only to discover that it was the biology exam, not the geometry test, that was being given that day. I sat through the entire three hours trying to wrack my mathematically-filled mind for some facts of life. The harder I tried, the less I succeeded. There was no knowledge to draw upon.

Now, sitting in the small, cluttered living room, I felt the same sense of frustration. Try as I might, I was unable to come up with even a vague notion of what terrible knowledge Majorski possessed or what had happened to the trainman. How ironic, I thought. I could solve complicated crossword puzzles all day without shedding a drop of perspiration, but give me a real dilemma and I couldn't get my mind out of first gear. I stopped my futile search for insight and turned my attention to the young woman sitting across from me.

Janet Pafko sat on the edge of the sofa, her deep green eyes focused on me, looking for a positive response, a sign of hope.

The intensity of her emerald eyes made me uncomfortable. What was it about her that was so familiar? Why was I so churned up about a woman I never met before who called me out of the blue to tell me her father hadn't come home from the railroad yard?

"I'm drawing a blank," I said. "Your father is obviously upset, but neither of us knows why. I'll do some checking at the train yard tomorrow. Maybe somebody down there knows something. I'll stop by tomorrow afternoon to tell you what I found. Meanwhile, if your Dad shows up or you hear from him, let me know."

I pushed myself up from the armchair and put on my coat. Janet walked me to the front door, her eyes still focused on my face, searching for some positive signal. At the door, I shook her hand, but had to force myself to make eye contact.

I knew too well that I had not been very reassuring.

The temperature had dropped into the twenties and the wind had picked up, but the snow had tapered off to a flurry. As I scraped my windshield I thought about Janet Pafko, her riveting eyes, her obvious desperation. She was so intense, yet so helpless.

My car started on the first try. I let the Honda warm up for a minute before putting it into gear. As I pulled away from the curb, my headlights swept over the cars parked on the other side of the street, illuminating them briefly. The fourth car up, a large dark colored Chevrolet had two dark figures in the front seat. I couldn't see their faces, but I noticed there was no smoke coming from the car's exhaust. I thought it was a little odd that two people would be sitting in a car without the motor running on such a cold night.

Driving home, I kept the driver's window open, hoping the cold air would shock me into some new insight——or at least numb my feelings of discomfort. The icy wind burned my cheek but didn't cool my feelings. I was still very frustrated. It was not just my inability to come up with a clever clue. Not even Sherlock, himself, could have figured out Majorski's whereabouts from the scanty information I had. It was more basic. I had sat there and promised this scared, helpless young woman that I would help her. I had raised her hopes by telling her I would ask around at the train yard.

What bullshit!

I was a graduate student who moonlighted, checking workman's comp claims, locating witnesses. I hadn't done any serious investigative work in four years. I should have been in the library working on my thesis, not playing super sleuth. What business did I have leading Janet Pafko on like this?

Just then an image of another frightened young woman with penetrating eyes formed in my mind and I knew why Janet Pafko seemed so familiar. In addition to their fear, both women shared another similarity——they both had beautiful deep green eyes.

Four years ago Sylvia Carling had come to the Onondaga Investigative Agency because she was concerned her estranged husband, Harold, might do something to her six-year old son, Jason. I had completed my apprenticeship at the Agency several months earlier and was assigned to the case. I conducted a background check on Mr. Carling and discovered he was a respected business man, belonged to a number of civic organizations, and was an active member of his church. The only persons who had anything negative to say about him were his ex-wife and his business partner, who said he had been acting a little strangely. According to the partner, Carling did not react when the judge issued a restraining order prohibiting him from returning to his former home. He simply smiled and said, "We'll see about that." He kept repeating the same phrase over and over, "We'll see about that. We'll see about that."

I didn't take the warning seriously. I figured Carling was just acting *macho*, trying to save face. Rather than provide additional surveillance, just in case Carling was serious, I tried to reassure my client. I tried to convince Sylvia Carling that she and her six-year old son were safe from harm, that she had nothing to worry about. I had a vivid memory of Mrs. Carling standing in her doorway, pleading with me to keep a close watch on her former husband. She told me he was desperate, he was going to do something terrible. I told her there was no danger. I was certain he wouldn't defy the judge's restraining order and risk being thrown in jail.

How wrong I had been.

The follow day, Mrs. Carling dropped her son at school. As he was getting out of the car she handed him his lunch and told him she would be a little late and he should wait for her. Harold Carling showed up at school just as the children were being let out. He coaxed his son to get in the car and drove away. The police conducted an extensive search but were not able to locate the boy or his father. The last memory Sylvia

Carling had of her son was watching him walk into the school, holding his Sesame Street lunchbox in his tiny hand.

The next week I submitted my resignation to the investigation agency. I met with Mrs. Carling and told her how sorry I was. She was very upset. She looked directly into my eyes and told me I should have listened to her; if I had paid attention to her warning Jason would still be with her. There was nothing I could do but agree with her.

A year later, still plagued with guilt, I called to see how she was doing.

She invited me into her apartment and offered me a cup of coffee. Sitting across from me at her small kitchen table, Sylvia Carling told me that when her son had been taken by his father she felt betrayed by me. Her anger toward me was so intense that when I came to see her shortly after Jason was abducted, she had to restrain herself from striking me. The intervening year hadn't dulled the pain of losing her son, but she was trying to get on with her life. She believed that one day her son would be found, and refused to change anything in his room. She told me she had been angry at me for a long time, but was now ready to forgive me.

It was more than I was prepared to do for myself.

The frigid air coming in through the driver's window finally got to me. I started to shiver and rolled up the window. This was crazy. Four years ago I had given up my job as an investigator because I had failed to help a woman who was worried about what was going to happen to her family. My ineptness in that situation had tragic consequences and I still had not gotten over it. So what was I doing now, telling this desperate young woman I had never met before I would help her find her father? Hadn't I done enough damage to Sylvia Carling?

I thought about turning around, driving to Janet Pafko's house, and telling her I couldn't help her. She should call the police in the morning and let the people who were paid to protect the public find her father.

It sounded like a good idea, but there was one flaw: I couldn't get myself to turn the car around.

Maybe a good night's sleep would help me think more clearly.

As I turned onto my street, I realized there was one small saving grace in this whole situation. At least I hadn't told her I was a licensed private investigator.

I noticed also that the parking space I had left this morning was still vacant. Unfortunately, the snow plows had created a new two-foot barrier of ice and snow, blocking the space.

Undaunted, I backed forcefully into the space, cringing only slightly at the sound of the tail light cracking as I passed through the frozen mound of snow. Climbing over the snow banks I cursed the Syracuse weather and asked myself why I had turned down Florida State's offer to enroll in their graduate program in psychology.

4

By morning the snow had stopped. The bright sunshine and clear blue sky meant it was very cold outside. Putting off my encounter with the winter elements, I decided to try my hand, once again, at organizing my thesis notes. Last night I had been too tired to do anything but work on last week's *New York Times* crossword puzzle. By the time I filled in the final word I felt like there were lead weights attached to my eyelids.

Today was different. I was determined to make progress on my thesis. I organized my notecards in neat piles on the small desk in my bedroom. Then I reached into my briefcase and pulled out the legal pad on which I had written the introductory paragraph. All I had to do was find a sharp pencil and I would be ready to begin.

Unfortunately the pencil in my briefcase had been worn dull yesterday afternoon in the library by my doodling. I had used the only other pencil in the room to work on the crossword puzzle and it also was not fit for serious writing.

Remembering that I had put a sharpened pencil next to the telephone I got up from the desk and crossed the room. As I picked up the pencil it occurred to me I hadn't checked for messages last night.

No harm in delaying my scholarly pursuits a few more minutes, I thought as I picked up the receiver.

I called the answering service and was pleasantly surprised when I was greeted not by Mrs. D's hacking cough, but by the sultry voice of Ms. O. In my more ribald fantasies, I imagined the operator to be continuously engaged in some Olympian test of the ability of the human voice to induce sensual arousal. I was convinced Ms. O would never make it through the first qualifying heat, but her failed sensuousness was preferable to Mrs. D's awful cough.

"Well good morning, Mr. Fenton," the operator breathed. "What can I do for you today?"

I stifled my first instinct. "Would you be kind enough to tell me if I have any messages?"

"Oh, certainly. It would give me pleasure. Your mother called and the man from the Norton Real Estate agency called, something about the rent. Now let me see if there's anything else for you."

Ms. O. always built to a climax.

"Oh, yes, a Mr. Lazard from Gladstone, Tyler and Perry asked if you would be kind enough to call him this morning."

I was surprised. Gladstone, Tyler and Perry was one of the most prestigious law firms in Central New York. I knew my landlord couldn't afford to pay the fees Gladstone would charge to intimidate me into paying the overdue rent. I didn't know anyone else who had litigious intentions toward me. And I was certain there was no rich old aunt who had included me in her will.

Professor Singleton was always trying to find investigative work for me, but Gladstone, Tyler and Perry was out of my league.

"Oh, Mr. Fenton," Ms. O. said, panting from excitement, "there is one more message for you."

I knew she would prolong the suspense for as long as possible. I decided to play the role that was expected of me.

"Let me guess. Was it the telephone company or the power company?"

"No."

"Was it a rich widow who wanted me to find her long lost hamster?"

"Don't be silly. You really know how to put a girl on."

"Okay, Ms. O., I give up. Who called?"

"You didn't even try very hard, Mr. Fenton. I know you can do better than that."

I began to reconsider the merits of an answering machine.

"I'll try to do better next time," I said apologetically.

Sensing that the game was over, Ms. O paused for a few seconds before speaking. "It was Ms. Tolliver. She would like you to call when you have a free moment."

"Thank you. As usual, you've been very helpful," I said, wondering why I allowed myself to be drawn into this ritual. Hanging up before Ms. O could reply, I quickly dialed Ollie's number.

I was about to hang up the phone after the fifth ring, when Ollie answered.

"Hello," she said, sounding short of breath.

I refrained from making a smart remark about interrupting her iron pumping. "Hi, what's up?"

"Oh, hi Marty. Want to see the new Bogdanovich film tonight?"

"Sounds good to me. What time should I pick you up?"

"Seven."

I was about to say goodbye when I remembered yesterday's conversation with Lou. "I'm sorry, Ollie," I said apologetically, "I promised Lou I'd go to the hockey game tonight." What was I saying? Less than twenty-four hours ago, Ollie had begun to bare her soul to me, admitting she shuts down when people get too close to her. Now she calls me, probably wanting to continue our conversation, or at least test my reaction to her revelation; and what do I do? I tell her I'm going to a minor league hockey game. I sure know how to inspire trust. "I could skip the game," I said, trying to reverse direction. "Lou wouldn't mind. He can go with one of his police buddies."

"No, that's okay," Ollie said flatly. "We can get together another time."

Way to go, Fenton. You've really screwed up now. "Maybe I'll stop by after the game," I said.

"Sure."

"Terrific. I'm looking forward to seeing you. By the way, how was your trip to Utica?" Talk about inane chatter.

"Good," Ollie replied.

Knowing she was not a premier telephone conversationalist, and I was digging myself into a deeper hole, I said goodbye and hung up the phone.

Not wanting to dwell on my failed social life, I dialed Lazard's number. I only had to speak to two women before I was put through to Mr. Lazard. He told me in a syrupy voice they were interested in engaging me for the purpose of handling a very sensitive matter. He said it would not take much of my time, but might prove to be lucrative and asked whether I could come to his office within the next hour.

I looked at the notecards on the desk. Then I looked at the pile of bills next to the telephone.

I didn't even bother to ask him where he had gotten my name.

The law firm of Gladstone, Tyler and Perry was located in the Carrier Tower, a tall glass and steel structure that offered panoramic views of Syracuse University and the surrounding countryside. The firm occupied two of the upper floors of the building, with an internal spiral staircase connecting the two levels.

The platinum blonde receptionist called the red haired secretary, who escorted me past the line of young, pretty secretaries ——mostly brunettes ——into Lazard's office. The attorney sat behind a large mahogany desk, framed by a view of Onondaga Lake and the factories that once soiled its clear blue waters. Malcolm Lazard was a short, husky man, dressed in an expensively tailored blue pin-striped suit. His straight black hair was combed across the top of his forehead, covering the first traces of a receding hairline.

Lazard's square face was filled with oversized features —large brown eyes, a broad flat nose, protruding ears—except for his small, thin-lipped mouth, which was fixed in a perpetual smile.

"Good afternoon, Mr. Fenton," the lawyer said, gesturing me to sit in front of the desk. "I appreciate your coming over so quickly."

"My pleasure, Mr. Lazard. It's not often that I get to take in this view."

The lawyer chuckled politely. "I know that you're probably very busy, Mr. Fenton. But, I wonder if you might have a little time to perform a small service for us."

I took a mental inventory of the large blocks of open time on my calendar and decided to ignore the lawyer's patronizing manner.

"We have a client with a minor problem," Lazard continued. "It seems that our client made a poor investment. About a year ago he was approached by his brother-in-law, a man of good intentions, but poor judgement. The brother-in-law has a rather dismal business record. He seems to have a reverse Midas touch when it comes to financial ventures. He has opened and closed a half-dozen business enterprises within the last ten years. Each one seems better than the last, but somehow none of them succeed.

"Now, this brother-in-law is not a bad fellow. He's pleasant and considerate and has always seemed to treat his wife—our client's sister—very well. So when he approached our client asking him to put a few dollars into a new enterprise, our client felt a little sorry for him. He agreed to become co-investor with the brother-in-law in this latest venture. That is when our client's minor difficulties began."

The lawyer rose and walked to the wall-length bookcase. Opening a cabinet in the center of the wall unit, he removed a cut-glass decanter and offered me a drink. Declining politely, I marvelled at the lawyer's ability to extend a dull anecdote into a suspenseful cliff-hanger and felt relieved that I wasn't a client of Gladstone, Tyler and Perry paying for each tick of the clock.

Taking a sip from his drink, Lazard returned to his story. "The brother-in-law explained that he had been asked to invest in a sure-fire venture, a new photo processing outfit that combined a computer-assisted developing system with a 'one hour print return or your money cheerfully refunded' guarantee. The company was offering a small number of limited partnerships to local backers. Stores in six other cities had produced an average return of forty percent in the first year for local investors. The minimum investment was eight-thousand dollars and the brother was short twenty-five hundred dollars.

"Unfortunately, the photo processing store turned out to be a front for a thriving kiddie-porn operation specializing in glossy eight-by-ten color prints. The fancy computer was programmed to offer—to a select group of subscribers—a coded list of hundreds of photographs depicting perverted and sordid acts involving innocent-looking youth.

"Through reliable sources we've found out the District Attorney and Police Department have been planning a surprise raid on the photo store."

Once again the lawyer paused dramatically. He savored the aroma of his drink before sipping slowly from the glass. Gazing down at the city below, Lazard continued.

"Our problem—and we are hoping you can help us with it—is our client's little act of family generosity made him a full-fledged investor in Photoflash, Inc. We need to discover how much of a liability this investment will become. We want you to find out if our client's name appears on any of the company's documents that might come into the hands of the authorities during legal activities that shall ensue."

"Mr. Lazard, I'm not certain why you called me. I think you may have made a mistake. You see, I am a graduate student in psychology. I have been trained to design and conduct research studies that may help us to understand and predict human behavior. Unfortunately, I am not clairvoyant. I have no special ability to know whether or not someone's name appears on an incriminating piece of paper."

Lazard twisted his face into a grotesque smile. "Let's not be coy, Mr. Fenton. I am well aware of your current status as a graduate student, and I admire your considerable courage in pursuing such a lofty goal. Science is indeed one of the strongest paths to truth. However, I am also aware that you have also been engaged in several other professions, one of which involved applying your intellect and skills to the art—or perhaps science—if investigation. So you see, Mr. Fenton, it is neither your skills as a researcher nor your powers of clairvoyance that I seek to utilize."

I wondered how this slick lawyer knew so much about me. Lazard certainly did not look like someone Singleton would hang around with. The professor was an extremely bright man—one of the most intelligent people I had ever met—but he was very unpretentious; more comfortable in a flannel shirt and corduroy slacks than a jacket and tie. Singleton was a down-to-earth person who abhorred phoniness in any form. No, this was definitely not a Singleton referral.

"It really does not matter how I know your background," Lazard said, anticipating my question. "What matters is that we have a simple assignment we believe you can successfully execute and, unless I'm gravely mistaken, your present position as a graduate assistant pays you slightly less than you require to maintain even a modest standard of living."

I had to admit, in this instance, Lazard's argument was compelling. Watching the lawyer swirl his amber colored drink, I cleared my throat.

"Mr. Lazard, I'm flattered that you've asked me to help you with your client's 'little problem.' But it's not clear what you expect me to do if I find this incriminating evidence."

"Nothing," the lawyer responded.

"Nothing?" I echoed, puzzled by Lazard's unusual request.

"That's correct. We merely want to discover whether our client will suffer any minor embarrassment when the Photoflash venture comes to the publics' attention. I think you can appreciate why we wish to employ you to handle this small matter, rather than using our own investigator, whose association with our firm might raise a few unnecessary questions."

I was annoyed with Lazard's pompous, condescending tone, especially his constant tendency to cleverly downplay everything. However, not being an individual who allowed personality considerations to interfere with business affairs—at least when I really needed the money—I agreed to accept this "small" assignment to do a "little" investigating.

Fortunately, the lawyer's annoying habit of downplaying everything did not carry over to paying for services. I graciously accepted his offer of four hundred-fifty dollars plus expenses for a job I was confident would take no more than a full day's work. Lazard handed me an envelope with ten crisp twenty-dollar bills and told me he would give me the balance when he received my report.

Coming down from Lazard's office, I leaned back against the rear wall of the elevator and thought about what a lawyer's life must be like. Seventeen years ago, when I was a senior in college, I had been faced with a career decision. My advisor was urging me to go to law school. In fact, I had been accepted to Cornell and St. John's. But I was fed up with academics and wanted to do something practical. So, with the mechanical aptitude and skills I had picked up hanging around my father's auto repair shop and an introduction from my roommate's well-connected father, I was able to get a job as an apprentice mechanic at the airport in Toledo, Ohio.

Having earned my credentials as a bona fide mechanic, I soon found myself bored with the daily routine of cleaning and mending the sterile mechanical birds. During this time I became friends with one of the air traffic controllers, whose description of the tension and stress involved in guiding the planes in and out of the airport fascinated me. I entered and successfully completed the initial six month training program to become an air traffic controller.

In September 1979, I began my first assignment navigating airplanes through the air lanes surrounding Hancock International Airport in Syracuse.

In the summer of 1981, Ronald Reagan declared war on the air traffic controllers of America.

The rest is history.

After my brief tenure as an air traffic controller, I tried a variety of vocations. In each case, the frustrations and constraints of working for an organization, with all of its rules and bureaucratic nonsense outweighed the satisfaction I got from trying to meet the challenges of the position. Having run out of viable job options I decided to enroll in a graduate program in social psychology, where I hoped to satisfy my interest in solving puzzles by conducting research on the critical social problems of our times.

As the elevator completed its descent, stopping at the first floor with a gentle bump, I briefly thought about my decision to not attend law school and wondered how often lawyers overdrew their checking accounts.

On the way to the Photoflash store, I stopped at a pay phone to call Janet Pafko. She had not heard anything from her father. The police had agreed to put out a bulletin, since he had not been seen for more than twenty-four hours. The desk officer's casual attitude had not helped. Janet sounded very worried.

I told her I would follow up with the police and promised to stop at her house later.

The Photoflash store was located on a major thoroughfare on the western edge of the city. Surrounded by fast food stores and decaying factories, Photoflash was housed in an old automobile service station that had been a casualty of the Arab oil squeeze of the mid-'70s. I parked in the small lot behind the building and walked around to the front entrance. Standing behind the formica counter was a tall, gaunt man who looked as if he had not seen sunlight for years. He was dressed completely in black——turtleneck sweater, polyester slacks and tasseled loafers.

"May I help you, sir?" the man behind the counter asked. His tone matched the color of his clothes.

"I hope so," I replied. "I'm looking for the manager, Mr. Paresi."

"Is there anything I can do to assist you?"

"Are you Mr. Paresi?"

"No."

"Then I'm afraid you can't assist me. Is Mr. Paresi here?"

"Just a minute," the man in black said, moving quickly through a door leading to the back of the store.

After a little more than the promised moment he returned, followed by a short, stocky man dressed in Levi jeans and a grey sweatshirt. "I'm Jimmy Paresi. What can I do for you?" the short man asked, reaching over the counter to shake my hand. He had a very firm grip.

"I wonder if I could speak to you privately?" I asked.

"Sure, come on back to the executive suite," the short man chuckled, pointing to the door behind the counter.

The executive suite turned out to be a stark, windowless room, not much larger than a broom closet. A file cabinet, small metal desk and a pair of folding chairs were the only furnishings.

"Now, Mr. ..."

"Fenton."

"Mr. Fenton, what did you want to talk about?" Paresi asked, gesturing for me to sit.

"Mr. Paresi, I have been hired to ascertain an individual's financial involvement in your business."

"And who is paying you to be interested?" Paresi asked.

I smiled. "You've watched enough TV shows to know that I can't answer that question. However, I am prepared to compensate you generously for your assistance."

"Generously?"

"One hundred and twenty dollars," I responded. I *was* being generous, I thought. I had only intended to offer a hundred, but sensed that Paresi might be reluctant to cooperate.

Paresi appeared to be considering the offer. "I don't suppose this information will be used for nefarious purposes?"

"Certainly not."

"And no one needs to know how this information was obtained, right?"

"Right."

The short, stocky man walked to the file cabinet, reached into his pocket for a key and opened the lock in the upper right hand corner. He slid open the middle drawer, and, after thumbing through the file, pulled out a thin, manilla folder, containing a single typewritten sheet. Handing the paper to me, he cautioned: "You have thirty seconds. Don't write anything down."

I quickly glanced at the paper. There were five names on the sheet. The third name on the list was the one I was looking for. I handed the paper back to Paresi. The entire transaction had taken less than fifteen seconds. I wondered if Paresi might give me a discount, but decided not to ask.

"Thank you, Mr. Paresi. It's been a pleasure doing business with you," I said, as I passed the money to the short man.

"The pleasure is all mine," Paresi said, pocketing the money.

We shook hands and walked to the door. Paresi told me there was a rear exit that led to the parking lot, and guided me down a narrow corridor lit by a red exit sign over the black fire door.

Stepping out into the sunlight I thought how easy this job had been. I turned toward the car and my head exploded in pain. The sky went black, my knees buckled and I slid to the pavement.

5

"Mr. Fenton, can you hear me?" I opened my eyes slowly. The bright fluorescent light made me wince.

"Mr. Fenton, are you feeling okay?"

This time I tried to lift my head, but the sharp pain made me wonder if someone had anchored my brain to the pillow.

"Take it easy, don't try to move."

After a minute I figured out that the woman in white standing over me was some sort of medical person and that I was in a hospital.

"You were found in a vacant lot in Westvale. A policeman saw you lying in a clump of bushes, unconscious."

"What time is it?" I asked.

The throbbing was only mildly unbearable, as long I he didn't move my head.

"4:45..in the afternoon. You've been here nearly an hour. You must have taken quite a blow."

"I guess so. The last I remember was walking out of the back door of Photoflash."

"There's a policeman waiting outside. He wanted to talk to you as soon as you regained consciousness. Do you feel up to it?"

"I guess so; though I don't know what I can tell him. Tell me Miss..."

"Dr. Hennessy."

"What? Oh yeah. Dr. Hennessy, can you tell me where I can find a phone. I had a late afternoon appointment. I would like to call to say that I'll be late."

"Very late, I'd like to keep you here overnight for observation."

I began to sit up, ready to protest, but reconsidered when the grenade exploded inside my head. "Okay, you win. Do you think there's any damage?"

"Maybe a concussion, but hopefully nothing serious. I'll know more tomorrow."

"All right. If you don't think making a phone call will short-circuit my brain, I'd like to call the person I'm supposed to meet. Then I'll be ready for the man in blue."

I considered calling Ollie, but something kept me from dialing her number. Maybe it was that I felt so foolish being cold-cocked in the middle of the day. Ollie never would have let that happen to her. Or maybe it was my frustration with our relationship. We were at a real impasse. I knew what I wanted, but Ollie wasn't interested. Our conversation at the Everson had confused me even more. I knew that Ollie would be worried about me if she didn't hear from me soon, but I couldn't bring myself to call her. I picked up the telephone and dialed.

Janet Pafko had not heard from her father. She seemed even more agitated than when we last spoke. I apologized for not stopping at her house, explaining that I had been detained unexpectedly. I did not tell her where I was calling from. I told her not to worry and promised to stop by tomorrow. As I hung up, I realized that my attempt to reassure her had not been very successful. This bothered me because I knew she was very concerned about her father and I was not in a good position to help her. It also bothered me because I found myself attracted to this young woman with the piercing emerald eyes even though that was the last thing I needed at the moment. My emotional life was complicated enough as it was.

I did not recognize the policeman standing beside my bed. The Syracuse Police Department had four hundred fifty members. I thought I knew most of them, but if pressed, I would have to confess that I recognized no more than one hundred fifty and was on speaking terms with fewer than fifty of Syracuse's finest. This one was tall, broad shouldered and not very communicative. He had a square, Irish face with blue eyes and gray hair, short on top, and combed straight back on the sides.

"Mr. Fenton, how are you feeling?"

"Like I have a three day hangover —without having enjoyed any of the benefits."

The officer did not appear to be impressed by my wit. He had obviously been a first-born child. "I have a few questions for you. Okay?"

I began to respond, but the big policeman did not give me a chance. "My name is Slattery. I'm the one who found you in the field. How did you get there? Who gave you the crack on the head? What kind of nasty business are you involved with?"

For a second, I considered suggesting to the officer that he might try for a job on *60 Minutes* after he put in his twenty, but thought better of it. Instead I opted for brevity.

"I don't know, Officer."

"You don't know what?" Slattery asked, with controlled anger.

"I don't know how I got to the field. I don't know who cracked me on the head, and I don't know what nasty business I'm involved with. I didn't even know I was involved with nasty business. I was leaving the Photoflash store, off West Genesee, after some routine business, when, zappo, the light went out."

"Routine business, Mr. Fenton?"

"Look, Officer Slattery, I wish I could help you. I would really like to know who coldcocked me. But, I can't think of anyone who would want to do me bodily harm. I'm not Travis Magee or Mike Hammer. I'm a graduate student who moonlights once in awhile. I handle divorces, insurance cases and an occasional minor scandal that someone wants to keep from the public. I don't deal with rough stuff."

Slattery looked disinterested. "What were you doing at Photoflash?"

"Asking some routine questions."

"What kind of questions?"

I sighed. The throbbing pain in my head was becoming worse. "Listen, let's save us both some time and aggravation. You ask me what kind of questions. I tell you the questions concern a client of mine. You ask me who is my client. I tell you that's privileged information. You tell me it can go easy or hard for me; that I should cooperate; that it's for my own good. I get my back up and say I haven't committed a crime, I'm the *victim*, so let me alone. You sulk a little and tell me we can talk now or later. Then I become completely outrageous and offer you the ultimate ultimatum: book me or let me go. And finally you stomp off, mumbling about how you won't forget me, while pondering what you're going to do about the big, tight knot in your gut."

Slattery glared at me for a moment. Just as I was beginning to worry that I had gone too far, the big policeman turned and walked away. Stopping at the door he spoke in a tremorous whisper. "You're a smart guy, a very smart guy, Mr. graduate student."

I let my better judgement prevail and kept my lips clamped shut. I had been given enough signals to know that this was not my day.

In the morning, I felt a little better, though not by much. With my solemn promise to go directly home to bed, Dr. Hennessy agreed to discharge me.

It was a promise I did not keep. I stopped at the first phone booth I

Mrs. D. greeted me with her usual raspy cough. She recounted her conversation with my mother, who wanted to know if I had called my sister and scheduled my yearly checkup. As always, Mrs. D. made a point of telling me what a fine person Ma was, how she was always looking out for me. Between coughs, Mrs. D. also sputtered that Lazard had called and wanted me to contact him at my earliest convenience. After some coaxing, Mrs. D. also acknowledged that Ollie had left a message asking why she hadn't heard from me. Mrs. D. always saved Ollie's messages for last. I don't think she likes Ollie; mostly out of loyalty to my mother who doesn't understand why Ollie hadn't jumped at the chance of marrying her son.

I thanked Mrs. D. before she had a chance to launch another coughing attack. As I hung up the receiver I wondered if all of the operators at We-Care were taking a course on how to make conversations with clients more interesting. I could picture the instructor giving them tips on how to add suspense to their message report.

Taking a quarter from my pocket I considered who to call first.

I decided that my head was not ready for a phone conversation with my mother and I was not quite ready to speak with Ollie. I dialed Lazard's number and was greeted by an efficient receptionist, "Gladstone, Tyler and Perry, please hold."

"Wait a second," I pleaded.

"I'll be with you in a moment, sir."

"But..." Click. Too late. The phone line was filled with the sound of Muzak.

Bad enough to have to deal with an officious receptionist, I thought. But canned music?

I hung up the handset, found another quarter and dialed.

"Ollie, I'm standing in a phone booth outside of Crouse-Irving Hospital. My head hurts like hell, I haven't eaten in twenty-four hours and haven't the vaguest idea where I left my car. No, I haven't been drinking. Yes, I need help. Please rescue me."

"Is that you, Marty?" she asked quietly.

At that instant I knew I was in serious trouble. "Of course it's me, Ollie. Who did you think it was, Mr. Wonderby?"

"I don't think sarcasm is in order, Marty," she said without inflection.

Damn it, I thought, I wish she would yell or curse at me. Even slamming the phone down would be better than this. The guilt was up to my chin and rising quickly.

"Ollie, I know I should have called you, but I couldn't. Well not exactly couldn't...I...I had a conflict."

"Spare us both, Marty. I'll pick you up in ten minutes. We'll talk later."

I listened to the click on the other end of the line, relieved to be done with our conversation. I knew that I was only postponing the inevitable, but at that moment my head hurt and I was very hungry. I was also grateful that Ollie had agreed to pick me up.

As I waited for Ollie it occurred to me how absurd my position was. I wanted a commitment from Ollie. I wanted us to live together, to have a stable, long-term relationship. Yet, I couldn't even pick up the phone to tell her why I hadn't kept our date. And when she didn't shrug off my inconsiderate behavior, when she let me know in her own way that she was concerned about me, what did I do? I became uncomfortable and froze up.

So much for being ready to make a commitment.

Two corned beef sandwiches and a short nap later, I felt much better. I sat at Ollie's kitchen table watching her chisel the facial features of a small stone statue of an expectant mother. "I'm sorry I didn't call sooner," I said. "Whoever hit me must have used a sledge hammer."

"That's okay," Ollie said continuing to chip away at the piece of sculpture. "I figured you were busy."

"Ollie, are you angry?"

"What makes you think that?" she asked, as she raised the heavy mallet above her head and delivered a forceful blow to the chisel she held in her other hand.

I stirred my coffee, searching the dark, swirling liquid for a good response. "I guess we didn't resolve anything the other night."

"No, we didn't."

Jesus, I thought, the strong, silent type certainly has its down side. "Listen, I know you like your freedom. I really don't want to push you. I can't help it. It's just that you're different from any other woman I've been with. Ollie——this is really hard for me——I think I'm ready for a permanent relationship. We've been together for more than two years. It's just...I..."

"Marty," Ollie said, putting down the mallet and chisel, "you're beginning to sound like a broken record. Give it a rest. You're making me feel like I ought to say yes just to make you feel better. That's not how a good relationship works. It shouldn't be so difficult. It's supposed to be a choice, not an obligation. If this is so painful for you, may-be...maybe we should call it off."

"That's not it Ollie. I want to be with you. If you're not ready to make a commitment, I can live with that. Take your time."

Ollie shook her head. "Why do I have such a hard time believing you, Marty. You tell me you accept my need for space, that you can accept the relationship as it is. Everything is fine——for about a day. Then you're back on my case, trying to persuade me to make a commitment. You're making me crazy, Marty!"

I looked into my coffee cup. No inspiration was forthcoming. "When we were talking the other day at the Everson you started to say something about becoming uncomfortable when people get too near to you...Do you want to talk some more about that?"

"I don't think so," she said.

I really wanted to know more about why she backed away from close relationships. Maybe it would help us work things out. But it was obvious that she was not about to open up to me at that moment. "I don't blame you for being angry at me," I said. "It was pretty inconsiderate of me. I guess I wasn't thinking very clearly."

Ollie started to say something, but changed her mind. She picked up the mallet and chisel and began chipping away at the stone statue.

"Can I ask one more favor, Ollie? Can I borrow your car?"

She reached into the pocket of her jeans, pulled out her keys and tossed them to me.

"Thanks," I said. Catching the keys in my left hand, I reached out to touch her shoulder with my right hand. She brushed my hand aside and resumed her sculpting. I decided not to push my luck.

I walked over to the telephone and dialed Janet Pafko's number. When she answered I told her I would be at her house within a half-hour. As I put on my jacket, Ollie called to me, "Where are you going, Marty? Are you on another job?"

She spoke without feeling, but her questions bothered me. Ollie didn't usually show much interest in my comings and goings. "Not really. The other day I interviewed this older man at the train yard. In the middle of the interview he took a phone call and never came back. Later that day his daughter called to tell me her father——this railroad guy——hadn't come home. She found my number and called to see if I knew where he was. She was real worried about him. I told her I'd ask around."

Ollie looked at me for a moment before she spoke. "Do you think your getting hit on the head has anything to do with this man's disappearance?"

"Nah. I can't see how it could be connected."

Again she paused before speaking. "Is this woman paying you to look for her father?"

"We really haven't talked about it," I replied, feeling even more uncomfortable.

"Then why are you doing this? Shouldn't the police be helping her?"

"I don't know, I can't explain why. It just seemed like the right thing to do."

"So is finishing your master's thesis. But you don't seem to feel the same moral obligation toward that."

I was getting in deeper and didn't know how to get out. Not only was Ollie annoyed at me for not letting her know I couldn't see her last night, it was also becoming clear that she was angry that I was helping Janet. The only thing I didn't know was whether she was jealous or just worried about me. This didn't sound like the Ollie I knew. "Is something bothering you?" I asked, not knowing what else to say.

"No, not really."

"You don't seem very happy."

"I guess I'm frustrated."

"With me?"

"Yes, with you. I don't understand you. One moment you want me to make a long term commitment to be with you. The next moment you can't wait to get away from me. You're off getting your head bashed in or trying to find some guy you met for fifteen minutes at the train yard."

I could have said the same thing about her but I didn't think that would be such a great idea——especially at this moment. She had just finished telling me how much she needed her own space. Now she was bothered because I was leaving her alone and doing my own thing.

Women were so complicated.

"I wish I could explain it to you," I said. "But I can't. At least not now." I wanted to put my arms around her, to feel her firm body against mine, to bury my face in her long red hair and breathe in her fresh, clean scent.

I knew that wasn't such a great idea, either. I restrained myself, and asked instead, "Do you want to come with me?"

"I don't think so...but thanks for asking."

I turned and reached for the door knob.

"Marty, be careful," she said, sounding concerned.

I considered asking for a hug, but thought better of it.

Ollie's 1970 Volkswagen squareback ran very well, but the pipes that carried hot air from the motor to the interior vents had long ago been rotted away by the road salt. The space between the door and the frame added to the arctic effect.

Pulling up my coat collar against the cold, I tried to figure out what I was doing wrong with Ollie. We seemed to see things so differently.

I could not understand how she could say that she liked me very much and wanted to be with me, but not want to commit herself to marriage or even move in with me. She felt frustrated that I needed a commitment to validate our relationship. She did not know why I couldn't accept her need to maintain some independence, why we couldn't just enjoy each other's company without formalizing our relationship.

In spite of my intense need for a more permanent bond, I had begun to realize that constantly prodding Ollie to make a commitment might backfire. I was afraid that the pressure I was putting on her would drive her away. I was trying hard to back off a little, to let the relationship take its own course for awhile. To make things worse, she became just as upset when I allowed her some slack. When I didn't call her constantly she took it as a sign that I didn't really care, that I was more interested in the *idea* of a permanent relationship than in actually putting forth the effort required to make our relationship work. While I knew she was wrong——I had never cared for anyone as much as I did for Ollie——I had to admit that it didn't look very good for me to not show up when I promised, then fail to call her until I needed someone to pick me up at the hospital.

It seemed odd that I could be so good at solving puzzles, but be so inept at working out my relationship with Ollie. Women were obviously much more complicated.

Driving along the plastic lined streets of Erie Boulevard, with its twin arches, white-haired colonels and other symbols of franchise America, I tried to piece together the sketchy information I had about Fred Majorski. He had called in response to my ad and agreed to be interviewed. We had talked briefly, Majorski had gone to take a phone call and had not returned. Majorski's daughter had contacted me and told me he had not come home. She said her father was very worried, but she did not know why he was so troubled. Not much to work with. I wished I could think more clearly. It was bad enough to have so few facts, but my throbbing head prevented me from tapping my rich reservoir of free associations. Sometimes I was able to put together two seemingly unrelated pieces of information to form a new idea or improbable clue that might just lead me somewhere.

But not today. The creative juices just weren't flowing.

As I approached the Majorski house, I had an uneasy feeling. Something was wrong. Not until I pulled into the driveway did I realize what it was.

The front door of the house was wide open.

I jumped out of the car and ran toward the house. I slipped on the icy walk, caught myself before falling and climbed the steps to the front porch. The living room lights were on and I could hear muffled words. As I rushed into the living room, two sounds converged: the familiar banter of Sesame Street's Ernie and Bert and the steady sobbing of a young child.

"Billy, what happened, what's the matter?"

The little boy was sitting on the sofa staring at the T.V. and crying.

43

He had obviously been crying for some time. His eyes were red and his sobs were faint. His gaze was fixed on the television screen, as if he were hypnotized.

"Billy," I called, "what's wrong?"

The boy finally noticed that someone else was in the room. "Mommy, I want Mommy," he cried.

I picked up the boy and held him. "It's okay, Billy. You're safe, I'm going to take care of you." He relaxed a little and put his head on my shoulder. After a moment, the child stopped crying.

"Where did mommy go?" I asked.

"She went outside," Billy replied.

What do I do now, I thought. My private investigator's correspondence course didn't deal with extracting information from frightened four-year-olds.

"Would you like to play a little game?"

"I guess so."

"Okay, here's how we play. I ask you a question, and you think real hard and try to give me the right answer. Each time you answer a question you get a point. If you get three points I'll treat you to an ice cream. Okay?"

"I guess so," the youngster responded, not showing much interest in my game.

Making a mental note to bone up on preschool interrogation, I plunged ahead. "Billy, did someone ring the doorbell or call on the telephone?"

Ten minutes and many questions later, I had a sketchy idea of how Billy had come to be alone, shedding crocodile tears in front of the T.V. Apparently, someone had knocked on the front door. Janet told Billy she was going to see who it was. That was the last time he had seen his mother.

My concentration was broken by a ringing telephone. I gently placed Billy on the sofa and picked up the phone.

"Hello, Pafko residence."

There was a brief silence. "Mr. Fenton, is that you?" the woman at the other end of the line asked. "Is Billy all right? I'm so worried about him."

"Janet, this is Marty Fenton. Yes, Billy's fine, he's here with me. But how about you? Where are you?"

"I'm not doing so well, but I'm better than I was. I'm at a diner in Liverpool. Uh, do you think you might be able to come to get me?"

"Sure, I'll be right there," I responded.

Being reunited with his mother seemed to revive Billy's spirits. The large ice cream sundae didn't hurt either. The three of us sat in a booth at the back of the old diner. Janet cradled the large white stoneware coffee mug in her hands, savoring the heat radiating from the hot cup.

"I had just come home from my job at the florist," she began. "I picked up Billy from Mrs. Cunningham, across the street. She watches Billy while I work. When there was a knock on the door, I figured it was her. Billy's always leaving something at her house. When I opened the door there were these two men.

"They told me they knew where my father was, that I could see him if I came with them. I said I wanted to call you first, but when I moved toward the phone they grabbed me and rushed me outside. I struggled, but they were too strong. They blindfolded me and pushed me into the back of a car. There was a third man, the driver. When I was seated in the back, between the other two men, he went back into the house. When he returned, he told me everything was okay, that he had told Billy I was going out for a little while."

"Did you recognize any of the men?" I asked.

"No, I've never seen the two men who grabbed me and the other man didn't sound at all familiar. He had a deep voice and spoke in short, clipped sentences.

"They started driving, making a lot of turns, not going very fast. After a few minutes the driver started asking me questions about Dad. Did I know why he had disappeared. Had he said anything unusual to me in the last few weeks? I couldn't figure out why he was asking me these questions. I tried to find out who they were, but he just kept asking more questions and getting angrier. Finally, the driver stopped the car and told me I wasn't being helpful. He said they wanted to help my father, but wouldn't be able to if I didn't cooperate."

Janet took a sip of coffee. She put down the mug and sighed "I didn't know what they were after. They didn't ask me where he was or if I knew what had happened to him. They were only interested in what happened before he disappeared. So I figured they knew where Dad was...and I was real scared."

"Where is Grandpa, Mommy," Billy asked, licking the rim of his ice cream dish.

"I don't know where Grandpa is, Sweetie. I wish I did, but I don't. And Billy, please use your spoon."

Billy shrugged and picked up his spoon.

"What happened then?" I asked.

"Nothing," Janet replied. "No one said anything for a moment. Then, one of the guys in the back opened the door and pulled me out of the car. Before they drove off the driver shouted something at me, but I couldn't understand him. By the time I pulled off the blindfold they were gone and I was standing in the middle of nowhere, scared out of my mind. I didn't know where I was. It wasn't far from the city, we hadn't been driving for very long. There were no houses or shops, just a lot of trees. Luckily, I could see some lights in the distance, so I started walking toward them."

"And you found this diner," I interjected.

"Yes. I was freezing when I reached here. I could barely put the coin in the pay phone. I was so worried about Billy." Janet reached over and touched her son's cheek. The boy looked up at his mom and smiled.

"Let's get you home and put Billy to bed," I suggested. "You're both exhausted."

Janet did not argue. She picked up the little boy and carried him to the car. In less than three minutes Billy was asleep, his head resting on Janet's shoulder. As we drove south on Route 81 toward the city, I looked over at the mother and son. They looked so vulnerable.

Janet began to tremble. "Mr. Fenton," she said in a quavering voice, "I'm very worried about Dad. I have this eerie feeling that he isn't coming back."

Looking at the frightened, tired woman with the intense green eyes, I couldn't think of anything reassuring to say. My immediate instinct was to drive to the Public Safety Building, turn Janet over to the police, who knew what they were doing, and go back to my thesis, which sorely needed my attention. But, in spite of the disturbing inconsistency of my behavior——which Ollie had painfully confronted me with a few hours ago——I knew I needed to stick around until I found out what happened to Fred Majorski. "Janet, I have a confession to make." She gave me a puzzled look. "Remember when I told you I was a graduate student, doing research for my thesis?"

She nodded.

"Well, that's partially true," I continued. "I'm also a private investigator...at least I used to be one, though I still have my license. What I mean is I still practice occasionally. Nothing significant; just small jobs that people don't feel comfortable doing themselves."

As I spoke, Janet's facial expression began to change. The worry lines on her forehead vanished and her eyes lost their fear. The corners of her mouth turned up into a broad smile. "Oh, Mr. Fenton," she said in a strong voice. "Will you help me? I would be very grateful. And I'll be glad to pay you."

Once again I was at a loss for words. I had already decided to help her, but I didn't want to raise her expectations.

"What is your fee? How much do you charge?" she asked.

"Uh, I don't have a standard fee. It depends on the case." I knew she didn't have any money, but if I took her on as a client it might make it easier for me to reconcile all the strange feelings I was having about Janet Pafko. At least I could tell Ollie I was working on a case. But if I did accept her offer I would be making a commitment ——another commitment. I wasn't sure I was up to this one, either.

"I'll pay whatever you say," Janet said. "I really need your help."

"Okay," I said, wanting to end this conversation. "How about twenty-five dollars a day. You pay me twenty-five dollars and I'll help you look for your father."

"I don't know, Mr. Fenton. Twenty-five dollars a day sounds very low."

"No, twenty-five dollars is my regular fee."

"I thought you said you didn't have a standard fee."

"I did, but I didn't make myself clear." Things were getting worse. "Twenty-five dollars. Take it or leave it."

"Okay, I'll take it. Twenty-five dollars a day...plus expenses."

I could see that I wasn't going to win. "Plus expenses," I agreed.

6

I stood by Olivia's living room window, taking in the signs of winter: white puffs of condensation exhaled by hunched-over pedestrians, like steam from a locomotive; snow covered cars sliding along the streets; glassy frozen crust covering day-old snow. Sipping hot black coffee, I wondered why in hell I lived in Syracuse. The local joke was that Syracuse had two seasons: Winter and the Fourth of July. Of these two, Independence Day was less reliable.

I felt stymied. Fred Majorski's disappearance did not make sense. He didn't seem to have any enemies and he certainly didn't own or control anything valuable enough to attract attention. Yet, he had been called off his locomotive to answer a telephone call and had not returned. Majorski's daughter was in a panic. A carload of mean guys were being very inquisitive. And I hadn't the foggiest idea what was happening.

Last night, for the first time, I sensed that this was more than an old man walking off into the sunset. This was not a simple case of visiting a secret girlfriend or going on a binge for a few days. The carload of mean guys had convinced me there was more to this case. But what?

Why were these thugs grilling Janet? If they were involved in Majorski's disappearance they would know more about where he was then she did. Unless they couldn't get anything from Majorski and figured she might know something. Or maybe they wanted to find out if she knew why they had taken her father. What if they hadn't taken Majorski?

This is crazy, I thought. I'm not getting anywhere. I took a last sip of coffee——by now it was lukewarm——put the cup in the sink, and considered my options. Somewhere outside this cozy apartment, hidden among the icicles and snowdrifts, was a baffling mystery, waiting to be solved. On the other side of the thin wooden door in front of me, Ollie was still in bed, warm and sleepy and very sensuous. I knew that she was angry at me, that I was at risk of losing her if I didn't stop pushing her for a commitment. I concentrated on what to do next, weighing the alternatives carefully. Finally I reached a decision. I put down my coffee cup and began to unbutton my shirt as I moved quickly toward the bedroom. Reaching for the doorknob, I reminded myself not to say anything about our relationship.

Fortified by my amorous interlude with Ollie and convinced that spoken language is not necessarily the best way of communicating, I was ready to take on the mystery of Fred Majorski. I picked up the phone and dialed Lou DeSantis' home number. I knew that Lou was probably sitting down to one of Angie's huge feasts——pasta, sausage and meatballs and more pasta——but I couldn't wait any longer.

"Lou, this is Marty."

"Hey, how are you doing, buddy. You missed a great game the other night. The Blazers were hotter than Dante's inferno. Incidentally, remind me to lend you my copy of Emily Post. You could have at least called to tell me you were going to stand me up."

"Sorry, my head was in the wrong place. I'll tell you about it later. Listen, I've got a difficult situation. Do you think I might pick your brain for a few minutes?"

"Now?" Lou asked.

"If at all possible. I really need some help."

The policeman hesitated for a few seconds. "Okay, Marty, but not on the phone, Angie's table is going to collapse if we don't start eating some of this food. Come on over and have a plate with us. Bring Ollie. We'll eat and we'll talk. Make it fast, though. My intellectual prowess begins to falter if it's not fed."

"We'll be right over."

Angie DeSantis was not your average Italian policeman's wife. She and Lou had met at the Hotel Syracuse fifteen year ago. He had been coordinating security for Senator Jacob Javits, who was speaking at a public policy conference at the University. Angie had been modeling evening wear for the manufacturers preview presentation of the Spring line at the Hotel. She had come up from New York City the night before the show, stopping in Utica to visit her Aunt Rose and Uncle Joe. They had driven her to Syracuse after dinner. She had waved goodbye to them and was walking toward the East Onondaga Street entrance when a teenager had snatched her purse. In trying to grab back the purse Angie had lost her balance, and literally fallen backwards, heels over head, tripping over the suitcase she held in her other hand.

Lou had heard her screams from his post inside the lobby. He chased the thief for several blocks, but could not keep pace with the fleet-footed youngster and lost sight of him.

When the policeman returned, Angie had regained her footing, but not her composure.

"I can't believe this is happening to me in Syracuse," she exclaimed. "I've lived my entire life in New York City and not once have I been robbed. I had to travel three hundred miles into the Yukon to have my purse snatched. Jesus Christ, this is unreal."

Lou stood awkwardly facing the svelte young model. He was awestruck by her beauty and embarrassed by his inability to catch the thief.

"I'm sorry this happened, Miss," he said. "This doesn't happen very often. I'm really sorry. Whomever did this is going to be sorry when I catch him."

"Whoever," the model said.

"What?" Lou asked.

"The correct word is whoever, not whomever. Who if the subject is he, whom if him. Remember the *m*."

"Whatever," Lou said, feeling like a real Neanderthal. "I just don't want you to think this happens all the time in Syracuse. And I meant what I said. I am going to get your purse for you."

Angie was struck by the policeman's sincerity. She also was becoming aware of the full reality of her situation. She had no money, no credit cards, not even any identification.

"Officer, I'm sure you mean well, but right now I'm not very concerned about the crime statistics for your town or even your gallant intentions to recover my treasured possessions. What I'm concerned about is what I am going to do right now. That young man left me without any visible means of support."

"Oh, don't worry about that, Miss. I know you're a citizen of good standing. You won't have any..." Lou stopped, realizing he had misunderstood her. "You mean that..."

Angie began to voice a smart retort, but held up. The policeman looked so helpless, so embarrassed.

"I don't mean to be giving you a hard time, officer," she said. "This has been very upsetting. I don't know what I'm going to do."

"Miss, I meant what I said. I'm going to recover your belongings. In the meantime, you'll be fine. The night manager of the hotel happens to be a good friend of mine. I'm sure he will be glad to extend credit for a room. As soon as you're checked in, we'll call the credit card companies. In the morning we'll contact your bank to put a freeze on your accounts. And if you need a little spending money, I'll be glad to make you a small loan."

Angie smiled. She was beginning to like this unsophisticated young man. Behind his awkwardness there was a rough-cut self assurance.

"What's your name, officer?" she asked.

"DeSantis. Lou DeSantis."

"No kidding. Another Italian. I'm Angie Tedesco, second generation Neapolitan. Listen, Lou DeSantis, I appreciate your offer to help and I'll be glad to accept it—except for the personal loan. I'm sure the company I'm modeling for will give me an advance. I would, however, love a good cup of coffee if you know where we might find one."

It was Lou's turn to smile. "Would you object to a great piece of apple pie with your good cup of coffee?" he asked. "I know a terrific all night diner not far from here."

"Why not," replied Angie.

Angie and Lou spent the next three hours sipping coffee and talking. Even though Angie found the apple pie to be as delicious as Lou had promised, she stopped at a half slice, concerned about putting unplanned bulges in the frocks she would be modeling. Lou limited himself to one and a half slices, afraid that Angie might think he was uncouth.

In fact, Lou had no reason to worry. The initial twinge of curiosity Angie had felt soon intensified. It puzzled Angie that she was attracted to this awkward young cop. But there was something about Lou that stirred some primitive feelings within her. At the time, Angie wasn't sure whether it was his large intense brown eyes or his big-boned Italian features or the pride he displayed so openly as he told her about his immigrant parents. It would be several years before she could articulate what it was about Lou that really turned her on. Only after their courtship, wedding and first year of marriage did she realize that it was the strong sense of integrity which Lou projected that attracted her. Lou did not speak eloquently about morality and high principles; nor did he flaunt his own virtues. But in his own simple and direct manner, Lou consistently communicated his honesty and decency. Somehow, while everyone around him was working so hard to be "up-front" and "actualized," Lou managed to be himself, without any apparent effort.

For Lou, there was never any doubt. From the moment he met her, after returning from his unsuccessful pursuit of the purse-snatcher, he had been completely enthralled. Initially impressed by her beauty and intellect, he soon came to appreciate her competence and passion as well. His only question had been why such an attractive and talented woman would be interested in him. Not being particularly introspective,

Lou did not spend much time pondering his doubts. Within a few months he stopped wondering and accepted the fact that this glamorous, sophisticated model from the Big Apple actually loved him.

They were married thirteen months after they met, in a simple ceremony in the home of her aunt and uncle in Utica. Angie continued to work as a model for the next year, but the strain of traveling caught up with her and she "retired" and returned to Syracuse to be with Lou.

Although her friends from the fast lane were skeptical about how she would do as a homemaker in primitive Upstate New York, Angie had no problems. She dove into her new role with enthusiasm and boundless energy. She renovated an old wood frame colonial on the East side and promptly filled it with polished refinished furniture and a series of cute little babies. Even with three children, Angie seemed to find time for numerous charitable and cultural organizations.

Culture. Angie's one link to the past was her involvement with the local performing and fine arts groups. Repertory theatre, the Everson museum, the Syracuse Symphony; she worked with all of them and attended every opening. She took Lou whenever she could drag him away from his work. What began as a desire to have his company soon became a plan for enhancing his Cultural Quotient. Finally, Angie's efforts on behalf of Lou became a full blown obsession with making him a sophisticated connoisseur of the finer things in life.

Lou resisted at first, but soon realized that she wasn't going to give up. So he took the path of least resistance, agreeing to attend one event per week. This satisfied Angie for a couple of years until she discovered the continuing education program at University College. Each summer she poured through the catalogue, looking for the right course for Lou. His erratic schedule gave him a welcome excuse for limiting her enthusiastic pursuit of knowledge for him to one course per year. She did, however, manage to slip in an occasional weekend seminar in the Adirondacks. After thirteen years of marriage he had accumulated an impressive record of courses in Medieval Literature, Latin American Politics, and macroeconomics.

Once in a while, usually late at night, while he was on a lonely stakeout, Lou would wonder about his beautiful wife's obsession with self-improvement. The closest he came to a plausible explanation was the semester he took a course in personality theory. He briefly entertained the idea that her zealous pursuit of culture and knowledge was the single thread connecting her to her former life in high society. Somehow that thin connection enabled her to adapt so well to the less glamorous life she now led. The thought made Lou anxious, however, and he quickly dropped it.

Ollie and I were greeted by the aroma of simmering sausage and the sound of Pavarotti singing an aria from *Rigoletto*.

"Hey Marty, when are you going to get a car with a heater," Lou chided, as he watched me rub my hands together.

"As soon as they perfect solar energy," I retorted. "As an entrepreneur from the private sector, I have to be very cost conscious —unlike some of my colleagues on the public payroll."

"Let's eat," Angie chimed in. "The linguini tends to become limp and soggy if it feels neglected; very sensitive, you know."

After stuffing ourselves with Angie's bountiful and delicious Italian feast, Lou and I left Angie and Ollie to discuss contemporary art, and retired to the back porch, which served as Lou's den. Pushing aside the small mountain of textbooks and journals, I gave Lou a full review of the puzzling event of the last few days. I finished by describing Janet's abduction.

"You really get involved in some winners," Lou said when I had finished. "Even Sherlock Holmes would throw in the towel on this one."

"The thing I don't understand," I said, ignoring Lou's remarks, "is how all these weird happenings can be related, though I know they are. I make a routine visit to an old railroad man and before we talk he disappears. Then I get sent on a wild goose chase by a sleazy lawyer. The chase ends with the goose getting me and all I get is a huge headache. Next my missing client's daughter is abducted by three men and dropped off outside of Liverpool."

"And you think all these things are connected?" asked Lou.

"Yeah. I can't tell you how, but I've got this strong feeling that it all fits together."

"Who's the lawyer, Marty?" Lou asked.

"Guy by the name of Lazard."

"Oh shit!" Lou exclaimed, dropping his eloquent pretense. "Lazard is not nice people. He's a real bastard. The word on the street is that he once brought his mother to small claims court when he found out that she had deducted his third grade milk money from his allowance. He accused her of wrongfully using his personal assets to fulfill her parental obligation. Claimed that she had violated his right to free and appropriate nutrition. Seriously, Lazard is a real sleaze. He gets most of his business from the folks who made kneecap repair a subspecialty at Upstate Medical Center. But he's also been known to offer his services to anyone willing to pay his fee. You might say his code of ethics is a little loose around the edges. In fact, it's more elastic than a rubber band."

"A rubber band, Lou? Did you get that from one of your creative expression courses?"

"You like that?" Lou said, "I thought it was pretty eloquent myself."

"You're a regular Mario Cuomo," I said, holding my hands up in a gesture of submission, "Now can we get back to Lazard? Why would he call me up to his office, give me $450, and send me out on a bogus case. Who would put him up to that? I don't travel in the $450-a-day circle."

Lou walked over to a small desk in the corner. He opened a small drawer under the top of the desk and pulled out a dog-eared brown leather address book. "Maybe he was sending you a message," Lou suggested, as he thumbed through the book.

"Sending me a message? What do you mean?"

Lou continued to turn the pages of the address book. "Somebody wanted to scare you," he said. "The lawyer provides a safe and effective way to deliver the jolt. You don't know who wants to frighten you off and the privileged information code assures anonymity for Lazard's client."

"So, how do I find out who wants to scare me?" I asked. "None of my cases involve high rollers. I'm dealing with nickels and dimes, not people who can afford to throw away $450 plus lawyers fees just to deliver a message."

Lou stopped shuffling pages, "I can't give you an answer, but I can tell you who might." He wrote a name and phone number on a scratch pad, tore off the sheet and handed it to me.

"What is a Mannie Bosco?" I asked.

"Mannie's a small time operator with a conscience."

"A conscience?"

"Yeah, he feels guilty whenever he passes up a way to make a quick buck. If he knows that someone is willing to pay for a piece of information he will make it his business to obtain and deliver that information posthaste."

"You think this guy might know who's spooking me?"

"If he doesn't know, he'll find out. Offer him fifty. If he balks, remind him about professional courtesy. If he wants me to let him keep practicing his profession, he'd better be courteous to you. Meanwhile, I'll send someone over to this Photoflash store. Check out what the kiddie-porn sleazebags know."

"Thanks for the tip," I said, stepping gingerly over the mounds of books and papers as I made my way to the door, "I'll keep you posted."

"All right, but if this thing gets too heavy, I expect you to turn it over to us bluecoats. I'm not kidding, Marty."

"Sure, no problem," I said, doubting my own sincerity. My head agreed with Lou's advice, but my gut told me I was unlikely to walk away from it——regardless of how heavy it became.

"Angie and Lou are such a great couple," Ollie said, as we waited for

54

my Honda to warm up.

I knew I was in trouble whenever Ollie spoke positively about another couple. It was a sure thing that she would soon be comparing their relationship with ours.

"You know what I really like about them as a couple?" she asked.

"No, not really."

"They're secure about their relationship. They don't dwell on how they're feeling about each other, or what might happen tomorrow."

"But they're married, Ollie."

"That's not the point."

I decided to quit while I wasn't too far behind. Besides, I had other things on my mind.

I dropped Ollie at her apartment, and drove to my place to call Lou's informant.

Mannie Bosco's voice had the mellifluous resonance of a chainsaw. Fortunately he was a man of few words.

"What you want?" Bosco rasped into the receiver after I had introduced myself.

I explained what I was looking for and made the offer Lou had suggested. There was a brief silence before Bosco responded.

"Okay, I'll call you tomorrow at 3:00 p.m. Give me your number and tell DeSantis not to worry. I'll deliver."

Convinced that Bosco had probably used his daily quota of words, I gave him the phone number and hung up. I did not feel very confident that the raspy-voiced man would produce any useful information, but at the present time I did not see any better alternatives.

Since there was nothing I could do on the Majorski case, I decided to work on the introductory chapter of my thesis. Knowing that I would become distracted by one of my puzzles if I stayed at home, I gathered my notes and drove to my office at the university.

Sitting at my desk in the cluttered space I shared with two other graduate students, I shuffled through my notecards. Looking for inspiration, I didn't need much, just enough to allow me to show how my study was the logical and inevitable outgrowth of the past ten years of research on social perception and birth order. Unfortunately, I couldn't keep my attention focussed on the notecards. My mind kept bouncing from Janet Pafko and her missing father to my frustrating encounters with Ollie. I could barely make sense of what I had written, no less convert it into a coherent rationale for my research project. My pen felt like a weighted iron shaft, held to the desk by a powerful magnetic field.

After two hours of struggling, I gathered up my cards and notebook and put them in my briefcase. I had doubled the length of my introductory chapter. It now contained two paragraphs. Hoping tomorrow would be a better day, I closed up the office, drove home and went to bed.

7

I woke up the next morning to find that the temperature had risen thirty-five degrees. After a leisurely breakfast of French toast and bacon, I scribbled on the back of an old envelope a list of errands that needed to be done: pick up sport jacket from cleaner; buy Ollie a jar of wheat germ; pick up light bulbs and vacuum cleaner bags at K-Mart.

Wading through the slush I cursed the winter weather. The January thaw was a mixed blessing in Syracuse. It was nice to have a reprieve from the bone chilling cold. But the wet trousers, cold feet and mud-spattered windshields that resulted from navigating the melted snow spoiled any illusions of tropical living. And the warm weather seemed to attract a particularly potent and tenacious breed of viral organisms.

I felt as if I were coming down with the flu. My throat was sore and all my muscles ached. Not feeling very confident that Mannie Bosco would deliver the information he had promised, I considered crawling back into bed and pulling the covers over my head. Instead, I took two Tylenol and hydroplaned my Honda through the slush to do my errands.

An hour and a half later, having succeeded in getting everything but Ollie's wheat germ, I returned to my apartment. The bottom of my trousers, and my shoes and socks were soaked. My body felt like it had taken several spins in a clothes dryer. I heated a can of Campbell's chicken noodle soup, and brewed a cup of herbal tea, a habit I had picked up from Ollie. The warm soup and tea made me feel a little better, but my energy level was still low. I lay down on my bed and picked up the most recent issue of *The Journal of Social Psychology*. Professor Singleton had suggested I get in the habit of keeping up with the research literature. The current issue of the *Journal* had an article by a researcher from UCLA who compared the responses of Asian Americans and Hispanics to unfamiliar social situations. The research seemed relevant to my thesis but I had a hard time understanding the author's theoretical rationale. After a few minutes, my eyelids began to feel heavy.

The harsh ring of the telephone woke me. Glancing at the clock, I saw that it was 3:05 P.M. I had been asleep for nearly two hours. Picking up the handset I was surprised to be greeted by Mannie Bosco's raspy voice.

"Hey, I got what you want."

"Okay," I responded. "How do we get to the punch line, Bosco?"

"The punch line is not a joke and it ain't free either. Come to Suburban Park at 9:30 tonight and bring a hundred bucks."

"I'll be there at 9:30. But I'll only have fifty. Lou DeSantis tells me you've got a special rate on punch lines for preferred customers."

"Jesus, you think I'm some kind of discount store or something? I'm just a workin' guy tryin' to make a living."

"Fifty bucks."

"Okay, okay, But you better be on time. I'm a busy man."

I hung up the phone and thought about calling Ollie. Our spontaneous moment of passion yesterday morning had been great. So simple and satisfying. If only the rest of our relationship could be like that. Unfortunately it was not and would not be as long as I wanted a commitment from her and she wanted to maintain her independence.

Since my resolve was not very strong at the moment, I decided not to call Ollie. Instead I opened the bottom drawer of my desk and pulled out last Sunday's *New York Times* crossword puzzle.

Suburban Park used to be a scaled-down amusement park, east of Syracuse in the town of Manlius. It was a family park; a small cluster of games and concession stand surrounded by a merry-go-round, ferris wheel, less-than-frightening roller coaster and several rotating rides. In its day, Suburban Park saw a lot of action. A nice place to take the family on a warm summer night.

Unfortunately, high tech had taken its toll on Suburban Park and its counterparts throughout the country. America's stimulation threshold rose at about the same rate as the nation's deficit, as Disney World and the other giant theme parks bombarded the senses of our young and not-so-young. Television, with its continuous flow of violence and sensationalism, had done its part, too. Before long, Suburban Park joined the phonograph and steam engine on the relic shelf.

Ironically, it was stimulus overload that was responsible for the rebirth of Suburban Park; not as an amusement park, but as an upbeat disco. The apparatus of the park——including the merry-ground——had been taken apart and reassembled in a large nightclub which changed its identity every time the leaves fell. Now it was a neon-filled play space for college students and yuppies. On a good night one could cross the entire floor in no more than twelve minutes.

The current version of Suburban Park was a large bar-like two story building at the eastern end of Erie Boulevard. The dance floor on the first floor was rimmed on three sides by a balcony where less aerobically inclined patrons could observe the flashing bodies below. Each floor had its own well stocked bar. Carousel horses, and ferris wheel seats hung from the ceilings. Brightly painted bumper cars lined one wall, providing cozy seating for couples taking a break from the frenzied pace of the dance floor. The club was filled with lights, multi-colored flourescents, twirling disco balls, blinking strobes. The Rolling Stones were trying to demolish the walls with the assistance of a twenty-four hundred watt Macrotech amplifier and an arsenal of J.B. Lansing speakers.

As I pushed my way through the crowd, I chastised myself for not wearing earplugs. I tried to concentrate through the noise, but the slow motion effect created by the strobe lights made me light-headed. After a moment, I stopped struggling against the intensity and began to make my way slowly through the crowd. I spotted a large, bald man with a plaid sport coat and black turtleneck standing in the rear, at the far end of the ground level bar. I knew immediately that it was Bosco. I squeezed through a small cluster of gyrating bodies and tapped the big man on the shoulder.

"Yeah," Bosco said, turning to look at me.

I could barely hear him. The music pounded in my ears. The blinking lights were making me dizzy. "Bosco, you sure know how to pick 'em. Nice intimate spot. Good place for a quiet conversation."

"Hey, for fifty bucks, what did you expect, the Persian Terrace?"

"Okay, I'd love to trade witty quips with you, but I'm beginning to experience permanent hearing loss."

"The money. Let's see the money."

I pulled out a small roll of bills and counted out two twenties and a ten. As the large man reached for the money, I noticed a small red spot just below his lapel pocket. I wondered whether the spot, which seemed to be growing, was an illusion created by the lighting. Before I could reach a conclusion, I was knocked backward into the bar as Bosco fell against me and slid to the floor.

Even with James Brown shouting about how good he was feeling and the slow motion effect created by the strobe lights, I knew this wasn't the latest dance step.

I knelt down and felt for Bosco's pulse. Nothing. I scanned the room, fighting the dizziness that was overcoming me. I closed my eyes, trying to regain control. James Brown was still feeling good. I wasn't.

When I looked up again, I caught a glimpse of a small, slender figure moving quickly along the balcony overlooking the dance floor. Before I could get a clear view, the figure disappeared behind a large merry-go-round pony suspended from the ceiling .

I pushed my way through the crowd. The tangle of dancing couples and blinking lights made it difficult for me to move quickly. I kept bumping into hard, sweaty bodies as I desperately tried to find a clear path to the exit.

Finally I found an opening and sprinted through the front door into the parking lot. There was no small man in sight. Two cars were pulling out of the lot; one turned left, the other had its right blinker on. I chose the first car, a dark Buick sedan. I raced after it, frantically trying to see the license plate, but the car was too far ahead. I stopped at the curb, gasping for air. A wave of nausea came over me. I dropped to my knees, trying to control my stomach. I had once read that a person who continued to breathe through his mouth would not throw up. I inhaled deeply.

After a moment, my stomach stopped churning. I was upset that I had not gotten a clear look at the man or his license plate. I made a mental note to write to the people who offered the correspondence course in private investigation. The module on identifying suspects just didn't cut it.

The wail of the police siren brought me back to the present. I watched the car turn into the parking lot, then walked toward the two uniformed men who emerged from the car and were moving quickly toward the noisy entrance of the disco.

"Lewis," I called, "wait a second."

The taller officer, a muscular black man, turned to see who had spoken to him. Ernest Lewis was a rising star in the Syracuse P.D. With less than five years on the force, he had already received three citations for exceptional duty and was the youngest black man in the history of the department to be promoted to Sergeant. He was ambitious, but he was also a damn fine cop.

The other officer was a short, stocky man with an unmistakably Irish face. I had not seen him before.

"Hey, Fenton," Lewis said. "What's happening here. We got a call that some guy was lying in a pool of blood in the middle of the dance floor. You know anything about this?"

"Unfortunately, I do, Ernie." I told them about my meeting with Mannie Bosco, the shooting and my unsuccessful pursuit of the elusive man in the Buick sedan. Mercifully, the policemen allowed me to tell my story before we entered the disco. I could not have competed with the blaring music.

As we moved through the crowd of dancers, who seemed to be oblivious to the real violence that had just occurred, the music pounded in my ears. I wondered if my hearing loss would be permanent.

The police officers briefly examined Bosco, concluded that he was, in fact, dead and called in the homicide team. While they waited I ordered a glass of ginger ale, hoping it would calm my stomach. I emptied the glass in two swallows. The carbonated drink burned my throat as it went down, but it made me feel better. So much for the virtue of whiskey. Give me a good shot of Canada Dry anyday.

It took about forty-five minutes for the police to complete their picture-taking and questioning. Fortunately, the management of Suburban Park finally realized it would be prudent to stop the music and clear the dance floor. I found the sound of silence very soothing.

After Bosco's body had been removed, Lewis invited me to Arby's for a cup of coffee.

"Marty, I know you've already answered a lot of questions and you're still upset about Bosco being blown away in front of you. But there's something about this case that really bothers me."

"What could that be?" I asked. "Besides the fact that some old train engineer disappears while answering a phone call and his daughter is abducted and dropped in the middle of nowhere. Besides the fact that I was smashed on the head while trying to find out if some schmuck's investment in a film developing store is being used to satisfy the needs of perverts who get off on seeing pictures of little kids doing lewd things. And besides the fact that some small time informant gets himself killed while selling me fifty dollars worth of information, I don't think anything bothersome has happened to me in the last few days."

"Take it easy," Lewis said. "I know you've been having a rough time. DeSantis called me while the homicide guys were doing their thing. He told me he was the one who put you in touch with Bosco. Lou was real upset. He said Bosco either had some very special information or he was paying back a favor he owed."

"What do you mean, paying back a favor?" I asked.

"Well," Lewis replied, "at first glance it looks as if the shooter really wanted to prevent Bosco from passing on this so-called 'information' to you. That's a logical inference given the scenario as it went down tonight. But what if we assume that everything didn't happen exactly as planned?"

"Meaning...?"

"Meaning, maybe the shooter was not such a good shot."

I felt my last bit of strength slip away. Using both hands, I carefully set the styrofoam coffee cup on the table. "You think he might have been aiming at me?"

"I don't know. Just a funny feeling I have. The shooter...or whoever hired him, must have known Bosco was coming to meet you. If he wanted to keep the information from reaching you he could have taken out Bosco sooner with a lot less risk. Suburban Park provides a little more exposure than your average dark alley."

"Jesus, if I wasn't paranoid before this little chat with you, I certainly am now."

"I hate to be technical with you, Marty, but paranoia is when you *think* they're after you but they're actually not."

"Thanks a lot, Dr. Lewis."

I slipped on my jacket and moved toward the exit. As I reached for the door, Ernie called to me. "Hey, keep in touch, huh?"

"Yeah, sure," I replied, as I pushed open the door and walked out into the unusually warm winter night.

I was not ready to go home. The numbness was fading, leaving in its place a vague sense of uneasiness. I had never seen a man murdered before. Sure, I had seen some pretty vicious fights, had even participated in a few. But the grim reaper had been fairly kind to me. My aunt Betty had died of cancer when I was fifteen, a high school friend was killed in Vietnam and then there was my father.

Dad had been a big, active man. At fifty-five, he played racquetball three times a week, bowled in the men's handicap league, and rode his bike with Ma every Sunday morning.

It was on one of those Sunday rides that Dad had suffered a massive coronary. The rescue squad responded quickly, but he was dead before they reached the hospital.

When my mother returned from the hospital, I was fixing a bologna sandwich in the kitchen. As soon as she asked me to sit down, I knew something terrible had happened. Immediately I broke into a cold sweat. But when Ma told me of Dad's death, I did not react. Her voice sounded as if it were coming from far away. I felt detached from my body. I was, as I learned later, in a state of shock.

It had taken me weeks to be able to react emotionally; months until I could get up in the morning without feeling sick; and years before I was able to work through the loss of my dad. The recovery process had been slow, but relatively complete. My only enduring scar was not noticeable. Since the day my father died, I have not eaten another bologna sandwich.

Now, faced with the mortality of a raspy-voiced man who had come to sell me fifty dollars worth of information, and confronted by my own vulnerability, I was confused and frightened.

My first impulse was to run, to get into my car and drive as fast and far as I could. I might have followed this impulse, except at that moment I was struck by another feeling of fear. I moved quickly to my car, turned the ignition key and backed out of the parking place. I turned left onto Erie Boulevard and right on Thompson Road.

As I pulled in front of the neat yellow frame house, my adrenalin started pumping. I ran up the path between the spruce trees and rang the doorbell.

"Mr. Fenton, what are you doing here?" the pretty green-eyed young woman asked, obviously surprised by this late night visit.

"Janet, I'm sorry to bother you, but I was...concerned."

"What do you mean? Do you have some news about my father?"

"No. I'm afraid not. I had a bad experience, tonight, and...can I come in for a few minutes?"

"Sure, I'm sorry. Come right in."

I looked over my shoulder before entering the house. No one was there. I was almost certain there wouldn't be, but in this situation reason was no match for runaway anxiety.

Over my second cup of coffee that night, I gave a detailed account of the evening's events. Janet sat on the edge of the sofa, elbows on knee, chin resting in her cupped hands. Her eyes were riveted on me. I found myself looking down at the floor to avoid her gaze, afraid I might lose my train of thought.

When I described Mannie Bosco's death, Janet squeezed her eyes shut for a few seconds, then resumed her unblinking stare. After what seemed like hours, but was in fact less than thirty minutes, I finished the story. I was drained, but felt better. Janet offered to refill my cup and I accepted.

As she was pouring the coffee into my cup, she stopped abruptly, spilling a little liquid on the rug.

"Mr. Fenton, I just thought of something. I don't know if it means anything, but, it came to me so quickly."

"What is it?" I asked, spilling more coffee as I rose from the chair.

"Do you remember when you first came to my house. I was telling you about how my father became really upset and told me he knew something terrible but refused to say anymore?"

"Yeah, you said he cried and went into his room."

"Well," Janet continued, "just now, as I was pouring your coffee, I remembered something else. After Dad went in his room and slammed the door, there was a thumping sound. Like he was kicking the baseboard or the chest of drawers. Then the thumping stopped and after a few seconds there was another sound, not as loud as the others. I figured he had sat down real hard on his bed or something like that. Just before that last sound, Dad said something in a really angry voice. At first I didn't understand what he was saying. Then I realized he was speaking in Polish, which he almost never did. *Niech szlag trafi tego rzeźnika*. That's what he said: *Niech szlag trafi tego rzeźnika.*"

"And what does that mean?" I asked, leaning forward.

"Well," Janet replied, "my Polish is not very good, but I think it translates to *Goddamn to that butcher* or *Goddamn that butcher*. It didn't make sense to me, so I guess I put it out of my mind."

"Goddamn that butcher," I repeated, straining to find some meaning in this seemingly inane phrase. I got up and started pacing.

Janet watched intently as I walked back and forth, my intensity increasing as I struggled with the engineer's words. She seemed frustrated; wanting to help me, but not knowing how. After a moment she stood and walked toward the kitchen.

"Can I get you another cup of coffee?"

I shook my head. My heart was beating rapidly and the adrenalin was still flowing. For the first time since Majorski had disappeared there was something to work on. Granted, the lead was flimsy——a Polish epithet, loosely translated ——but at least it gave me something to pursue.

"Janet, think hard. Does that phrase mean anything to you? The neighborhood meat man? Someone named Butcher? Tell me the first thing that comes into your mind."

Janet paused, her coffee cup just below her lips. Her mouth slowly formed into a crooked smile.

"Mr. Fenton, I know that investigators use a lot of modern scientific techniques, but I didn't realize psychoanalysis was in your bag of tricks."

I was so intent on following the lead that, for a few seconds, I didn't absorb what she had said. When I finally grasped her message, I began to laugh.

The tension was broken.

"Good point. I'll try not to get carried away. Maybe we can use a little logic. Do you have a phone book?"

She went into the kitchen and returned with two books.

"White or yellow pages?" she asked.

For the next twenty minutes we poured through the telephone books, searching for a familiar name or place. Janet found the store where she once bought some great Italian sausage and remembered that the receptionist at her dentist's office was named Hazel Butcher. But neither this information nor any of the other butcher references we came across held any meaning for her. She couldn't make any connections with her father. He did all of his food shopping ——including meat ——at the small family grocery store around the corner from their house. She couldn't think of anyone named Butcher that her father knew. He didn't even go to her dentist.

I closed the phone books and stretched my arms above my head. "Let's quit for the night. We're not getting anywhere and I'm tired as hell."

Janet nodded her agreement. She walked to the closet to get my coat. As she reached to hand my coat to me, her eyes suddenly welled up with tears and she began to sob. I instinctively put my arms around her and began to gently pat her back.

"Oh my God," she gasped, "I'm so scared. I know something terrible has happened to my Dad. Billy keeps asking, 'When is grandpa coming home?' and all I can tell him is I don't know. Jesus, isn't there anything we can do?"

I knew that words couldn't comfort her at this moment. I continued to hold her, pausing only to hand her my handkerchief. Janet clung to me, tears streaming down her face.

After a couple of minutes, she stepped back and dabbed her eyes with my handkerchief.

"Do you think my father is dead?" she asked softly.

I shrugged. "I don't know. I'm not really very experienced in this line of work. What I do know is that a small time operator was killed tonight either to stop him from giving me information or...because the killer didn't aim very well. Either way, it's obvious that some pretty heavy hitters are involved. I wish I could give you a more optimistic response, but I can't."

Janet gazed up at me. Jesus, I thought, those damn green eyes. I feel like she's got her own x-ray machine. An image of Sylvia Carling flashed in my mind. She was standing in her doorway pleading for me to keep an eye on her ex-husband. I pushed the painful scene out of my mind. "Listen, Janet, I really wish I could be more helpful to you. If you want somebody more experienced to help find your father, I'll understand. Really, I can even give you some names."

For the second time that evening, she smiled.

"Mr. Fenton, you're a funny man. I wouldn't think of having anyone else help me. You're my one and only detective."

I blushed.

"Okay. I'll give it my best shot." I looked at my watch. "It's getting late. Why don't you get some rest. I'll call you tomorrow."

When Janet didn't object, I picked up my coat and left.

Driving home, the events of the evening caught up with me. I felt very tired. I thought about my fatal meeting with Mannie Bosco and the unsuccessful pursuit of his killer. I reviewed my conversation with Ernie

Lewis and the chilling revelation that I might actually have been the shooter's target. And I thought about the young woman with the penetrating green eyes.

I had seen several sides of Janet Pafko which I had not previously known: the extraordinary intensity she projected and her vulnerability. So different from Ollie whose strength and self-sufficiency often made me feel as if she didn't need me.

In the course of the evening, I also had become more aware of my own vulnerability and I was now even more convinced that I had to help Janet Pafko find out what happened to her father.

Ollie was not there when I arrived at my apartment. She didn't like to be there alone, so I wasn't surprised that she had gone home. Actually, I was relieved. My final few moments with Janet Pafko had stirred up some strong feelings. Having Ollie at my apartment would have made me uncomfortable. It was hard enough sorting out my feelings without Ollie being there. She had left me a note on the kitchen counter saying she had an early appointment the next morning and had left at 11:30 p.m. when I hadn't returned. She also mentioned that Lou had called and wanted me to call him.

I glanced up at the kitchen clock on the wall over the stove. It was one-fifteen a.m. Ordinarily I wouldn't have returned a phone call at that hour, but I knew that Lou was probably reading one of those self-improvement books Angie had bought for him or studying for an evening course she had encouraged him to take.

Lou answered on the second ring.

"Sorry to bother you. I got this message that you had called."

"You bet your ass I called. What am I going to do with you, Marty? I let you move beyond the perimeter of my vision and you come frightfully close to negotiating a permanent appointment with the Grim Reaper."

"What course are you taking this semester, Lou, Essential Elements of Saying Less with More Words?"

"Very funny. I see that your encounter with your own sense of mortality has sharpened your rapier-like wit. Listen, Ernie Lewis called me. He told me about Bosco taking a bullet and he shared his theory about the shooter maybe having bad aim. Are you okay, buddy?"

"I've been better. It happened so quickly. I'm still trying to catch up with myself. Christ, Bosco is dead, I'm on the verge of paranoia, scared that somebody wants to kill me, and I still don't know a damn thing about why Fred Majorski disappeared or what's happened to him."

There was a brief pause. I heard Lou slowly let out his breath.

"Marty, I feel terrible about what happened tonight. Mannie Bosco acted like a tough guy, but he was really a big teddy bear. He used to help around the convent; changed washers when the faucet leaked, helped the nuns move heavy furniture. That kind of thing. Even did some grocery shopping for my Mom when she was laid up. I don't mean that he was a saint. Mannie did his share of mean deeds, but it was all lightweight stuff. Intimidating late payers for the Northside sports brokers, fencing T.V.'s for the discount chain on wheels...I feel kind of, you know, responsible for what happened tonight. Not just for Bosco, but for you too."

That made two of us who were feeling the uninvited burden of responsibility. "But, Lou," I said, "I asked you to help."

"Hey, give me a break. How often do I let down this thick-plated character armor and expose my fragile emotions to the cruel light of day? Anyway, you can count me in. I'm on the case. Tomorrow morning I'll start asking around. I can't do anything official; homicide has its stamp on this one. But I'll try to pick up some information."

"Great. I really appreciate it."

"Sure, no problem."

"And Lou,"

"Yeah?"

"Don't worry. Your fragile emotions are safe with me. My lips are sealed as tight as Sigmund Freud's."

8

At seven-thirty the next morning, I opened my bedroom window and discovered the January thaw was over. Judging from the blast of cold air that hit me, I guessed it was between fifteen and twenty degrees Fahrenheit.

I filled a saucepan with water, put it on the top of the stove, and lit the burner. Then I reached for the telephone.

Ms. O. was working the early shift at We-Care Answering Service. She breathed hoarsely into my ear and informed me that my mother had called last night. I asked if there were any other messages. Ms. O. did some more heavy breathing, gave me a not-so-convincing imitation of Marilyn Monroe trying to make small talk and finally told me no one else had called.

I wondered whether saving eight dollars a month was sufficient reason for continuing to retain the We-Care Answering Service.

My mother answered on the first ring. "Hello Martin, I'm glad you called now. I just finished making my morning list. Let's see, there's something here for you..."

"Ma, you called last night. Is everything okay?"

"Just a minute, Martin, I'm checking my list. Oh, here it is. In this week's issue of *Modern Living* there's an article on the benefits of oat bran. It prevents cancer, reduces cholesterol, it's kind of a miracle food."

"Ma, is that why you called?"

"No, Martin. I called to remind you to call your sister, Grace, in Milwaukee."

I counted to four before responding. I would have counted to ten, but was afraid that my mother would start up again.

"Last time you told me to write to her," I said.

"And did you?"

"No," I admitted.

"Precisely my point, Martin. I read recently that correspondence is a dying art. Young people don't write letters anymore. They prefer to use Ma Bell. So, I thought maybe my son——who is certainly a modern man——might be more inclined to pick up a telephone and call his only sister."

"Okay, Ma. You win."

"When?"

"What?" I asked.

"When are you going to call, Martin?"

I knew she would not quit until I gave her a specific commitment.

"Eight forty-five P.M.," I responded. "I'll call her at eight forty-five tonight. Okay, Ma, satisfied?"

There was a brief pause before she spoke. "Your time or hers?"

Two cups of instant coffee——bad as it was——helped me to gain some distance from my mother's phone call. I had learned to control my response to her constant nagging. I no longer gave in to my urge to tell Ma to mind her own business when she told me——in great detail——how to lead my life. Still, her phone calls never failed to leave me feeling tense and irritated ——as much with myself as with her. I put on a pair of navy blue corduroy slacks, a grey and white plaid cotton shirt and a maroon wool crew neck sweater. I pulled on my lined black boots, grabbed my nylon parka from the closet and left the warm apartment to go out into the cold Syracuse morning.

I knew Lou wouldn't be in his office for another hour and probably wouldn't have a chance to check for information before noon. I decided to so some exploring on my own.

I remembered reading somewhere ——perhaps in one of my correspondence course manuals ——that one should always begin at the beginning. This made as much sense to me as anything else, so I started driving east, toward the railroad yard, where this strange series of events had begun.

When I arrived most of the yard workers were busy with a freight train that had just pulled in. I walked up behind one of the workers, a stout, gray haired man. The railroad man was wearing a gray striped denim jacket and coveralls. An old blue baseball cap was perched on his head.

"Pardon me," I said. "I was wondering whether you could help me."

The railroad man turned slowly. One look at his face convinced me that this man had not spent much time behind a desk. He squinted at me through dark brown eyes set deeply in a face covered with skin that was the texture of leather. The deep wrinkles in his brow seemed to be permanently stained with a dark mixture of dirt and grease.

"How might I help you young man," the railroad man responded in a voice that was surprisingly cheerful. "You look like you're lost."

"No, I'm not lost. I'm looking for some information about a man who worked here."

The railroad man smiled. "You wouldn't be from the Internal Revenue Service, would you? I happen to know that Uncle Sam is very curious. He goes to great lengths to find out about people."

"I'm not from the I.R.S. My name is Marty Fenton. I'm a graduate student in psychology. Fred Majorski asked me to come out here to meet him. Before he told me what he wanted, Mr. Majorski disappeared. His daughter is very worried about him. She asked me to help her find him."

The railroad man frowned. He removed his baseball cap and ran his fingers through his thick gray hair.

"Well, Marty Fenton, I'm glad you're not a Fed. You're a nice looking young man. But I feel very sad about poor Freddie Majorski. I always liked Freddie. He was kind of quiet, but a helluva nice guy and a real good worker."

"What do you think happened to him, Mr. ...?"

"Campbell, Malcolm Campbell."

I extended my hand and Campbell responded with a very firm handshake.

"Mr. Campbell," I continued, "you said he *was* kind of quiet. What do you mean?"

"Marty Fenton, you're some clever fellow. If I'm ever in need of psychological services, I will certainly request your assistance. For now, however, let's cut the chit-chat. Freddie Majorski was not the kind of person to wander off. You could set your watch by him. Punched in at exactly 7:30 every morning. Punched out at 4:15. Not 4:14, not 4:16. Someone told me once—I don't know if it's true—they said that Freddie not only went to the supermarket the same day and same time every week, but he also walked up to the check-out line to pay for his groceries at exactly the same moment every week. So, with that kind of precise regimen do you think he would willingly toss aside his time table and walk away? I don't. I think that Freddie Majorski is in big trouble. No, I take that back. He's not in big trouble. Freddie Majorski is almost certainly dead."

"What do you base that conclusion on?" I asked.

Campbell reached into the pocket of his coveralls and pulled out a pack of Skoal. He took a wad of tobacco and pushed it into his mouth. He glanced at the men working on the freight rain and discharged a stream of brown spit in the same direction. Turning to me, he said, "My conclusion, as you call it, is based on a very bad feeling I have in the pit of my gut. Now, if you want to know the basis of that feeling, I'm afraid I can't be very precise."

Campbell released another glob of dark phlegm. I inhaled, trying not to reveal my reaction to his tobacco chewing.

"What I can tell you," Campbell said, "is that Freddie had been acting more than a little bit funny for a couple of weeks. Sometimes when he was driving one of the big freight engines, he would drift off, lose his concentration. Once, he missed a signal and nearly ruined a boxcar. At lunch, he usually had two or three sandwiches, an apple and a piece of cake. But lately he would sit on the slope over there, and just stare off into space."

"Sounds pretty odd."

"Yeah, it wasn't at all like Freddie to act that way."

I noticed that Campbell was fingering the buttons on his jacket. "Mr. Campbell, are you his supervisor or his friend?"

"Oh no, nothing like that," Campbell replied. He continued to play with his buttons, but did not speak. I waited, sensing the train man had more to say. When Campbell finally spoke, his voice was quieter, not as bold. "I liked Freddie, but he really wasn't my friend. No. It was my sister. Freddie and my sister, Gladys, were sort of close. Not intimate or anything like that. At least, I don't think they were. But they were good friends.

"After Freddie's wife died, Gladys sent in covered dishes for him several times. Freddie wanted to thank her. He asked me to bring her to Danzers' so he could buy us dinner. Gladys——she's a widow——didn't feel comfortable going out to a restaurant, but she invited him over to dinner. With me, of course.

"It was quite an experience. Neither of them said more than a half dozen words. By the time dinner was over I was exhausted. You ever try to sustain a three-way conversation with two people who are obsessed with the patterns on their dinner plates?"

I smiled. "Better you than me. I have enough trouble conversing with Dale Carnegie graduates."

"Anyway," Campbell continued, "neither of them said anything afterwards. I tried to pry, but Gladys simply said 'he's a nice man': Freddie grunted a few times and went back to work. I figured that was it. But they were sly devils. They would get together once or twice a week, usually at my sister's house; always when I was playing cards or off at some sporting event. I don't know what they did——studied dinner plate patterns or something —but they seemed to enjoy each other's company."

"Do you think your sister might know anything about Majorski's troubles?"

"I really don't know. Gladys has kept to herself even more than usual since Freddie disappeared. She won't even answer the phone some days. She's pretty shook up."

A locomotive whistle signalled the arrival of another freight train. Campbell expelled some tobacco juice onto the ground. He extended his hand to me. "I've enjoyed our conversation, Marty Fenton. I wish you success in your quest. Unfortunately, I'm afraid you're too late."

"I hope you're wrong, Mr. Campbell. I hope you're wrong."

"Well, the whistle calls for me," Campbell said. "By the way, my sister lives in the 2700 block of Hawley Avenue. Gladys Blazek, 476-8329."

I watched Campbell move toward the incoming freight train. He walked with a bit of a strut. More like a cocky teenager than a sixty year old man who looked after his widow sister. I liked him. I was drawn to his wry sense of humor, his engaging smile. I especially liked Campbell's candor. I only wished I could find a reason to doubt the railroad man's certainty about Freddie Majorski's fate.

I looked at my watch: 11:45. By the time I found a pay phone, Lou might have some information. I turned into a stiff wind and walked to my car.

The enclosed shopping mall has to be counted among the top five advances of modern civilization. Especially in Syracuse, in mid-winter. Shoppingtown Mall, in DeWitt, the suburb bordering Syracuse on the east, was a particularly fine example of the genre. Prior to being enclosed, Shoppingtown had been a bland, easy-to-pass-by string of shops, anchored by a local department store. Now, protected from the elements by a skin of brick, metal and tar, the expanded mall was the hub of this community. It offered food, entertainment, health care and almost every form of consumable goods to the bored and restless citizens of the east side. Lately the mall had even become a recreational arena, providing senior citizens with a safe and comfortable place for aerobic walking.

I found a parking place six spaces from the entrance. My lucky day, I thought, as I locked my car and walked toward the mall. Inside, there was a row of pay phones just to the right of the entrance.

The policeman who answered the telephone asked me to wait while he fetched Lieutenant DeSantis from the records room.

"Sherlock Fenton, I presume." Lou said, when he finally came to the phone. "I hope you have discovered some obscure but significant clue in the course of your morning meanderings."

"I was hoping that you might have gotten some information, Lou."

"Nothing worth publishing in the *Journal of Police Science*," Lou responded. "I spoke to a few street scholars. They were long on theory and short on facts. The only thing I learned was that Majorski was seeing a woman who lives on Hawley."

"Gladys Blazek."

"Marty, you are a veritable sleuth. I'm impressed."

"Ninety-nine percent speculation, one percent inspiration and a healthy dose of serendipity, to paraphrase Thomas Edison. I ran into Gladys Blazek's brother at the railroad yard. Did your scholars have any thoughts about what Mannie Bosco knew that made him such a good candidate for termination?"

"No, their knowledge base on that subject appeared to be fairly shallow. I have a few more sources to query and I've sent a couple of men out to Photoflash. I'll get back to you later."

"Thanks, I think I'll call on Mrs. Blazek."

I replaced the receiver and walked over to the mall directory. I was hungry, but didn't know what I wanted. The list of fast food restaurants was disappointing. The same grease filled joints that could be found in every shopping mall and commercial strip in Onondaga County, and almost any other town or county.

I turned and walked toward the exit leading to the parking lot. I decided to dine at Mother's Cupboard. If I was going to saturate myself with grease, let it at least be good local grease.

Feeling properly bloated from two jumbo cheeseburgers and a large order of french fries, I set out to find Gladys Blazek.

Hawley Avenue had seen better days. Once a solid, lower middle class family neighborhood, the area just north of Erie Boulevard was euphemistically described as transitional. Those who could, had moved out to the suburbs —Baldwinsville, Liverpool, Camillus, DeWitt. Those who couldn't, coped with or succumbed to the constant onslaught of drugs, violence and prostitution. Without the cohesiveness found in more stable neighborhoods, the residents were unable to mount any resistance to the continuous infusion of group homes, half way houses and rehabilitation centers. These residential settings were established for that sizable group of individuals—those with mental disabilities, substance abuse problems and criminal records—whom society had previously institutionalized far from their natural homes, but who were now being "mainstreamed" back into the community, even if it was not their community.

In one of the ironic twists of social progress, the agencies most concerned about normalizing life for these people, who had been shut out for so long, were unwittingly constructing an institutional ghetto. And the ghetto was being produced within a neighborhood that was already doing more than its fair share to produce clients for these service programs.

It was not a great place to live.

I scanned the street looking for Gladys Blazek's house. I was convinced that she must live in the best looking house in the neighborhood. When I spotted the small gray house with dark blue trim across the street, I was certain it was hers. The neatly trimmed hedge surrounding the postage stamp yard was exactly what I had imagined. I bet that beneath the snow covering the lawn there was not a single leaf or piece of trash.

I crossed the street and walked to the narrow path leading to the front steps. Next to the door were four small blue wooden numbers. Two seven three eight. Beneath the numbers were a row of smaller wooden letters. I had to take several steps up the front walk before I could see them clearly. They spelled BLAZEK.

Before ringing the door bell, I wiped my shoes on the mat. It was that kind of house.

I had never heard door bell chimes playing bagpipe music. I was not a whiz in ethnicity, but had a pretty good idea that Blazek was not a Scottish name. It must have been the Campbell influence. After a moment, the door opened. I was surprised that I had not heard any footsteps. In the doorway stood a short, slightly built woman. Her gray hair was pulled back into a bun. She wore a charcoal gray cardigan sweater over a light blue and white plaid housedress. The dress was long, coming almost to the top of her black ankle-high shoes which laced all the way up the front.

She did not look directly at me. Her hands, which were exceptionally large for her size, were clasped in front of her. Her eyes scanned the floor between me and herself, as if she were trying to find the right place to focus her attention. It was hard to judge her age. She dressed and stood like a very old woman, but had the smooth cream colored skin of a forty year old.

"Excuse me, are you Mrs. Blazek?" I asked.

She responded in a quiet, high pitched voice, sounding almost like a little girl. "Yes, I am."

"I'm sorry to bother you, Mrs. Blazek. My name is Marty Fenton. Your brother, Malcolm, told me where you lived. I meant to call first, but I was in the neighborhood."

"I see." Her voice was even quieter.

"I was wondering if you might have time to answer a few questions. I promise not to stay very long."

The tiny woman continued to survey the floor.

"Ordinarily I wouldn't come knocking on your door in the middle of the day, but it's kind of important. I understand that you know Mr. Fred Majorski."

I noticed that her knuckles turned white as she clasped her hands tighter.

"Oh, don't worry, I'm not going to hurt you...or Mr. Majorski. Actually, I'm a...an acquaintance of his daughter, Janet Pafko. I met Mr. Majorski just before he, uh, disappeared. Ms. Pafko asked me to help her find her father. I'm studying psychology at the university, but I used to work as a private investigator. I just thought you might be able to help me figure out what happened to him.

Gladys slowly lifted her gaze until she was looking at my face. She had pale blue, almost gray eyes. She unclasped her hands and held her right hand, palm up, in front of her chest. My first impulse was to reach out and take her hand. But I quickly realized that was not what she wanted. "I'm sorry," I said reaching into my back pocket. "My mother would be quite upset with me." I handed her my Syracuse University identification card and investigator's license which she scrutinized very carefully. Finally, she handed back the I.D. card and license and stepped back into her house.

At first, I thought she was going to close the door on me. I wondered what I had done to frighten her. Was she suspicious about my identification? Did she believe I had something to do with Majorski's disappearance? As I considered these possibilities, I realized that Gladys Blazek was not moving. She was waiting for me to come inside.

The woman is a master of subtle communication, I thought, as I quickly stepped through the doorway before she changed her mind.

The inside of the house was as neat as the outside. The living room was sparsely furnished. A dark brown upholstered sofa faced a tiny brick fireplace that looked as if it hadn't been used for a long time. In front of the sofa was a low rectangular coffee table, flanked by two matching arm chairs, which faced each other. There was a single magazine, neatly centered on the dark walnut coffee table. The magazine was *Readers' Digest*.

I stood awkwardly at the entrance to the living room trying to pick up some signal from Mrs. Blazek. Unable to find even a small cue, I decided to plunge ahead. "Mrs. Blazek, your brother tells me that you and Mr. Majorski were...uh, seeing each other."

Silence.

"Well, I was wondering if Mr. Majorski might have mentioned...might have said something that made you wonder if he was in trouble. Not that I believe he did anything wrong, I just thought he might have..."

The tiny woman held up her hand and slowly pointed to the arm chairs. Grateful for a break in my monologue I moved quickly to the far chair and sat down. Gladys Blazek walked slowly to the chair facing me.

"Mr. Fenton," she said, in a surprisingly strong voice. "My brother has a big mouth. He shouldn't have told you about Fred and me. It's none of his business. It's none of your business."

"I'm sorry. I can't agree with you. Fred Majorski is missing. You may know something that will help me find him."

Gladys clasped her hands together, placed her elbows on the top of her knees and leaned forward. "You seem like a nice man. I don't want to offend you, but I do want you to understand my position. I am a private person. That probably doesn't surprise you. My relationship with Fred is not something I wish to share with anyone. But, if there is anything that can be done——and I do mean *anything*——to help find Fred, I will do it. Do you understand me, Mr. Fenton?"

I now saw this fragile looking woman much differently. She was definitely not helpless. "I understand what you're saying. Now, I'd like you to try to understand my position. I am doing everything I can to find Mr. Majorski. But I don't have anything to work with. I need some help."

"How do I know?" Gladys asked.

"Excuse me."

"How do I know you're really interested in finding Fred. Maybe you're just running up your time, trying to collect a big fee."

Assertiveness was definitely one of this woman's strengths, but trust was not.

"Listen," I said trying to control my anger. "Last night a man was shot and killed just as he was about to give me some information about Fred Majorski. Another two feet to the right and the bullet would have hit me. Believe me, if I wanted to make a lot of money, there are easier ways. Now, can we stop playing games and get on with trying to find out what happened to Fred Majorski?"

The tiny woman sat very still, hands clasped in front of her. She looked directly into my eyes. "I apologize, Mr. Fenton. I needed to know if your interest was genuine. You have shown me that your intentions are sincere. Now, let's get on with this. I'm very worried about Fred."

For the next forty five minutes, I questioned Gladys Blazek, trying to uncover some information or clue about Fred Majorski's disappearance. I guided her through their relationship, from the silent dinner with Malcolm Campbell, to the last time they were together ——the night before he disappeared. I probed and Gladys responded as we desperately searched for something Fred might have said that would shed some light on why he was so worried. But nothing emerged.

Finally, Gladys stood up and shook her head. "Enough. I can't think clearly anymore. I appreciate your efforts, but I'm afraid I can't be very helpful now. Maybe I'll think of something tonight."

"Okay, but let me ask you to do something. Please write down every name and place that you recall Mr. Majorski mentioning. Don't worry about why or when he said it, just make a list of what he said."

"I'll try. But I really don't think there's anything that I haven't already told you."

I stood and took Gladys's hand. "Fair enough," I said. "I'll call you tomorrow morning."

Gladys walked me to the front door. She held the door open as I passed by her, she tugged on my sleeve. I leaned toward the tiny woman, and she rose up on her toes and kissed me on the cheek. "You're a nice young man, Mr. Fenton. I hope you're as smart as you are nice."

I hoped so, too.

I was tired. The effort to jar Gladys Blazek's memory had taken its toll. I had not yet recovered from last night's shooting at Suburban Park. I decided to return home for a brief rest.

It felt strange, resting in the middle of the day. The last time I had been in bed in the afternoon —alone —had been seven years ago when I was stricken by a tenacious Asian virus that had knocked me on my back for three days.

I stripped down to my underwear and shirt. Drawing back the covers I stretched out between the cool sheets and wished that Ollie was there with me. Just as I was pulling up the down comforter, the telephone rang. Feeling annoyed that my beauty rest had been interrupted before it had begun, I reached over to the night stand and picked up the telephone receiver.

"Hello, Fenton here."

"Fenton, you are one persistent son of a bitch." The man at the other end of the line had a deep, harsh voice. "Don't you know how to take a hint. Bug off before you get hurt."

"Who is this?," I asked, gripping the phone tightly, trying to contain his fear.

"Never mind who I am, asshole. Just listen to what I'm telling you. You're in over your head. If you don't stop probing around, something real bad might happen to you."

In spite of my fear, I began to feel angry. "What about Majorski. I want to know what happened to Fred Majorski, and I'm not backing off 'til I find out."

"You're dumber than I thought, shithead. This has nothing to do with Fred Majorski. This has to do with you minding your own business, or getting hurt real bad. Suit yourself, asshole. It don't make no difference to me."

"You can't intimidate me," I exclaimed, lying through my teeth. "I want to know what happened to Fred Majorski."

There was a click at the other end of the line.

I started to shake. I had to use two hands to set the receiver on its base. Getting up from the bed, I put on my jacket. I didn't know who or where the caller was, but the deep voiced man at the other end of the line knew exactly where I was. My mind raced. Was this guy trying to scare me away? Was the caller trying to find out what I knew? Or was he trying to flush me out, to make me an easy target?

I was too nervous to analyze all of these options. My instincts told me to get out and get away—fast. My brain sent another message.

I turned and picked up the telephone. After three long rings the receiver was picked up. I broke in before the voice at the other end had completed its formal salutation.

"Give me Lieutenant DeSantis. It's an emergency."

Clink. The sound of the phone bouncing reverberated in my ear. Damn, I thought, next crisis I'll try to be more civil.

"DeSantis, here."

"Lou, I'm really glad I found you."

"Gee, Marty, your unabashed expression of positive feeling is very touching."

"Cut it out. I just received a very spooky call. I need some advice."

After hearing my story, Lou instructed the dispatcher to send a patrol car to pick me up and bring me to headquarters. We spent the next hour trying to figure out what was happening. When we were finished neither of us was closer to understanding the telephone call, but I felt a little better.

Lou asked me to come home with him. He had tickets to the Syracuse-Georgetown basketball game. We would have a little pasta with Angie, take in the game at the Dome, have a beer or two at The Orange Grove. Given what had just happened to me, I jumped at the chance to be away from my apartment, in the company of friends.

On my way to Lou and Angie's I realized I hadn't talked to Ollie since the murder at Suburban Park. Being the astute psychology graduate student that I was, I knew that my failure to call her was more than simple oversight.

9

Carrier Dome was a political gift to the Syracuse community. Normally a Republican stronghold, the City of Syracuse and the County of Onondaga in the early eighties, gave a fair share of support to an underdog Democratic candidate who was elected Governor of New York. To return the favor, Mario Cuomo arranged financing for the largest indoor collegiate sports arena in the country.

Located in the southeast corner of the campus, Carrier Dome loomed over the academic quadrangle like an enormous space ship. Fifty thousand spectators could view a football game. More than thirty-two thousand avid fans jammed into the Dome to see the Orangemen play one of their Big East rivals. At times, the roar of the crowd seemed as if it would lift the domed roof off the helium filled arena.

Lou found a parking place on Irving Avenue. We trudged up the steep hill leading to the Law School. "That guy really got to me," I said, as I struggled to catch my breath at the top of the hill. "There was something about his voice; it really spooked me."

"It's normal. Your research subject disappears from under your eyes, the guy standing next to you gets blown away; not really conducive to tranquility."

"I know, but I've been through rough times before and never reacted the way I did today."

"How old are you, Marty?"

"What's that have to do with anything?"

"I read in one of my psychology texts that people entering mid-life, usually in their thirties, start to become hypersensitive to their own mortality. They become real aware that someday they are going to die and it really spooks them. The book said a lot of folks start acting strange. Some go out and have affairs, try to reaffirm their potency. Others quit their jobs, go off and build boats and try to sail around the world, some other crazy shit like that. Some guys just get real jittery."

"If you're trying to suggest I'm going through a mid-life crisis, you better go back to that half-assed excuse for a college and ask for a refund. I know a correspondence school that will cost you only fifteen box tops from your favorite cereal and will give you a better education."

"Hey, I was only trying to be helpful," Lou said defensively. "If you don't want advice, don't ask for it."

I knew that I had hurt Lou. He was a very tough skinned guy, except for two things: his wife and his self-improvement efforts. In the beginning Angie DeSantis had been the prime mover behind Lou's educational and cultural enrichment program. But over time the rough-edged policeman had become genuinely committed to his own personal growth. He took pride in being able to quote Bertrand Russell or recognize one of Bach's concertos. He liked being the tough Italian guy who was as familiar with Michelangelo as with Michael Jordan.

"Listen," I said. "I didn't mean to jump on you. I know you're trying to be helpful."

"Forget it. I deserve it for trying to play amateur psychologist with a full-fledged bona fide psychology graduate student." Before I could think of a clever retort, Lou changed the subject. "By the way, you might be interested to know what my men found at the Photoflash."

"Yeah?"

"A nice old woman who said she never heard of Marty Fenton and thought it was disgusting that people would take lewd pictures of little children."

"But there wasn't any woman in the store. Only two seedy looking guys. Maybe she works a different shift."

"That's what my guys thought, too. But it turns out that this woman——Mrs. Cunningham——and her husband, who own the store, are the only ones who work there. And Mr. Cunningham is in the hospital recovering from back surgery. In fact, the day you were clobbered, Mr. Cunningham was being operated on. Mrs. C. closed the store and spent the day in the hospital."

"So, this guy broke in and pretended to be working there?"

"Looks that way..."

"Which means that Lazard knew it was a setup."

"Probably."

"Probably, my ass. He had to know it. He deliberately sent me down there to get whacked... But why? I've never met the guy before. I don't have any serious enemies——at least not the kind who would pay several hundred dollars just to have me whacked on the head... The only thing I can think of is Majorski. Somebody knows I'm trying to help his daughter and they want to discourage me."

"Could be," Lou said matter-of-factly.

"Oh shit," I said. "That means the bullet that hit Mannie Bosco was probably intended for me."

"Also a possibility," Lou said in the same nonchalant tone.

"What the hell is the matter with you?" I said, anything but nonchalant. "These guys are trying to kill me and you act as if we're discussing Gothic architecture."

We proceeded up the steep incline, in silence. At the top of the hill we merged with the crowd flowing toward the Dome.

"You hear about the new small forward they got, the kid from Spain?" Lou asked. "He's some kind of exchange student. They say he's got a mean corner jumpshot and he holds his own under the boards."

"You mean Hernandez? Yeah, I hear he's pretty good," I responded. "I sure hope he can shoot foul shots."

Lou chuckled. "I never understood how a team with so much talent can be so piss-poor from the line. Man for man they were the best team in the country last year. But they still didn't make the Final Four."

We reached the line approaching the entrance. Dome folklore held that if all the doors were opened at once, all of the helium would be sucked out and the dome would collapse. Tonight, we were lucky. The door we were standing in front of was open and the line was moving quickly. As we shuffled toward the ticket taker, I heard a loud, deep voice behind us.

"Lou, hey Lou, hold up. I gotta speak with ya."

The voice belonged to a tall, broad shouldered man in a green hooded loden coat who was rushing toward us, waving his arms. He pushed through the crowd like a fullback going through the middle of the line, oblivious to the people standing in his path.

Lou held up his hand. "Jerry, slow down. I'm not going anywhere."

The large man continued to plow through the crowd, coming to a stop within inches of Lou. "Geez, talk about lucky breaks," he said, breathing heavily. "You're the one guy I really need to see, DeSantis, and here you are, in the flesh. How the hell are you?"

"I'm great. Listen, say hello to my friend, Marty Fenton."

"No shit," Jerry exclaimed. "This is Marty Fenton? Sweet Jesus, this is *really* my day. Hey, Marty, good to meet you." Jerry thrust a big, beefy hand toward me.

Lou shook his head. "Jerry, your manners are abominable. It is customary, in virtually every culture in the contemporary civilized world for a person upon first meeting another person, to reveal his identity to the other person."

"You slay me," Jerry chortled. He squeezed my hand, very hard. "Pardon my primitive manners, Marty. The name is Jerry Bullard."

"Also known as the Bull," Lou added. "Lieutenant Bullard looks like a big lug, but he's actually the central nervous system of the Onondaga County Sheriff's Department. Jerry runs the information systems unit for the Department. He makes those computers do things that would make Steve Job jealous."

"Steve who?" I asked.

"Steve Job," Lou responded. "The guy who started Apple Computers. Maybe if you educated yourself, you wouldn't come off as being so ignorant. For a graduate student you're not very well informed. Anyway, I remember one time these guys robbed the Syracuse Savings Bank. Got about $200,000. One of the tellers noticed that one of the robbers — a young guy — had on an American University ring. Jerry hooked into their computer system and pulled out a list of recent graduates of American from Central New York. Then he ran that list against the Department's file of recent arrests. He found two matches. One was a two hundred eighty pound young lad who had been caught shoplifting in a health food store. They found the other American U. graduate at home — with fifty thousand dollars in new hundred dollar bills stuffed in the cookie jar."

"Hey, cut it out, Lou. You're embarrassing me. Listen, I surveyed my information network regarding Mannie Bosco. Nothing very solid, but one data bank had some interesting little bytes on his recent affiliations. Seems that Mr. Bosco was spending more than a little time doing odd jobs for Mr. George Hartman..."

"George Hartman, venture capitalist, extraordinaire?" Lou interjected.

"The same," Bullard responded. "Real estate baron, wine merchant, and — most important — senior partner in the Central New York Sports Book. Which, incidentally, you won't find listed on any of your legitimate financial markets."

"That surprises me," Lou said. "I knew Mannie did work for some of the small time bookies. But Hartman is in a different league. He does a good job of hiding behind his legitimate business fronts. We've never been able to link him to the gambling operation. Why would he use someone like Mannie?"

"You think Hartman had something to do with Fred Majorski?" I asked.

"It doesn't make sense to me, but nothing about this case does," Lou replied.

Lieutenant Bullard was becoming restless. "Hey, I've gotta go. I'm meeting my wife at the next gate. She's got the tickets. She's a fanatic

Orange fan and might just go into the Dome without me if I'm late. I'll keep my terminal open, Lou and let you know if anything comes up on the screen. Nice meeting you, Marty."

Before I could respond, the big man was pushing his way through the crowd, leaving in his wake, a line of fans trying to regain their balance.

Lou and I made our way into the arena. It took us a few minutes to find their seats.

"Not bad," I said. We're at least twenty rows below nose bleed level. Where did you get this from, one of your full professor buddies?"

"Nah, just a guy who's tithing his salary to the Orange Booster Club for a pair of season tickets."

"What do you make of the Hartman-Bosco connection?" I asked.

"Not much, yet. I'll make some more inquiries tomorrow. Nothing more I can do tonight. Sit back and relax. Enjoy the game."

The first half was very close. Georgetown shot well from the outside, hitting seven of ten three pointers. The Orangemen had a slight edge on the boards and took advantage of their speed to put together several breathtaking fast breaks. Fortunately for George-town, Syracuse did nothing to damage its reputation as terrible foul shooters, missing eight of thirteen from the line. Halftime score: Georgetown forty-seven, Syracuse forty-six.

We decided to stretch our legs. We worked our way down the crowded aisle, reaching the main level directly across the court from the Syracuse bench. In front of us the sportswriters were putting together their first-half summaries. On the court, the cheerleaders were performing a very acrobatic routine, complete with human pyramids and soaring co-eds. Scanning the floor, I noticed two very well dressed men standing behind the Orange bench. The shorter man was wearing a form fitting gray silk suit. His thinning black hair was combed across his forehead. The other man, taller and thinner, was wearing a dark chocolate colored flannel suit.

"Lou, you see that short guy in the fancy suit, behind the bench?"

Lou squinted, as he peered across the court.

"That's Malcolm Lazard," I said, "the lawyer who sent me on the wild chase after the kiddie porn investment."

"That's funny. You know who the other guy is?"

"No."

"That, my friend, is none other than Mr. George Hartman."

"No shit. That's Hartman. I'll be damned. Hey, let's go talk to them, see if we can find out what their connection is."

"I don't know. I'm not sure that's a good idea."

I did not heed his caution. I hurried along the perimeter of the court, weaving through the crowd in pursuit of Lazard and Hartman. Lou hesitated for a second, considering his options. Then, fearing what I might do, he took off after me.

Just as I reached the corner of the court, a small phalanx of security personnel moved into the aisle, blocking my way. I squeezed between two officers and crossed the aisle seconds before the Syracuse team trotted out of the tunnel leading from the locker room and passed in front of the security men onto the court. Glancing over my shoulder I saw only a wall of blue uniforms and a herd of tall men with short haircuts streaming onto the court. No sign of Lou.

As the sound of the crowd grew to a loud roar I searched frantically for the lawyer and the bookmaker, but I couldn't find them. Catching a glimpse of a dark brown suit a dozen rows above the court, I plunged into the stands in pursuit of Hartman and Lazard. The brown suit belonged to an overweight woman with an orange and white megaphone. I continued to scan the stands, but could not find the two men I had seen talking with each other behind the bench. Looking down, I saw Lou at the base of the stands, craning his neck.

"Hey, Lou, up here."

Lou spotted me and waved for me to come down. He didn't look happy.

"They weren't there," I said when I reached him. "I looked around, but I couldn't see them anywhere."

"Do you think they saw you?"

"I don't know, but I doubt it. This crowd is pretty thick."

"You're telling me. I got hung up in the half-time procession; thought I'd never get through."

"You're just getting old; old and slow."

"Son of a bitch, I'll show you who's getting old," Lou said, reaching for me. I jumped back and tripped over a young boy who was re-enacting Michael Jordan taking it to the hoop. Trying to regain my balance, I stumbled and fell into the lap of a buxom blonde co-ed. The boy glided gracefully on toward the imaginary basket.

I removed myself from the young woman's lap—slowly—and apologized.

"Smooth, very smooth," Lou said, putting his arm around my shoulders and guiding me to our seats on the other side of the court.

The second half was classic Syracuse-Georgetown basketball. The Hoyas were smooth and consistent; the Orangemen were flashy and sporadic, playing hot for a few minutes, then going absolutely flat. Their only consistency was their foul shooting; for every one they made, they missed two. Fortunately, Hernandez, the Spanish kid, had a hot streak with five minutes remaining, hitting two three-pointers and a pair of driving lay-ups. With the Orangemen up by nine, Georgetown put on a clinic on catch-up basketball, but had the bad fortune of running into

Jerry "Jammer" Webster. The Big Easts' leading shot blocker swatted away Ronnie Milton's driving jump shot from the key with four seconds left on the clock.

Final score: Syracuse 88, Georgetown 87.

"Why can't they shoot foul shots?" I asked, as we walked down the hill to Irving Avenue.

It had begun to snow; big wet flakes.

"I hear that each player takes fifty shots every practice," I said. You'd think they would improve, at least a little."

"Maybe its psychological."

"Come on. Give me a break."

"I'm serious," Lou said. "According to some research I read last month, performance declines if one concentrates too much on the task. The researchers found that distracting the subjects from the designated task actually led to increased mastery."

"Great. Maybe you should share your scientific insight with Coach Boeheim. I'm sure he would be very appreciative."

"I'd love to share more empirical wisdom with you, Marty, but I think we should direct our attention to more mundane matters. I don't like the smell of the Hartman-Lazard connection. Sort of like clamping together the loose leads of a booster cable attached to a live battery."

"So, what are we going to do?" I asked.

"We aren't going to do anything now, but go home and go to bed. Tomorrow morning I'll ask Bullard to stroke his computer, see what he can find out about the dynamic duo. Meanwhile, you should stay put in your apartment. Don't want you to run into your friend with the winning telephone personality."

"What about the beer you promised me?"

"Not tonight, buddy. It's been a long day. Besides, the Orangemen beat Georgetown. That's more than I promised."

Compliance had never been my strong suit. That was one of the reasons I liked working on my own. No one to chew me out when I didn't follow "established procedure." No disappointed supervisor to appease when I threw out the game plan and responded to my own hunch. Just solve the problem and stay within the rules——at least, most of the time.

When I awoke in the morning, my fear had subsided. The disturbing events of the past few days—Bosco's death, the chilling phone call—no longer seemed so vivid. Time had blunted their edge. Lying in bed my thoughts returned to Ollie. Why did she need to be so damned independent? It wasn't as if I crowded or stifled her. I felt as if I gave her plenty of space. Granted, my anxiety sometimes made me do things

that might be construed as intrusive. Like the time I insisted on
escorting her home from work after there had been a series of purse
snatchings outside the museum. In hindsight I realized the gesture had
been a little foolish since Ollie was more capable of protecting me than
I was her. But those incidents didn't occur very often and I was learning
how to control my anxiety. At least I thought I was.

I felt frustrated on two counts. My inability to persuade Ollie to make
a commitment bothered me constantly. At the same time, I was upset by
the intensity of my own feelings toward her. I had always considered
myself to be a rational person. I tried to approach life the way I
approach puzzles; with logic and patience. My relationship with Ollie
during the past year didn't fit that pattern. With Ollie I was emotional
and impatient, pressing her to say yes even when I knew that was the
worst thing I could do. In all of my jobs I had let events unfold. In my
relationship with Ollie, I felt compelled to guide destiny, to speed up
that which couldn't be hurried.

The worst part of it was that I was fully aware of what I was doing.
I just couldn't stop myself.

Why couldn't relationships be more like puzzles. Doing the *New York
Times* was a helluva lot easier, and a lot less painful, I conceded as I
pulled myself out of bed.

The snow had stopped during the night and the sun filled my tiny
apartment with warm light.

I dressed quickly, had half of a cup of coffee and hurried out of the
apartment. I considered calling Lou, but decided against it, not wanting
to contend with his objections.

Leaving the building, I looked both ways—my anxiety had not
completely subsided. Finding no menacing figure on the street, I walked
briskly to my car and hastily brushed the snow off the windshield.
Relieved that the engine started on the first try, I pulled out of my
parking space, circled the block completely, glancing at the rear view
mirror each time I made a turn. When I was convinced no one was
following me, I drove cautiously into the center of the city.

The two women guarding the entrance to Lazard's office were as
beautiful as they had been on his first visit. The redhead conferred with
the blonde, who smiled at me as she retreated to the back of the office.
When she returned, she smiled at me again before whispering into the
other woman's ear.

"Mister Lazard is with a client," the blonde said, showing me her
pearl-like teeth. "But, he will be able to see you in twenty minutes, if
you have the time to wait."

With this scenery, it would be a pleasure. "No problem, I don't have another engagement until eleven."

I scanned the magazines on the end table. *Modern Maturity, Forbes, National Review.* Pretty conservative. Not your typical hit man clientele reading fare.

Fifteen minutes later, a tall gray haired woman in a well tailored suit emerged from Lazard's office and walked briskly past me. She appeared to be in her late fifties or early sixties but was remarkably well preserved. I noted that she certainly would have given the blonde and the redhead a run for their money several years ago. Even today she looked very good.

"Good morning, Mrs. Kaston," the blonde said, giving her the same smile she had given me. "I hope you have a nice day."

I was disappointed. The smile hadn't been meant exclusively for me.

A few minutes later, the redhead escorted me into Lazard's office. The short man with the oversized features was dressed in a pale gray sharkskin suit, obviously custom made by a tailor with a European inclination. His wide collared Egyptian cotton pin striped shirt and blue and red paisley tie had clearly not been blue light specials at K-Mart.

The lawyer extended his diamond studded hand. "How nice to see you, again, Mr. Fenton. I must admit to being a bit surprised, however, to be blessed with the pleasure of your company so soon after your last visit."

I started to respond, but Lazard, seeing the redhead with her hand on the doorknob, getting ready to leave, called out, "Cynthia, would you be kind enough to do a small favor for me. Please call Mr. B and tell him the package will be ready in fifteen minutes." Turning his attention back to me, he asked, "Now, what can we do for you today?"

I looked intently at Lazard's eyes, hoping to see a sign of anxiety or discomfort. But the lawyer's gaze was steady, revealing no emotions. There was a dull, flat quality to his eyes, in direct contract to the exaggerated grin he formed with his mouth.

"I'll come right to the point," I said. "In the last few days I have been clubbed on the head while walking on the street, stood next to a man as he was shot to death in a disco, and been threatened over the phone in my own home. I have the distinct impression that you have some connection to each of these very ugly incidents."

Lazard looked bored. "In my profession, we deal with facts, with hard evidence, not with 'distinct impressions.' Would you be kind enough to share with me the factual basis for your 'impressions?'"

"Certainly." I found myself becoming obsequious in the presence of this slick lawyer. I had come to Lazard's office to confront this man. I wanted some answers and knew I would have to be firm in order to elicit the information I needed. Now, within the first minute of our conversation, I felt the balance of control slipping away from me as Lazard took the offensive. "Here are some facts," I said, trying to be assertive. "The clubbing I received occurred as I left the Photoflash, a store to which I had been sent by you to follow a lead on a case that doesn't seem to exist. The man who was killed while trying to give me some information worked for George Hartman, who appears to be a close buddy of yours..."

"And the threatening phone call," Lazard interjected, "how might I be connected to that incident?"

My mind was racing, but I couldn't find the track. I felt foolish and helpless as I struggled for a response. In my gut, I knew Lazard was in the middle of this mess, but I couldn't translate my intuition into a plausible argument. Once again, the old reliable private investigator correspondence course had shown itself to be lacking.

"I am confident that you are very adroit at your profession, Mr. Fenton. Why else would you have been recommended to me? But I'm afraid you've strayed a tad from your recognized area of competence. Please do not misconstrue the context of my observations. I mean no disrespect. I appreciate the discomfort you have experienced and would, if I could, assist in rectifying any injury or injustice you have suffered. Unfortunately..."

My anger finally overcame the self doubt that had been consuming me. "Listen, Lazard. You may be one slick son-of-a-bitch lawyer, but you aren't fooling me one damn bit. Please do not misconstrue the context of *my* observations. I know you are involved in this. I know you are linked to my bashed head, to Mannie Bosco's death, and to the creep who called me yesterday morning. And when I get done putting all this shit together, I have no doubt that I'll find your greasy fingerprints all over Fred Majorski's disappearance."

I thought I detected a faint twitching of Lazard's left eye. Was I actually getting to this master of control or had I simply read into Lazard's facial expression what I wanted to see.

"I can see that you are slightly upset," Lazard said condescendingly. "Perhaps it would be best if we curtailed our little conversation for now, before your accusations lead to a regretful consequence."

Jesus Christ. What's this bastard going to do, sue me? "I like your choice of words, Lazard——*regret*. Very appropriate. Except that you're the one who will have regrets when this is over. It's going to give me great pleasure to place your testicles in a cold steel vise. It will give me even greater pleasure to turn the crank and watch the metal jaws of the vise come together."

This time I was fairly certain the lawyer actually flinched.

"Perhaps you should consider changing professions," Lazard said.

"With your graphic ability to use language, I am confident that one of the noted literary journals, such as the *National Enquirer* would consider putting your talents to work. Unfortunately, my aptitude for vocational counselling is somewhat limited." Lazard glanced at his gold Rolex. "And, I seem to be a little late for my next appointment."

Realizing that it would be difficult to make my point more vividly, and sensing that Lazard wasn't going to divulge anything, I walked toward the door. As I passed Lazard I was tempted to do something menacing, like lifting him by his large ears, but thought better of it.

Lazard offered his hand. Overcoming the excellent socialization training I had received from my mother, I refused to take it.

"A word to the wise," Lazard said to my back. "Checking on whether alleged whiplash victims become disco dancers after dark may not be very glamorous work, but may be more suitable for a man in your position."

"And what position is that?" I shot back.

"I think that is self-evident," the lawyer responded.

Self-evident, my ass. I passed by the redhead and the blonde, and both of them smiled at me, seductively. I punched the elevator button and waited. Maybe I am in the wrong profession. Maybe I should take a few of Lou's night courses and learn to say self-evident and misconstrue. Then I could open my own office and hire some beautiful office help. Better yet, I could ask Lazard's ladies to come to work for me. They couldn't resist me.

The elevator announced its arrival with a ring. I walked in and pushed the button for the lobby. The elevator stopped at the ground floor and the doors slid open.

Filling the doorway were two very large men. They were not smiling.

10

"Marty Fenton?" The smaller large man asked in a voice as deep as he was big.

"That's what they call me," I responded, swallowing hard. I considered bolting, but the eclipse created by the two giants standing in the doorway discouraged me.

"Would you please come with us," the larger large man requested politely.

"What are my other choices?" My mind was racing. If I went willingly, I might be volunteering for my own execution. If I resisted, the commotion might attract enough attention to allow me to make a graceful exit. As I weighed my options, the smaller large man reached into his coat. My pulse quickened.

"Mr. Fenton, my name is Manelli. This is McPhail." He flipped open his wallet, revealing a police identification badge. "Lou DeSantis asked us to find you. He figured you might be seeing that creep shyster, Lazard. Not a bad guess."

I took a deep breath and exhaled loudly. I made a mental note to buy Lou a beer——and to lay off jokes about his night school education.

"Lou said you might be in some kind of danger," McPhail said. "He didn't tell us much, just find you and bring you to him."

"It's a long story, guys," I said. "When the elevator door opened and you bruisers were filling the doorway, I thought *you* were the danger. You scared the hell out of me."

Manelli grinned. "I guess we are kind of imposing. Sorry we spooked you. Better us than them, huh. Whoever *they* are."

"Let's get on the road, Gene." McPhail said. "You ready?" I nodded.

The two men flanked me as we left the building. Even tucked between the large policemen, I felt nervous. On the street I glanced both ways, looking for an unknown danger. Only when we had pulled away from the curb in the unmarked police car and I saw through the rear window that no one was following, did I feel safe.

"What the hell do you think you're doing?" Lou bellowed as we entered his small office.

I looked up at the two men escorting me. "He talking to you?" I asked.

"Don't be a smart-ass, Marty," DeSantis said, pushing himself up from his chair. He walked around his desk and stood in front of me. "You know damn well what I mean. After what's happened how could you wander off by yourself. It's not bad enough that you walk off without protection, but you stroll into that snake lawyer's office like Little Red Riding Hood visiting the Big Bad Wolf's lair."

I considered commenting on Lou's mixed use of animal allusions, but thought better of it. I knew he was right. "I'm sorry. I really am. I just thought..."

"That's problem number one," Lou quipped. "Let me do the thinking on this one. You're out of your league."

"*Mea culpa*," I said, pounding myself on the chest. "Now can we get back to business. What did you find out?"

Lou noticed that the two large policemen were still flanking me. Pointing to the door, he said: "Thanks, guys. You did good. I'll fill you in later."

Manelli looked at his partner, shrugged, then turned and left. McPhail followed.

Lou returned to his desk, lowering himself into the wooden chair. He opened the top right hand drawer and pulled out a pipe and a pouch of tobacco. As he tamped tobacco into the pipe's bowl, I noticed that Lou was looking more and more like a college professor. I knew he was coming up on the magic twenty year mark. Maybe he would turn in his shield and try a new profession. With all the courses he had taken, the University should at least give him a Masters degree, if not a Ph.D. Lou could teach at Onondaga County Community College. Medieval literature or cultural anthropology, or some other intellectual subject. Wouldn't Angie be proud. Unfortunately, even with all of those courses, Lou was still a couple of semesters shy of his Bachelor's degree. Maybe they would let him teach at the regional police academy.

Lou lit his pipe and took a deep drag. The bowl of the pipe emitted a red glow. He rarely smoked a pipe, only when he was struggling with

91

an exceptionally difficult case. It helped him relax and focus.

"I asked Jerry Bullard to make some magic with his computer," Lou said between puffs. "He pushed all the buttons, trying to find connections: Lazard...Hartman... Mannie Bosco...Majorski."

"And?"

"And, he came up with zilch."

"But we saw Lazard and Hartman together at the basketball game."

"Yeah, I know. But according to Bullard there's no connection, at least not officially. Hartman has a string of lawyers on retainer, but Lazard isn't one of them. Jerry confirmed that Bosco occasionally did some work for Hartman, but we already knew that. As for Majorski, he had no traffic with any of those high principled gentlemen."

I sighed. "Which leaves us where we were——no where."

"Not exactly," Lou said. He leaned forward, elbows on the desk, looking at the pipe cupped in his right hand. "The Bull is a tenacious son-of-a-bitch. Give him an assignment to get some information and he takes it as a personal challenge. Won't stop until he retrieves something worthwhile. 'Juicy bytes,' he calls them."

"So what did he find?"

"I'm not sure. Jerry said he milked his information network until it was dry. Just before he was ready to shut down the system, he noticed something odd in Fred Majorski's file. Apparently someone has tampered with his personnel record."

"How did Bullard know that?"

"The latest in data security technology. With all of the computer hackers snooping around, the electronic wizards have devised a system for detecting unauthorized entries, even attempted entries. The best detection systems can even give clues about the hacker's point of origin."

"That's incredible. What did the system tell us about Majorski's hacker?"

"Nothing. Zippo. Jerry says it's really strange. He can tell that someone broke into the file——the computer makes some kind of mark on the record ——but that's all. There's no indication of who entered, or what they were looking for. The weird thing is this security system can sometimes trace where the hacker is coming from: a government agency, private computer, in-state, out-of-state. That kind of information. In this case, Jerry says it looks like the file was entered from within the system. But he doesn't understand why someone would want to break in to Majorski's file from inside."

"What about Majorski's file. Anything promising?"

Lou reached into the inside pocket of his sports jacket. He pulled out a folded computer printout and unfolded it. "Looks pretty ordinary to me, but I thought you could show it to his daughter," he said, leaning across the desk and handing it to me.

I scanned the paper. Name, date of birth, address, number of years with the railroad. Nothing special. Nothing to justify kidnapping an old man. "I'll run it by Janet Pafko's house. Maybe she can see something we can't."

"Okay," Lou said, reaching for the phone. I'll have Gene drive you over."

I started to protest, but the image of Bosco crumpling to the floor of the disco brought me up short. "What's the matter, you don't like me any more? Can't McPhail come with us, too?"

The ride to Janet Pafko's house was uneventful. I discovered that Gene Manelli was a basketball fanatic. We played hoops trivia, starting with Dolph Schayes, Paul Seymour and the old Syracuse Nats of the 1950s and finishing our ride with speculation about who would be in the Final Four in March. Our most heated exchange was a debate over who was the greatest player to put on an S.U. uniform, with Manelli favoring Dave Bing and me casting my vote for Billy Owens.

As we pulled up in front of the house, I saw Janet turning the corner. She was walking toward us with a brown paper sack in her arms and Billy hanging on to her coattail, kicking at the snow piled along the edge of the sidewalk.

"Mr. Fenton," Billy called when he spotted us. "You wanna make a snowman with me?" The little boy ran directly at me, his hands reaching out and up. I grabbed Billy under the arms and lifted him above my head. He squealed with delight.

"The snowman will have to wait, Billy," I said looking up at the little boy. "But how about a quick airplane ride?" I shifted my right hand to the boy's right leg and, holding the boy horizontally above my head, twirled around several times, dipping and raising Billy as we turned.

Billy squealed even louder.

Gently lowering Billy to the ground I asked Janet, "Would you please look at something for me?" I pulled the printout from my pocket and handed it to her. "This is your father's personnel record. I need to know if there's anything unusual about it."

"But, what does Dad's work record have to do with all of this?"

"I don't know. That's why I want you to check it."

Janet shrugged. "Okay, I'll take a look at it." A cold blast of wind made her shiver. "Can we go inside while I read this?"

I took Billy's hand and started up the path. Manelli and Janet followed. Just before we reached the front door, another strong gust of wind blew Billy's cap from his head and carried it out toward the street. Janet turned and ran after the cap. As she stooped to pick it up, she caught a glimpse of a large black four-door sedan cruising past the house. Two large men filled the front seat.

"It's them, it's them," she screamed, pointing at the black sedan. "Those are the men who grabbed me and drove me out to Liverpool."

I let go of the little boy's hand and started to run after the sedan. Manelli ran in the opposite direction, toward his own car. "Come on, Fenton, let's catch those bastards."

I pivoted and slipped on the icy pavement. Recovering my balance, I hurried to Manelli's car.

The driver of the black sedan floored the accelerator, the car lurched forward, made a sharp left turn and sped east on Grant Boulevard. Manelli pulled away from the curb in pursuit of the black sedan.

Manelli's car hit a patch of ice, the tires spun and the rear end fishtailed. By the time he regained control of the car, the black sedan was out of sight.

After several blocks, Manelli gave up and pulled over to the curb. "Did you get the license number?"

"No, I thought that was your job."

"Hey, don't get smart, guy. We blew it. We were a little too slow and they were a little too fast. I'll own my screwup. How about you?"

I looked at the big policeman. Up to this moment I had seen him as nothing more than a tough, invulnerable bodyguard, an oversized security blanket. Now I was seeing another side: the wrinkles on his forehead, the disappointment in his voice. "Okay," I said, raising my hands in surrender. "So I won't qualify for the Olympic two hundred meter dash. Big deal."

Manelli gave me a friendly punch on my upper arm; I winced. He put the car into gear, made a U-turn and drove back to Janet's house.

Manelli decided to wait outside in the car, in case the black sedan returned. The rest of us entered the warm house. Janet fixed some coffee for us and poured a glass of milk for Billy. After setting out a plate of cookies, she sat down and began to read her father's personnel record.

"Majorski, Fred...railroad engineer Grade 3...Date of employment, September 16, 1954...Date of birth, March 7, 1927...Place of birth...Bialogard, Poland. Hmm, that's funny."

"What's funny?" I asked, finding myself riveted, once again, by her beautiful green eyes.

"They misspelled the place where Dad was born. Maybe they abbreviated it. He was born in Bialystok, a city in northeastern Poland. He came over here as a young boy during World War II. His parents sent him and his older brother to England just before the Nazis invaded Poland. They stayed with an uncle in Manchester for a few months before coming over to live with family friends who had moved to Buffalo in the 1930s. Dad's parents died in a concentration camp. He was raised by the family in Buffalo."

I interrupted my eye contact with her and returned to the personnel record. "Notice anything else on the printout?"

Janet scanned the computer sheet. "No, nothing unusual, just basic information: address, family members, work record. It all looks okay to me. What are you looking for, Mr. Fenton?" she asked.

I took a sip of coffee and held the cup in both hands, feeling its warmth. "I wish I knew, I wish I knew." I walked over to the small bookcase on the wall behind the sofa. I scanned the titles, not knowing what I was looking for. *Reader's Digest Condensed Books*, an old *Time-Life* series, several volumes of the *Britannica* encyclopedia, a few hard covered novels. Must have gotten one of those four-for-a-dollar Book of the Month Club deals, I thought, running my finger along the spine of a dusty leather bound volume of the Harvard Classics.

"Did your father do any writing——a journal, letters? Was there anyone he corresponded with regularly?"

Janet considered my questions for a few seconds, then shook her head. "Dad was as good at writing as he was at talking. Ronald Reagan had no reason to worry about Dad challenging him for the title of Great Communicator."

I replaced the Harvard Classic in the bookcase and walked to the sofa. "Janet, I don't want to be intrusive, but I'm wondering whether you've made any effort to locate any clues to your father's disappearance. You know, looked through his dresser drawers, cleaned his dresser drawers. That kind of thing."

She raised her eyebrows in surprise. "No, I...I just didn't think of it. Dad is such a private person..."

"I know this is difficult for you, but we're really in a blind alley. We need more guidance and it's possible there may be something in the house that will help us. I think it's time to do some searching."

I went out to tell Manelli we would be awhile. Hoping to appease him, I brought him a hot mug of coffee. Manelli grumbled, but agreed to stay put for awhile——if I brought him a donut to go with his coffee.

Janet and I went through Majorski's belongings. I was surprised by how impersonal the trainman's room was. There were few signs of personal identity: no pictures or mementos, only a handful of correspondence, none more intimate than a Niagara Mohawk electric bill. After a half hour of futile searching, Janet replaced the last pair of her father's undershorts in the dresser and pushed in the drawer. "That's it. We've gone through everything. Did you find anything useful?"

"I'm afraid not. Your father's room isn't exactly a rich source for a biographer."

Janet started to smile, but her lip began to quiver. Her eyes welled up with tears and she began to cry. She sat on the edge of her father's bed and put her hands to her face. Her body began to shake.

Once again, I found myself feeling helpless and confused; angry with myself for reactivating her grief, frustrated because I was no closer to understanding Majorski's disappearance than I had been when I first realized the railroad man was missing. And bothered by the increasing intensity of my feelings for the young woman with the beautiful green eyes.

Life used to be simpler, I thought, as I tried to comfort Janet Pafko. Though, at that moment, I couldn't remember when.

As I sat on the edge of the bed with my arm around Janet's shoulders, I suddenly recalled something she had said when I came to her house the night Bosco was murdered. I jumped up and started pacing.

"Do you remember the other night you were telling me about your father becoming upset and cursing in Polish? 'The goddamn butcher' or something like that."

Janet nodded.

"You said just before he said that, there was a sound, like he was sitting down hard on the bed."

"That's right," Janet said, composing herself.

"Maybe he wasn't sitting down on the bed. Maybe he had lifted the mattress and was dropping it back onto the bed."

Janet stood up and turned around. Bending over, she reached under the mattress and began to lift. "Will you give me a hand, Mr. Fenton?"

Together we pushed the mattress up on its side, letting it rest against the wall. Stepping back, we noticed it at the same time.

There, in the middle of the box spring, was a single sheet of white, lined paper, folded twice.

We took Janet and Billy to her best friend's house for safekeeping, then headed for the Public Safety Building.

We drove downtown in silence. Manelli concentrated on driving while I stared through the side window trying to figure out what Majorski's note meant. We drove past Ollie's apartment and I was tempted to jump out of the car, run up to her flat and insist we complete the conversation we had begun in front of the Everson. If only I could understand what drove her away from close relationships, I was sure we could work things out. Unfortunately it was mid-afternoon and Ollie was still at work. I made a mental note to call her as soon as I got home.

Manelli pulled into the underground parking deck and parked in the section reserved for the police. We entered the building at the basement level, pushed the elevator button, and waited. Stepping inside the empty elevator we moved to the rear and rode up to the eighth floor. We walked briskly along the corridor, turned into the Special Services suite and knocked on the door of Lou's office.

"Come in, come in," Lou called. "The suspense is killing me." As soon as I entered the room, Lou reached across the desk. "Give it to me, Sherlock," he said, snatching the paper from my hand. He unfolded and read the note. Then he read it again. When he was finished, Lou put the paper on his desk. He scratched behind his right ear, then picked up the paper again. He shook his head as he tried to make sense out of Fred Majorski's cryptic note.

Szmalicovniki
Dodge
NIO 58

"What the hell does this mean?" DeSantis asked, waving the paper in front of my face.

I shrugged. "Beats me. His daughter knows some Polish, but she didn't recognize the first word. Hell, I can't even pronounce it. Looks like he may be describing a car. Those numbers may be part of a license plate."

Lou picked up the telephone, switched on the intercom line and pushed the number two button. Almost immediately an attractive, tall blonde woman opened the door and walked into Lou's office. She was dressed in a crisp white blouse with a blue tie and slacks that accented the nice curve of her hips. She was undoubtedly the most beautiful policewoman I had ever seen.

"Julie, I need some research. Call Motor Vehicles and ask for a list of all license plates starting with NIO 58. And ask communication to locate Buddy Fedorski. Have him come in ASAP."

"Is that all?" she asked. He nodded.

The policewoman waved to Manelli, gave me a brief smile and left.

"I would have introduced you," Lou said, "but I didn't want to get Ollie angry at me. She might decide to use my neck as a hand grip exerciser. Besides, Julie's married to a former Syracuse linebacker."

The three of us discussed the events at Janet Pafko's house. We went over the details several times: the men in the car, Majorski's note, the connection to Janet Pafko's abduction. Each time we drew a blank we became more frustrated. When we heard the knock on DeSantis's door, we were relieved, grateful for the interruption in our dead end search.

"Hey, Lou, what's up?" The man in the doorway was a striking contrast to the large, imposing policemen I had recently encountered. He was short and thin, with narrow shoulders and a small head. He looked youthful in spite of his full head of gray hair. I guessed he was in his late fifties. If he were not wearing a police uniform, he could easily be mistaken for one of the jockeys at Vernon Downs.

Lou introduced me to Buddy Fedorski and the two policemen chatted about each other's families. When they had exchanged updates, Lou picked up the piece of paper on his desk and handed it to Fedorski. "What's this word on the top mean, Buddy?"

The small policeman pulled a pair of half-frame reading glasses from his shirt pocket and placed them on the middle of his nose. Holding the paper at arms length he studied the Polish word. After a few seconds, he handed the paper back to Lou, removed and folded his glasses and placed them back in his breast pocket.

"Strange, Lou, very strange," he said looking puzzled. "This isn't a common word. In fact, it isn't used at all, now. Hasn't been used for more than forty years. *Szmalcovniki* describes a group of sleazeballs who operated in Poland during the Holocaust. These guys used to prey on Jews who lived in the ghetto. Sometimes they promised them special favors, like hiding their children from the Nazis or helping them escape. Other times they threatened to turn in the frightened ghetto dwellers unless they came across with whatever the *Szmalcovniki* wanted. The payment they demanded came in many forms: money, jewelry, sex. Once they got what they wanted, these animals almost never delivered on their promises. Some of the scumbags killed their victims with their own hands after they had gotten everything they could from them. They were your basic low-life extortionists. Blood-sucking blackmailers."

"What happened to these guys?" I asked.

"Some of them were dealt with by the post-war government, a few found justice at hands of the Jewish resistance fighters. Most of them got away clean, faded back into the community and found some other sleazy way to exploit helpless people. I think the Israelis managed to locate a few of the more notorious thugs, but I'm afraid most of them got away."

"Real charming individuals," Manelli said, curling his lip in disgust.

"Did any of them leave Poland?" I asked.

Fedorski shrugged.

"What are you getting at, Marty?" Lou asked. "You don't think Majorski was mixed up with that group, do you?"

I shook my head. "No, and I'm pretty sure he isn't Jewish. They have all kinds of Blessed Virgins and crucifixes in their house."

"Maybe Majorski saw one of these guys," Lou said. "He could have known him in Poland and run into him somewhere. He might have threatened to turn him over to one of those Jewish groups that track down Nazis all over the world. Or maybe he decided to give this guy a little of his own medicine. Hit him up for some big bucks in return for keeping quiet."

"I don't know about the extortion bit," I responded. "Majorski didn't strike me as that kind of guy. But the rest of it seems to fit. His daughter said he was very upset before he disappeared; seemed to be struggling with some awful dilemma. And I remember his daughter telling me that when her father was banging around his room, she heard him muttering in Polish. 'Goddamn that butcher,' or something like that. Sounds like a pretty accurate description of the kind of thug Buddy was telling us about."

Lou turned to Fedorski. "Ring any bells, Buddy?"

Fedorski scratched his head and thought for several seconds before responding. "I don't know. I don't know. This may be off the wall, but I remember Ma talking about a small group of deluxe sleazeballs in her hometown. There were three of them and they specialized in young Jewish women, who were often no older than sixteen or seventeen. They would promise to help the women and their families. Hide them on a farm, arrange for them to leave Poland. In return, these goons would demand to have sex with them. Not ordinary sex, real kinky, perverse stuff. Once the goons got what they wanted, they changed their story from a promise to a threat. Told the girls that unless they kept coming across, they would turn them over to the Polish police, who were even worse than the Nazis."

Before Fedorski could continue, there was a knock on the door. "Come in," DeSantis called. The door opened slowly and the attractive young policewoman poked her head into the room.

"What's up, Julie? Find anything?" Lou asked.

"Not much. There are only seven cars with license plates that begin with NIO 58. All of them were registered in Putnam County, in the Hudson Valley. All but two still list their current address in Putnam. Neither of the other two reside in Onondaga County. We're going to run criminal record checks next."

"Thanks. Stay with it," Lou said. The policewoman backed out of the room, pulling the door closed. Lou turned to Fedorski. "Anything more on the 'Polish Princes'?"

"These three thugs were nicknamed the Butcher, the Baker and the Candlestick Taker. The Candlestick Taker had a thing about silver: coins, jewelry, anything he could get his hands on. The Baker was obsessed with the ovens of the concentration camps. He loved to torment his victims with graphic descriptions of what it would be like for them if they went to the camps. The Butcher... well, he was the worst of all of them."

"You said your mother talked about these three creeps?" I asked.

"Yeah, that's right. She always told stories about the old country."

"Let's go talk to her," I suggested. "Maybe she can give some clue about the Butcher."

Fedorski looked down at his shoes.

"No good, Marty," Lou said. "Buddy's mom died last year."

"I'm sorry," I said.

"No problem," Fedorski responded.

Lou rose from his desk, and walked over to the gray haired police-man. He placed his hand on Fedorski's shoulder. "I appreciate your coming in, Buddy. We're still in the dark, but at least we know there's a light switch somewhere out there. Okay if we call on you again?"

"Anytime. Later, guys," Fedorski said, waving to Manelli and me as he moved toward the door.

"Hey," I called, as Fedorski reached for the doorknob. "What town in Poland did your mother come from?

"Bialystok," Buddy replied. "She was born and raised in Bialystok."

11

As soon as Lou finished dialing the number he knew his telephone call was in vain. This was Wednesday and Wednesday night was when the City-County Employee Bowling League played. Jerry Bullard was a bowling fanatic. He always went home early on bowling night. Rumor had it that Bullard mapped out his team's strategy for the evening on his home computer, but no one had ever caught him in the act.

After two rings Lou returned the handset to its base. "That's it. Let's call it a day." He reached back and lifted his jacket off the old wooden coat tree. Putting on his jacket, Lou walked around to the front of the desk and perched himself on top of a pile of daily reports.

"Okay," I said before Lou could speak. "Let's skip the lecture. I know it's a jungle out there. I know the guy who threatened me is probably connected to the lump I took on my head and to Mannie Bosco's murder. And I know you're concerned with my safety and well-being. But I'm too old for a babysitter. It's time to give Manelli a break. I promise to be careful, Lou."

"Sure, no problem. You're a big boy now. Listen, I've got to cover a fund raising dinner for the Democratic Party tonight. Black tie, speech by the Governor, rubber chicken, the whole bit. Want a free meal?"

"Nice try, but I think I'll pass. I haven't seen Ollie in a few days. Don't worry. She's not as big as Manelli, but she's pretty tough."

Lou held up his hands in surrender. "As you said, you're a big boy. Remember how you felt yesterday though. After you received that threatening call. Be careful."

"I will. I'm your basic arm chair investigator. None of this macho stuff for me."

"I'm serious. I don't want to see that good brain of yours experience any unnecessary trauma. I'll call you in the morning. Between Jerry Bullard and Fedorski's Polish relatives we should be able to get a lead on this butcher guy."

Ollie greeted me with less than unbridled enthusiasm. She was annoyed and upset that I had once again failed to contact her for several days. My explanation about not wanting to worry her wasn't well received, especially since she had heard on the news that I was standing next to Mannie Bosco when he was shot to death. After several futile attempts at convincing her that my lack of contact had been in her best interest, I changed my tack. "So, how about a pizza. Wouldn't you like to share a special at Twin Trees. Or if that's too far we can drive up to Cosmo's on Marshall Street. Maybe they have one of those old movies you like playing on campus tonight."

"I don't think so, Marty."

We were standing in Ollie's living room, just inside the entrance to her apartment. I still had my coat on. Ollie was dressed in a pair of loose fitting blue cotton shorts and a grey hooded sweatshirt. She had just finished a light workout. I had a strong urge to throw my arms around her and squeeze very hard; to kiss and make up. But seeing Ollie standing in front of me, arms folded across her chest, cold eyes focused on my face, I controlled my impulse. Rejection by itself would be bad enough. Being flipped on my back was more than I could handle. I took a step backward.

"Just because I don't want to marry you doesn't mean I don't care about you," Ollie said. She was trying hard to hold back the tears that were welling up. "Damn you, Marty. Why didn't you call? I was worried sick about you, not knowing where you were or what might have happened to you."

I was shocked. I knew that Ollie was capable of having strong feelings, but I had never seen this side of her. I had seen her anger and her passion, even her tenderness. But I had not seen her so visibly upset and worried, so vulnerable. "I'm sorry, Ollie. I'm really sorry. I didn't know you would be so bothered. I figured you're tired of me pestering you. With all that we've been going through lately, I thought you might appreciate some distance." I didn't add that I was caught up in trying to help Janet Pafko find her father and was more than a little concerned about my reaction to Janet, not to mention Ollie's reaction if she discovered the real reason I was putting myself at risk.

The tears were streaming down Ollie's face, now. I took a step toward her, but she held up her hands to let me know I shouldn't come any closer. "You're such a jerk, sometimes," she said to me as she turned to go into the bathroom. I didn't argue with her.

In a few minutes, Ollie emerged, her face washed and her eyes dry. She walked up to me and briefly touched my cheek with her fingers. "I've got an opening, tonight. A traveling exhibition of Eskimo art just arrived at the Everson. There's a small reception for the Board and patrons of the Museum. You want to come?"

The last place I wanted to be, this evening, was an art museum filled with the rich and super rich of Onondaga County. The only person I wanted to be with was Ollie. The choice was not difficult.

"Sounds fitting, Eskimo art in mid-February. Maybe we can catch a pizza afterward?"

"We'll see," she said, smiling as she headed toward the bedroom to change.

I was always amazed by the amount of wealth in Syracuse. For a small, upstate city, Syracuse had a large number of well-to-do families. Though it still stacked up as a poor community in relation to Rochester, its neighboring city to the west, Syracuse had its fair share of spending power.

Looking around the exhibition area in the Everson, I recognized a number of industrialists and professionals, dressed in tuxedos and formal evening gowns. There were philanthropists, power brokers, the people who made things happen in the Salt City. Italians, Irish, Eastern Europeans; Catholics, Jews and WASPs; even a small number of blacks could be counted among the elite of Onondaga County.

They were a handsome group of people, looking healthy and fit for the most part. Even in the middle of winter many were tan, having recently returned from trips to Florida or the Caribbean.

As I scanned the crowd of well-dressed people, I noticed a particularly striking silver-haired woman in a long black peau de soie gown. She was tall and slender, but it was her face, with the prominent high cheek bones and pale blue eyes that made her stand out. Many of the younger women, attractive as they were, paled by comparison.

There was something familiar about the tall, elegant woman. I knew I had seen her before. She was not a woman I would forget, but I couldn't place her. I surveyed the crowd, trying to find someone I might associate with the silver-haired woman.

On the other side of the room I spotted Lazard, my favorite lawyer, wearing a black satin dinner jacket. Seeing Lazard jogged my memory. The elegant woman had been in Lazard's office while I was in the waiting room.

"Who's that tall woman?" I asked Ollie, pointing in her direction.

"Shouldn't you be more discreet," Ollie responded, poking me in the ribs. "If you're interested in another woman, at least have the decency to keep it to yourself."

"I'm serious," I pleaded, stepping back and folding my arms across my ribs.

"Relax. I might feel threatened, but I know she's already spoken for. That's Emma Kaston. She's active in refugee resettlement. She's also involved in the art world; very interested in permanent acquisitions for the Museum. Brings a few assets of her own to the marketplace."

"She is kind of attractive, now that you mention it," I quipped. This time I didn't cover my ribs quickly enough. "Ouch! Take it easy, Ollie." Her poke hurt, but it pleased me that she had reacted as she did.

"Mrs. Kaston has other assets as well. She's married to Paul Kaston, Chairman of Atlas Industries."

"Isn't that the conglomerate that just bought the Healthfirst Pharmacy chain?" I asked.

"That's the one."

"Jesus, she could probably buy the entire Everson Museum. Now I'm really confused. What's a classy lady like her doing with a sleaze like Lazard?"

"What do you mean?"

Realizing I hadn't told Ollie about the first time I had seen Emma Kaston, I briefly explained how I had seen Mrs. Kaston leave Lazard's office while I was waiting to see the attorney.

"That is puzzling," Ollie said. "Lazard is not as much of a lightweight as you would like to believe——though he is a little slick around the edges. But, I'm certain Emma Kaston has access to the best lawyers in the city."

"I think I'll ask Mrs. Kaston about her choice of attorneys," I said, stepping toward the tall, elegant woman.

"Marty, not now."

"What's the matter?"

"We're here for an art reception, not an interrogation. This is not the time or place to ask Mrs. K about her taste in lawyers."

Remembering her displeasure with my immersion in work during the past few days, I decided it would be better to postpone my inquiry into Mrs. Kaston's relationship with Malcolm Lazard. I would ask Lou in the morning.

"So what's so special about Eskimo art?" I asked.

"You want to go, Marty?"

"Uh huh."

"Okay, give me a minute. I want to make sure everything's okay."

"Yeah. Better turn down the heat. Recreate the natural habitat of the soapstone seals."

Ollie glared at me. "Sit on an iceberg, Fenton."

Bob Cohen

It had begun to snow again. Big wet flakes floating down from a dark grey sky. Heavy flakes, splattering on the windshield, shrinking slowly as the air from the defrost warmed the window. Peering through the splotched windshield, I was mesmerized by the thick stream of white flakes continuously flowing into the twin beams of the car's headlights. The snow was so pretty. Too bad it was such a nuisance. Pulling myself out of the trance, I looked over at Ollie. She was sitting very still, her eyes closed. I wondered whether she was sleeping or lost in fantasy. I hoped I was playing a major role in her reverie, but feared that I had no part at all. Given my extended absence without contact and my inane explanation, I was fairly confident her fantasies were more likely focused on Eskimo sculpture than upstate New York graduate students.

She looked so serene. Maybe she had forgotten she was annoyed at me. I really wanted this evening to have a happy ending.

The absence of parking spaces in front of my apartment building didn't bode well for the evening's outcome. I turned the corner and found a space between two Toyotas. I gently nudged Ollie. She rubbed her eyes, then stretched. When she looked over at me, I thought I detected a hint of a smile.

There was still hope.

The wind had picked up since we had left the Everson. I turned up my collar. Ollie pulled the hood of her parka over her head. We quickly crossed the street, hunched over to avoid the wet, wind-driven snow. As I stepped onto the curb, I heard footsteps coming toward me. A man called my name. I didn't recognize the voice and it didn't sound friendly.

Instinctively, I raised my arms and hunched my shoulders protectively. Unfortunately my instincts were too slow. A large fist crashed against the side of my head, I felt my knees buckle. I fell hard against the fender of a car and slid to the pavement.

I must have lost consciousness for a few seconds because I didn't recall sitting down on the sidewalk. When I looked up, I saw two large men standing above me. Before I could react, I heard a thud and saw a blurred figure catapult off the hood of a car, pass over me and kick out at the man standing closest to me. The large man slammed against his partner, and both men fell to the ground. The man who had been kicked stumbled to his knees and lunged at the figure who had delivered the powerful kick. The fast-moving figure leaped away from his grasp, managing to get behind him. Grabbing the large man by the hair, the leaper pulled him off his knees, planted a foot on the small of his back and sent him sprawling face first into the bushes in front of the apartment.

The other man managed to get to his feet and move behind my agile defender. Unfortunately, I was too dazed to respond, other than utter a

105

muted grunt. The leaper turned in time to see the large man lunge. The lithe figure dropped to one knee, reached up and flipped the assailant over on to his back.

Before turning to help me, Ollie delivered one final kick, jamming the toe of her right boot squarely into the crotch of the man lying on the sidewalk. The large man folded like a jackknife. Hugging his knees, he rolled onto his side and began to groan.

Then Ollie grabbed me by the wrist and pulled me to my feet. Sensing that I was still dazed, she took my face in her hands and drew me toward her. "Listen to me," she yelled. "We've got to get out of here quickly." She yanked my arm and began to run. I slipped on a patch of ice, regained my balance, and followed Ollie. As we turned the corner, the man on the sidewalk called out.

"I'm going to get you, creep. I'm going to stomp your pitiful ass, dickface."

Something about the man's voice was familiar. I had heard it before. It sent a chill through my body. It was the man who had threatened me on the telephone.

After running two full blocks, Ollie and I stopped and looked around. No large men; only a short old woman walking an overweight beagle. Not much hope for protection there.

Since the probability of finding public transportation was slim—buses rarely ran after 10:00 P.M. and taxicabs didn't cruise in Syracuse—we decided to walk to Ollie's place. By weaving through side streets and alleys we were able to cover the mile between my apartment and Ollie's in slightly more than twenty minutes.

The snow was still falling in large, heavy flakes. Ollie and I were both wet and tired.

"Jesus, you were fantastic," I said, kneading her shoulder muscles with my fingers. I was kneeling at the back end of the old claw footed tub as Ollie soaked in the warm, sudsy water. I never realized you were so fast, so...oh, you know what I mean."

Ollie rolled over onto her stomach and pulled herself up to the rear edge of the tub. Resting her chin on her forearms she gazed at me, her mouth set in a crooked smile. "Careful, big boy, I might need to hone my skills on your ample equipment."

"Ollie!"

"I'm sorry," Ollie said, sliding back into the water. "I'm glad I was there. Those guys were pretty mean. To tell you the truth, I was kind of worried."

"You were worried!??"

"Yeah. I was fairly confident I could handle the two big lugs, but the snow made it difficult to see. I didn't know if they had weapons or if there was a third person; a driver or back-up man."

"You talk as if this is old hat to you," I said, resuming my shoulder massage. "You sure you're not some kind of undercover agent. C.I.A. Fine Arts Division or Museum of Modern Art Secret Police."

Ollie chuckled. "No, I've had some kung fu training, but only to keep me in shape. I don't make a habit of attacking large men. Only when there's a cute guy in distress."

I was grateful for her assistance, but I was also uncomfortable having been rescued by a woman. As liberated as I was, it was embarrassing for me to sit on the sidewalk and watch my girlfriend take out two thugs who were intent on doing me harm. After all, I was a private investigator and she was a sculptor who earned a living managing a museum gift shop. "Give me a break," I said.

Ollie started to say something, but she must have sensed that I had already experienced more emotional confrontation than I could handle. She opted for a more subtle approach. She decided that distraction would be a more effective way to deal with my discomfort.

She reached back and ran her hands down my arm. Gently taking hold of my wrists, she arched her back and guided my hands over her shoulders, onto her breasts.

"Marty, I've had enough of this bath. I sure could use some help drying myself."

12

The distraction approach proved to be effective. I awoke in the morning feeling much better. Aside from having a sore jaw, I was in good shape physically and my psyche appeared to be healed.

It had been a scary night. The surprise attack had shaken me. Hearing the voice of the telephone terrorist had been bad enough. But being pummeled by two goons in front of my own apartment had really gotten to me.

Then there was the small matter of my masculine pride.

Fortunately the evening had ended well. Now I felt rested, ready to plunge back into the murky mystery of Fred Majorski's disappearance. There were still too many questions without answers. But the bits of information we had gathered yesterday held some promise: the gang of Polish thugs with the unpronounceable name scribbled on the paper they found under Majorski's mattress; Fedorski's description of the three super sleazebags——the Butcher, the Baker, and the Candlestick Taker; the odd coincidence that Majorski and Buddy Fedorski's mom had been born in the same town in Poland; Emma Kaston, the stunning older woman who was somehow connected to my favorite attorney, Malcolm Lazard. And finally, the familiar voice of the man who attacked me in front of his apartment.

I dialed Lou's number, hoping he had gotten some new information from Fedorski. He picked it up on the second ring.

"Hey sport, how was your quiet evening away from the job," Lou asked.

"You really don't want to know," I responded. I proceeded to tell him about being attacked in front of my apartment, glossing over the details of how I escaped from the two thugs.

Lou pressed me for descriptions of the two men, but I was not able to provide many details beyond their large size and the fact that one of the attackers was the same person who had threatened me on the phone. Lou said he had a lead on additional information about the Polish gang. He told me he would pick me up in thirty minutes and directed me to stay inside until he arrived. He suggested it might be good if Ollie spent the day with Angie. I passed along this suggestion to Ollie, but she declined, saying she had a lot of work at the museum. After some heated exchanges between Lou and Ollie, with me serving as relayer and interpreter, Ollie reluctantly agreed to ride into work with us. After work, Lou would pick her up and she and I would have dinner at the DeSantis' house.

I was a little uncomfortable about leaving Ollie, but after her performance on the street, last night, I was convinced she needed less protection than me.

On the way to work Ollie dropped her VW squareback at the gas station near my apartment. It was due for inspection and this station had a reputation for being lenient. And 1970 Volkswagens needed all the help they could get. As we left Ollie at the museum, I recalled the attractive silver-haired woman at the reception.

"Lou, what do you know about Emma Kaston?"

"The wife of the guy who owns Atlas Industries?"

"Yeah."

"Well, besides being an incredibly stunning woman, she has a reputation for being very diligent in fulfilling her civic and charitable responsibilities. I've heard she has a special affinity for the refugee settlement program."

"Why would such a classy woman associate with a sleaze like Malcolm Lazard?"

"I don't know, but I presume it has something to do with her philanthropic endeavors. Even nattily attired barristers need a good tax writeoff."

"Jesus, Lou. Are you taking one of those vocabulary building courses? Can't you just speak plain English?"

Lou looked over at me with disdain. "I won't dignify your ignorant outburst with a response." Then he gave me a quick jab in the ribs.

We turned west on Erie Boulevard and then north on Geddes Street. We passed through a run down commercial section lined with small manufacturing plants and warehouses, struggling to survive or, in some instances, already dead and abandoned. Soon we were in a residential area, also old, but not decaying. The small single family wood frame houses were not attractive, but were well kept. Last night's storm had covered the ground with a fresh coat of white snow that added to the neat, clean appearance of the neighborhood.

Most of the homes were occupied by older couples and widows, their children grown and living in the suburbs: Camilus if they wanted to stay close to their roots; Liverpool or North Syracuse if they went to work for General Electric; DeWitt or Fayetteville, in the east, if they really wanted to get away from home.

We had not spoken since our exchange about Lou's vocabulary. Now Lou broke the silence. "Kind of an odd coincidence."

"What's that?"

"Last night, at that Democratic fund raiser I attended. Emma Kaston's brother was there..."

"Her brother?"

"Yeah, Carl Dodge, the Deputy Mayor."

My body stiffened. Being aware of a blood connection between Emma Kaston and the Deputy Mayor made me feel uneasy. I couldn't explain why this knowledge made me so uncomfortable, but a fuzzy image was beginning to form in my head. This image, as blurred as it was, obscured another connection that was taking shape in the back of my mind. This second connection was buried so deep in my mind that it would take some time before it reached the light of consciousness.

"What are you pondering, Sherlock?" Lou asked, noting my blank look.

"I don't know. I got this real spooky feeling when you told me Carl Dodge is Emma Kaston's brother. There's just too much coincidence: Lazard and Paul Kaston; Lazard and Emma Kaston; Kaston and Dodge. Put them all together and you've got a lot of clout. What I can't figure out is what all that power has to do with Fred Majorski. They're definitely in a different league than the train man."

"I think you're reaching. Spooky feelings are okay for psychics and TV detectives, but they don't often solve crimes in real life." Lou turned into a parking space in front of a small neighborhood tavern. A green and white vinyl awning hung over a narrow glass brick panel. The building was painted bile green. It was the last building on the block. The entrance was on the corner. Lou pushed on the heavy brown wooden door, and we stepped into the tavern.

As soon as we entered, I was struck by the darkness. The only visible light was an old fashioned blue and red flashing Miller beer sign hanging over the bar.

"Hey, Lou," Fedorski called from the rear of the tavern. The policeman was standing next to a booth waving at Lou and me. Walking toward the rear booth, I noticed that Fedorski was wearing a windbreaker, tan khaki pants, and dark brown ankle-high leather boots. The policeman looked even more slightly built than when he wore his uniform. "Glad you guys could make it. How about a beer?" he asked, motioning us to sit at the booth.

Lou slid into the seat against the rear wall, leaving room for Fedorski. As I sat on the bench opposite the two policemen, I noticed a small, older man already seated next to the wall. The man had a large head. He was bald, except for several long scraggly strands of gray hair at the back of his head. He wore a loose fitting black wool sportcoat and a white oxford buttondown shirt with a thin black tie.

"Guys, meet the Professor," Fedorski said. "The wisest man this side of Salina Street."

The older man extended his hand across the table. Lou reached out and shook it. When the older man did not move his arm, I leaned over and awkwardly grasped his hand.

"Pleased to meet you," the older man said. He spoke with a European accent. "I am Arthur Paulson. I hope that I may be of some help to you."

My eyes had become accustomed to the dark. I now noticed two things about Arthur Paulson that I had not initially seen. Paulson had several deep scars running from his cheek bone down to his jaw line. The scars, which disfigured both sides of his face, resembled the African tribal markings I had seen in *National Geographic*. The only difference was that Paulson's scars were thicker and more jagged.

The other thing I noted was the older man kept his head very still, his eyes constantly staring straight ahead.

Looking into the professor's eyes, I saw that Arthur Paulson was blind.

"The professor knows a lot about everything," Fedorski explained. "But he especially knows a low about Poland, and what happened there during the war."

"That is correct," Paulson said with a note of sadness in his voice. "I was born in Lódz in central Poland. When I was a young man we moved to Sokólka, a small city about fifty miles from Bialystok. I was a student at the university when the atrocities began. My parents were very brave. Our family was Catholic and many of our friends were Jewish. My mother and father helped many of these friends find a safe place, but eventually the authorities discovered what they were doing and sent them to Treblinka. I never heard from them again.

"The professor was no slouch, either," Fedorski added. "He did his own share of rescue work. And he paid a price for it."

"This is not important," Paulson interjected. As he spoke he moved his left hand to the side of his face. "What is important is helping these men discover what happened to Fred Majorski."

"Did you know Fred?" Lou asked.

"I met him once at a function at the Polish-American Club. But I did not know him personally."

"Professor Paulson, is there anything you might tell us?" I asked, hoping that the brave scholar might give us information that might help us figure out what happened to Majorski.

Paulson smiled. "Gentlemen, please do not be misled. I am not now and have never been a professor. I am a simple merchant. At least I was until I retired six years ago."

"Don't let him fool you, guys," Fedorski answered. "The professor may not have any fancy college titles, but he knows more about Poland than any teacher on the Hill or any other damn university."

"Please, Buddy, let us not waste the time of these gentlemen. It is true, that I have studied my motherland. It has been my way of staying in touch with the past. It is also my way of keeping watch."

"I don't follow you, Mr. Paulson," Lou said.

"It is difficult to explain. The terrible things that happened in Poland, in all of Europe; it is possible they could occur again."

"But, what about the changes that are taking place now?" Lou asked. "The removal of the Communist dictators, the rise of democracy."

The old man shook his head, slowly. "There is still hatred. There is still danger."

I was becoming restless. Under other circumstances I might have enjoyed a philosophical discussion about political tyranny. Now, however, I was anxious to find a clue to Fred Majorski's disappearance. "Have you ever heard of the three thugs from Bialystok known as the Butcher, Baker, and Candlestick Taker?" I asked.

Paulson sighed. "Yes, I know about these animals. Bialystok was only a short distance from Sokólka. Their reputation for brutality was very well known."

"What happened to them?" I asked.

The professor took a sip of beer before responding. "The Candlestick Taker, a swine named Lutz, became a wealthy man from the precious goods he took from his victims. He fled to Argentina just before the Russians invaded Poland. With all of his money, he lived very well—until 1962. Then he suffered a massive stroke which left him paralyzed. He died a few years later." The Baker did not fare too well. He also left Poland before the allied forces invaded. He went to Brazil. Because he had not acquired the same wealth as his partner, Lutz, he had to take a job to support himself. Ironically, he found work in a bakery. Unfortunately for him, one of the Baker's victims recognized him and notified one of the groups who were searching for Nazis who had relocated to South America.

"This was before Simon Wiesenthal and the other Nazi hunters returned their bounty to Israel to stand trial for war crimes. This group brought the Baker to the kitchen of the bakery in which he worked. The self-selected tribunal conducted a very brief trial. They found the Baker guilty on all counts, proclaimed sentence upon him and quickly administered his punishment. They placed him in a large oven, set at four hundred fifty degrees, and baked him for ninety minutes."

"That's what I call poetic justice," Lou said.

"I've been told the Baker laughed ecstatically as they put him in the oven," Paulson added. "The ultimate thrill."

The professor amazed me. How did he know all of these details? "Mr. Paulson, what about the Butcher? What happened to him?"

The old man took another sip of beer. Once again, he stroked the side of his face with his left hand. "The Butcher was the worst of all of them. He was a cold-hearted sadist. His name was Josef Sikorski, the same last name as Poland's prime minister in exile during the German occupation."

Suddenly images began to form in my mind, the same images that had filled my head when Lou had told me that Emma Kaston and Carl Dodge were sister and brother. This time my vision was much clearer.

I reached into my pocket and pulled out the wrinkled piece of paper. Unfolding it, I laid it on the table and searched its contents.

Szmalcovniki
Dodge
NIO 58

"Not a car," I said to myself, tapping the paper with my index finger. *Image number one.*

"What's the matter?" the blind man asked, sensing the shift in my attention.

"Sikorsky——ain't that the guy who invented the helicopter?" Fedorski asked.

"Sure is," Lou responded. "He was an aeronautical engineer from Russia. Came to the United States after World War I. Built the first helicopter in 1939."

"Igor Sikorsky was a brilliant engineer," Paulson exclaimed. Wladlyslaw Sikorski was a great statesman, a Polish hero. Josef Sikorski was a sadistic swine!"

Aha. Who would have believed that my experience as an air traffic controller would come in handy. *NIO 58 was not a license plate number for a car. It was the registration number for a helicopter.* All helicopters registered in the United States had identification codes that begin with the letter N, followed by a series of numbers and letters. What appeared to be the letters I and O on Majorski's note were probably numbers —1 and 0.

Image number two.

I was torn between wanting to find out more about the Butcher from Arthur Paulson and wanting to track down the link between Fred Majorski and the awkward flying machine. Mostly I wanted to learn more about the Polish connection that seemed to be emerging. How long and how strong was it? Josef Sikorski, Fred Majorski? Emma and Paul Kaston? Carl Dodge? I knew the Kastons and Deputy Mayor Dodge were related. I had seen Emma Kaston in Malcolm Lazard's office. Janet Pafko had described how her father had cursed the Butcher, in Polish, just before he disappeared. And I had Fred Majorski's crumpled piece of paper, with three bits of information which, until now, had made no sense to me.

Szmalcovniki —the brutal gang of sadists, which counted among its members Josef Sikorski, the Butcher. Dodge —not the car, but the man: Carl Dodge. And the helicopter registration number.

My train of thought was interrupted by Fedorski. "Professor, what happened to Sikorski?"

"I assume you mean the Butcher not the prime minister," Paulson replied, turning up one corner of his mouth into a wry smile. "Unfortunately, I cannot help you very much with that question. Sikorski remained in Poland. After the war he moved to Warsaw. With the money he accumulated from his helpless Jewish victims he started a small business, a security agency. Ironic, isn't it? He provided security services for several large industrial firms. There were rumors that Sikorski used his position within these companies to gain information that might be damaging to the top executives. Bribery to government officials, cheating on spouses, that sort of thing. Using this knowledge, the Butcher would extort large amounts of money from both the officers of the company and the government employees who had been involved."

"Jesus, talk about repeating patterns," Lou interjected. "this sleaze did the same thing to the Polish bigwigs that he did to the poor Jews in the ghetto."

"Apparently with the same success, also," Paulson continued. "Even those wealthy executives and high ranking government officials were too frightened of Sikorski to take any action to stop him."

"How long did this go on?" Fedorski asked.

"For several years," Paulson said. "Until the Israelis became mobilized. Apparently Sikorski terrorized enough people to keep his identity from the allied personnel who were investigating war atrocities. But when the Israelis began tracking war criminals, Sikorski realized he was vulnerable. He knew the Israelis were incredibly thorough and tenacious. Eventually they would get to one of his victims——ghetto or corporate.

"The Butcher sold his security agency, moved to Warsaw and changed his identity. Josef Sikorski literally disappeared. Whether he assumed a new name and blended into the crowded masses of Warsaw or used his wealth to find refuge in a safer country, I do not know. I once heard he had worked his way up the ranks of the Communist party and had become a supervisor in the section that investigated crimes against the Party. Another time I was told he found his old partner, Lutz, the Candlestick Taker, in Argentina. He threatened to kill Lutz if he didn't share his wealth; became a silent partner, of sorts."

The old man took another sip of beer. He wiped his mouth with his sleeve. "Neither of these stories is based on reliable information. Knowing what I do about the Butcher, both are believable."

Lou and I looked at each other. We both sensed there was nothing more to be gained from this conversation. The Professor was an incredible resource. With his enormous storehouse of knowledge about painful experiences and tragic events, he had helped us fill in a few of the blank spaces of this frustrating puzzle. We now knew who the Butcher was. Through Buddy Fedorski's side trip into historical trivia, I had discovered that the letters and numbers on Majorski's note referred to a helicopter, not a car.

What next? Was Carl Dodge or one of the Kaston's connected to Josef Sikorski? To Fred Majorski?

"Mr. Paulson," I said, reaching across the table and grasping the old man's gnarled hand. "Thank you very much, you've been extremely helpful. I've enjoyed meeting you and I'm in awe of how much you know."

"You are very kind, young man. I hope you are able to find out what happened to Mr. Majorski. I shudder to think that the heinous monster, Sikorski, is still operating. If there is any way I can contribute to his detection and capture, I will go to my grave a happy man."

Paulson squeezed my hand. I was surprised at the strength of the old man's grip.

Driving back to the Public Safety Building Lou and I squabbled over how we should proceed. Both of us agreed that any inquiries about Deputy Major Dodge had to be handled very discreetly.

What we disagreed about was how to approach the Kastons. I wanted to confront the Kastons; to sit down with the industrialist and his wife and ask them what they knew about Fred Majorski...Josef Sikorski. I wanted to grill them about their relationship with Malcolm Lazard.

Lou was not thrilled about this direct approach. He knew Paul

Kaston had a lot of political juice. Waltzing into his office or home to ask some pointed questions would probably not be well received. Lou didn't mind taking a little heat from downtown. But not when he didn't have any evidence to justify intruding into a solid citizen's privacy.

We finally reached a compromise.

"I'm going to concede that your idea has some meat," Lou said. "Having an opportunity to speak directly with the Kastons would be beneficial. But I think you'll have to concede that my line of reasoning is also persuasive."

"Yeah, what's that?"

"If you choose to visit the Kastons —even if I am not present —the displeasure that Mr. Kaston will communicate to the City Fathers will find its way to my desk. I, in turn, will be obliged to find suitable expression for my frustration. An administrative review of alleged inappropriate behavior by a private investigator is one possible vehicle for reducing frustration. Naturally your investigator's license would have to be suspended during the investigation."

"You wouldn't," I exclaimed with a twinge of uncertainty.

"I'm glad you understand my perspective," Lou responded. "To show my appreciation for your empathic response, I intend to assist you in seeking more information about Mr. and Mrs. Kaston. Let's go see the Bull."

"I'm disappointed in you, Lou. You've become a real bureaucrat." I wanted Lou to believe I was disappointed. In fact, I was quite pleased with the outcome. Bullard's computer would be able to provide us with useful background information without tipping off the Kastons. Besides, I might learn something about the helicopter.

I felt mildly guilty that I had kept my knowledge about the helicopter from Lou. But not guilty enough to reveal my insight. There were advantages to collaborating with the police. And I certainly valued my friendship with Lou. One had to set limits, however.

Perhaps I would share my deduction with Lou at a later date. For now I would pursue my own search for a link between the helicopter and Fred Majorski's disappearance.

Jerry Bullard was hunched over a keyboard, typing furiously. I had expected a large room filled with a giant main frame computer, lights flashing, reels of tape spinning. Instead we found the hefty policeman sitting in a small, windowless cubicle. The only furniture was a computer desk and a swivel chair. On the desk was an IBM microcomputer with a VGA color monitor.

"Be with you in a minute, guys," Bullard said, keeping his eyes on the monitor's screen. "I'm just editing the monthly management report."

I scanned the titles of the books on the shelf above the computer:

Lotus 1, 2, 3, . . . The ABC's of Wordperfect . . . Not exactly typical reading matter for a policeman. I wondered how Bullard had chosen this line of work. The guy certainly had the physique of a street cop. Obviously his brain was in a different league, though. Hell, working with a computer was a lot safer than patrolling drug infested inner city neighborhoods. Maybe I should get some training in data processing. My imagination kicked into second gear as I visualized the new ad in the Yellow pages. *Have disc, will travel . . . modem for hire . . . graduate student fully armed with forty megabytes in each drive.* The possibilities were endless.

"Okay, guys," Bullard said, pushing himself away from the computer. "What can I do for you?"

"We need to check on a couple of people," Lou said. "Background information, personal profiles. Routine data."

"Some high rollers, huh," Bullard responded.

I was surprised at Bullard's perceptiveness. "What makes you say that?"

"Easy. If they were ordinary dudes or your basic criminal types, you would have gone through regular channels. You obviously don't want anyone to know you're snooping around."

"Thanks for the lesson in deduction, Bull," Lou said. "Maybe if I hang around you long enough University College will give me course credit."

"This about the missing railroad guy?" Bullard asked, ignoring Lou's sarcasm.

"Yeah," Lou replied. "Emma Kaston's name keeps cropping up in connection with this matter. We want to learn a little about Mrs. Kaston and her husband, Paul."

The Bull crossed his arms and leaned back in his chair. He looked at Lou, then me, waiting for one of us to say something. When neither of us spoke, Bullard began to grin and shake his head, slowly. "What about Carl Dodge?"

"Huh?" Lou responded, his jaw dropping.

"You know, the deputy mayor. Emma Kaston's brother."

I was impressed. "You know, Bull, you're definitely more than a pretty face." I made a mental note to check on correspondence courses for information technology. Maybe the school that gave the course on private investigation offered one on computers.

After a brief discussion Bullard agreed to discreetly check on the Kastons and Carl Dodge. Lou and I went to lunch, promising to bring the Bull a super Italian hoagie as payment for his services.

When we returned the door to Bullard's office was locked. Lou knocked, the door opened a few inches and the Bull peeked out. He silently beckoned us into the room, closing the door behind them.

"Interesting. Very interesting," Bullard said, after Lou and I were seated. "All three of them are originally from Poland. Carl Dodge and his sister are from Bialystok. Paul Kaston lived in Wasilkov until he was sixteen."

"Jesus," Lou exclaimed, blowing air out through his mouth. "These coincidences are becoming too damn much. Either the whole town of Bialystok migrated to Syracuse or we have ourselves one incredibly intricate network of unlikely relationships."

"That's not all," Bullard said. He reached into his pocket and pulled out a key ring that held almost a dozen keys. Then he leaned over and unlocked a drawer at the bottom of the computer desk. He rifled through the drawer for a few seconds before pulling out a single piece of paper. It was a computer printout sheet —the perforated feeder strips still attached —and it was folded in thirds. Bullard handed the sheet of paper to Lou.

Lou unfolded the paper and studied it carefully. After a moment he re-folded the printout sheet and began tapping it against the palm of his left hand. He stared at the ceiling, his brow furrowed in concentration.

I got up and reached for the paper, but Lou pulled it away, stood up and started pacing. "Come on, let me see that paper. What does it say?"

Lou continued pacing. "Bull, are you certain this is accurate?" The large man nodded. Lou resumed tapping the paper against his hand as he paced. "We may have stepped into something very big. I hope to Christ we don't drown in it. Frankly, this frightens me more than a little."

"Are you going to tell me what this is about?" I asked. "Or would you prefer to play twenty questions?"

"Not here," Lou responded. He turned toward Bullard. "What are the chances that someone else has put together this information?"

The large policeman squirmed in his chair, trying to strike a pose that reflected confidence with a subtle undertone of modesty. "I really don't think so. Of course, it's possible. But not likely."

"Can I keep this?" Lou asked, holding up the sheet of computer paper.

"Sure. But be careful. This could be treacherous."

"Thanks, Bull. I'll try." Lou motioned me to follow him. He led me down the corridor to the elevator and pushed the Down button. To my surprise, he got off at the ground floor rather than going to the garage level. He turned right onto State Street and began walking quickly. The thick grey cloud cover and heavy air gave a warning that snow would soon follow. At Jefferson Street, Lou crossed State Street and walked west to Warren Street. As usual, a half dozen homeless people patrolled the street, looking for handouts.

At the public library he stopped and turned to me.

"Roll up your sleeves. We're going to do a little research."

"Wait a minute. I'm not going anywhere until you fill me in on what you found out from Bullard."

"Okay, let's get a cup of coffee," Lou said, reluctantly. "I don't know why I'm being so accommodating to you. I am the duly authorized official investigator for the peoples' government. While you, you are merely a private citizen with an entrepreneurial interest in this case."

"Bullshit. You wouldn't have a case without me."

Lou shook his head. "This never happens on television or in the detective novels I use as primary source material for my personal growth program. At best, the policeman and P.I. have a peripheral, but respectful working relationship. Who every heard of a co-equal partnership between the public and private criminal justice sectors?"

"You always get wordy when you're nervous, Lou. Let's get that cup of coffee."

13

We found a booth at the back of a Greek coffee shop on East Fayette Street. The coffee wasn't great. But it was hot.

Lou cradled the white porcelain mug with both hands. "About a year and a half ago, maybe a little longer, there was a big scandal in City Hall. A couple of building inspectors were taking money from some of our city's finest slumlords. Seems as if they were overlooking code violations in some run down tenement houses on the south side. Might have gotten away with it if one of the buildings hadn't burned down. The insurance company suspected arson. When their investigators took a close look they discovered faulty electrical wiring, along with a number of other violations."

"Pretty sleazy."

"It gets worse. In the rubble of the fire they found two charred bodies: an elderly woman who apparently had been sleeping, and an eight month old boy. The baby's mother, a single parent worked the four to midnight shift. Her next door neighbor, a licensed practical nurse, sat for her before working the night shift at Crouse-Irving Memorial Hospital. On the night of the fire, the baby's mother was held over for forty-five minutes. She called the nurse, who said her supervisor had threatened to fire her if she was late one more time. The baby was a sound sleeper. They both thought it would be okay if he were left alone for a short time. They were wrong."

"Jesus." I looked down into my coffee cup, trying to imagine the mother's reaction, what the neighbor must have felt.

As if he had read my mind, Lou said: "The baby's mother was

devastated. It was her only child. She was in her mid-thirties, had wanted a child for a long time. After the funeral she went to pieces. Ended up being committed to the acute care unit of Hutchings Psychiatric Center. She was released after a month, but I understand she never really recovered."

"What about the neighbor?"

"She was pretty upset, also. Stayed home for a few days, trying to pull herself together. When she went back to the hospital, her supervisor fired her."

"One of life's little ironies."

"Yeah. She eventually got her job back, but not without considerable hassle. I don't know what happened after that. Lou paused and took a sip of his coffee.

"What happened to the landlord and the building inspectors?" I asked.

"The landlord was convicted of manslaughter and a slew of building code violations. Public pressure was so great they actually sent the bastard to prison. He's serving a few years of very hard time at Auburn. The civil suits are still pending."

"The system actually works, sometimes," I said, signaling the waitress for more coffee.

"Once in awhile. The building inspectors are another story. The District Attorney brought some heavy duty charges against them. He even had them up for manslaughter, accessory before the fact. Then, suddenly the whole thing disappeared. The Feds became involved, there was some talk of culpability at higher levels of city government, immunity in exchange for testimony, that kind of crap. The next thing I hear the D.A. has backed off, the building inspectors have disappeared, and the Feds have thrown a large blanket over the whole case."

The waitress refilled their coffee cups and asked if we wanted some baklava. I declined. Lou asked for a small piece. He had a hard time turning down Greek pastry.

When the waitress returned with the pastry, I accepted her offer of a second fork. She must have anticipated my change of heart: the piece she brought was rather large.

The baklava was delicious. We were mute as we ate. I took the last bite, put down my fork and wiped my mouth with a paper napkin. "I suppose that is where Deputy Mayor Carl Dodge enters the picture."

The corner of Lou's mouth curled up in a wry grin. "Afraid not," he said, shaking his head. "As a matter of fact, it's Paul Kaston, not Carl Dodge, who enters the picture here."

"What!"

"The computer printout Bull gave me had excerpts from several data sources," Lou explained. "He knows how to tap into computer systems the way Willie Sutton used to break into bank vaults. When he ran a background check on Kaston he tapped into a U.S. Justice Department data bank. Kaston's name showed up among a list of people involved in the tenement fire case."

I leaned forward as Lou removed the paper from the inside pocket of his sports jacket. He unfolded the paper and began to read: "County of Onondaga, Northern District of New York. Incident involving suspicious fire and possible malfeasance on the part of city officials. Individuals under suspicion: Lindquist, Michael——that's the landlord; Keaton, Ernest and Rinaldo, Donald——the building inspectors; Kaston, Paul... That's all it says. I guess this is some kind of internal memo."

"Anything else on the paper?"

"Just some background information: occupation, date of birth, social security number, that sort of thing." Lou folded the paper and put it back into his jacket pocket. He caught the waitress's attention and motioned for the check.

"What now?"

"As I said in front of the library, time for a little research. I want to look at back issues of the *Post-Standard*. Find out who covered the tenement fire. Maybe the reporter can shed some light on why the Feds hushed up the case."

"Okay, but that's not a two man job. Why don't I catch up with the Professor. See if he knows anything about Kaston. How about giving Buddy a call? See if he can arrange a meeting."

"Nice try, Marty. I'm not letting you out of my sight, today. You've had too many close calls. Besides, a little time in the library will do you good."

"What are you, my mother?" I protested. I picked up my jacket and followed Lou to the cashier. "How much do I owe?"

"I've got it," Lou said.

"Thanks, Mom. Does this come out of my allowance?"

Speak of your mother and she will appear. I had managed to convince Lou that making a phone call would not put me in imminent danger. While Lou scanned microfilm, I checked with the We-Care Answering Service.

Mrs. D had an exceptionally resonant cough, today. She barely managed to say hello before she was overcome by a fit of coughing. As I held the receiver away from my ear, waiting for her to finish, I once again had second thoughts about my choice of answering services. I wondered how long Sam Spade would put up with Mrs. D's consumptive cough. Hercule Poirot would certainly not tolerate the crass seductive tone of Ms. O. But then, neither of those esteemed investigators would have permitted himself to be babysat by a police lieutenant in the public library.

At last, Mrs. D's coughing fit subsided.

"Mr. Fenton, your mother, is very worried about you," she said. "You should call her right away."

I had to struggle to keep from responding. I wondered if We-Care would be charging me extra for family counseling. "Anything else, Mrs. D?"

Mrs. D broke into another coughing spasm. To my relief, her attack lasted only a few seconds. "A man called. He wasn't a very nice man. He didn't leave his name. He said you would know who he was."

A wave of fear surged through my body. I clutched the receiver tightly in my fist and pressed it hard against my ear. I tried to control my breathing as I spoke: "What else did he say, Mrs. D?"

"Not much. As I said, he was not a nice man. Frankly, Mr. Fenton, I did not care for him, at all."

"Mrs. D, what did he say?"

"Oh, he muttered something about catching up with you later."

I squeezed the receiver even harder. My knuckles turned white. "Anything else?" I asked, speaking in barely more than a whisper.

"I don't think so. Except he did say he would call again."

"When he calls, Mrs. D, be sure to get a number from him." As soon as the words were spoken I knew how inane I sounded. I hung up the telephone, pried my fingers from the receiver and went to find Lou.

He had found the articles about the tenement fire and its aftermath. They were written by Mary Beth Flynn, a hard hitting reporter with a reputation of being thorough and accurate. I told Lou about my conversation with Mrs. D as we walked back to the pay phone.

Ms. Flynn was at her desk writing a feature story for the next day's edition when Lou called. Yes, she remembered the fire and the Lindquist trial. Lou asked if she could spare a few minutes to provide them with some background information. She agreed to see us for ten minutes if we came to her office immediately. She was working on a 5:00 P.M. deadline and it was already 2:30.

Lou decided to drive to the Post Standard office, even though it was only a few minutes walk. He said we would be able to follow up on any leads quickly if we took the car.

Walking back to the Public Safety Building garage, Lou told me what he knew about Mary Beth Flynn, which was not very much. She had won several awards for investigative journalism. One of the awards had been given to her for discovering a welfare scam within the County Department of Social Services. A supervisor had managed to enroll a half dozen of his relatives on the welfare roles, giving false information about their income. The supervisor, who worked in the income maintenance section, was smart enough and influential enough to be able to short circuit the routine checks and balances within the Department.

Ms. Flynn was tipped off by an anonymous source that there was a scam being run within the Department. The source was apparently ambivalent about being a snitch. He refused to give her any details. After six months of laborious research she discovered a discrepancy in basic information reported for the same individual on eligibility determination forms for two consecutive years. Through dogged determination she was able to trace payment to a prosperous merchant who happened to be the supervisor's first cousin.

After she broke the welfare scam, her coworkers rewarded her with the nickname "Bulldog."

Mary Beth Flynn did not look like a bulldog. She was tall and thin, with straight blonde hair at shoulder length. I guessed she was in her early forties, though her fair, smooth skin and warm, open smile made her look younger. She had intense blue eyes which bore into my eyes when we were introduced, as if she were searching for some inner secret that might be used in her next story. She invited us to sit on two molded plastic chairs opposite her desk and launched into a rapid fire account of the building inspector scandal.

She recalled being stunned when the Feds had intervened in the case. All of her usual sources of information had dried up. Every place she looked she drew a blank. She became very frustrated. She could not even find out the name of the city official who was under suspicion. Finally, after several weeks of futile investigations, her editor pulled her off the story.

Sensing that Ms. Flynn had shared everything she knew and was giving us some not so subtle signs that she needed to return to her feature story, Lou prepared to leave. "Thank you for giving us time on such short notice," he said, pushing his chair back. "If I find anything newsworthy I'll remember you."

She gazed at him, looking for a sign of credibility. "I appreciate your offer, Lieutenant. I'm sorry I haven't been able to be more helpful." Then she grinned. "I don't suppose you might tell me something about the case you're working on?" she asked.

"'Afraid not," Lou replied.

I had an urge to ask the reporter about Paul Kaston, but knew that Lou would be upset if I did. As I shook hands with Ms. Flynn, I weighed my options. After a few seconds of deliberation I chose to suppress my urge, but decided to take one last shot at testing the reporter's memory. "Did you come up with any hunches or speculations that sounded plausible to you? Anything that might not have had supporting evidence but couldn't definitely be ruled out?"

Ms. Flynn's forehead wrinkled as she pondered my question. She walked over to a file cabinet and pulled out a thick green folder. Rifling through the folder she came to a sheet of handwritten notes. She scanned the paper, dropped it back into the folder and returned the folder to the file.

"It's funny you should ask me that. I didn't think there was anything I had forgotten, but your question triggered a fuzzy recollection. That's what I was checking out in my story file."

"And?" Lou asked.

"There was a rumor," the reporter said. "It was never verified, but there was talk that Lindquist had a silent partner, someone with a lot of money."

"Come on, Lou, let's stop farting around," I said as we left the newspaper building. "What more do you need, a signed confession? It's pretty damn obvious that Paul Kaston has been in some fairly deep shit. I don't know how he's tied into Majorski's disappearance, but there's no doubt in my mind he's connected somehow. Let's confront the son-of-a-bitch."

"It's not that simple," Lou responded.

"I don't care if the guy has a lot of clout. He's dirty and we aren't going to get anywhere unless we find out how he's involved."

"Okay, chill out. Let's think this through. A...uh...actually I agree with you. It's just that we have to be careful."

"I don't want to get you in trouble. Why don't I go to see him. I can use some ploy——insurance claims investigator or something like that to get through the door. Once I'm in I'll find some way to bring the conversation around to Majorski. What do you think?"

"I think you ought to change cereals."

"Huh?"

"You're not getting enough value for your box tops. You can get a better grade detective comic book from Wheaties."

"Very funny. You have a better idea?"

"As a matter of fact, I do. Why don't you leave the police work to us. Go home, have a beer, bake yourself a nice quiche."

We had reached the car. Lou unlocked the door on the driver's side and slid behind the wheel. Before he unlocked the passenger door, he picked up the microphone from the police radio and had a brief conversation.

I shifted from foot to foot, waiting impatiently for Lou to open the door. Looking up, I noticed the thick moisture laden mass of dark clouds still floating low in the sky, ready to dump precipitation on the city. The air temperature had risen a few degrees, bringing it above the freezing mark.

When Lou finally opened the door, we started up where we had left off. I chided him for his cowardice and Lou reminded me about the limitations of a private investigator. Beneath the surface of our lighthearted banter was a strong undercurrent of anxiety and tension.

I was so caught up in the verbal sparring match I did not notice where we were going until Lou pulled over to the curb. We were in front of my apartment.

"Hey, what's going on?" I asked, pivoting in the seat to confront the lieutenant.

"Not you, buddy. Last stop for today," Lou replied.

Just before I was about to deliver a stinging retort, there was a tap on the window behind me. Turning to see what had made the noise, I saw a huge figure leaning against the door, eclipsing the light from the passenger side of the car. The figure bent down until its face was at the same level as mine. The man on the other side of the window smiled.

Detective Manelli was bigger and uglier than I remembered.

Lou reached over and unlocked the passenger door. As Manelli opened the door Lou spoke: "I know you don't appreciate that this is for your own good, but it is. I'm going to do some checking downtown. I'll call you when I'm finished. Meanwhile, Manelli will guard the gate to your palace."

I was too angry to speak. Grudgingly I allowed Manelli to escort me upstairs to my apartment. The big detective watched me enter the apartment and close the door. Then he went downstairs. His surveillance had two purposes: to monitor any suspicious persons who might want to visit me and to make sure I didn't leave before Lou returned.

My only consolation was that I had not acted on impulse to let Lou know I had de-coded Majorski's note about Carl Dodge and the helicopter. Let him find his own clues.

I called Ollie at the museum and was told she wasn't in the gift shop. I made a note to remind her to be careful, but knew it would be fruitless. Once again I was frustrated by her independence but had to admit it was one of the qualities that attracted me to her. I picked up the telephone book and thumbed through the pages until I found a listing for Atlas Industries. I dialed the number for general information, and when the operator answered, asked for the transportation division.

"Hello, this is Mr. Roland of the Hartford," I said when the secretary answered. "We're preparing a bid for the general liability contract for Atlas. I misplaced my transportation assets inventory list and wondered if you might help me fill in some gaps."

"What do you want?" the secretary asked.

"Well, I've got all of the large ground transportation items and most of the aircraft. I just need a little help remembering a few miscellaneous items."

"Yeah."

She was quite a conversationalist. "Could you give me the make and model of all company owned vertical axis rotor aircraft."

"Vertical axis?"

"Helicopters. I'm trying to compile a list of helicopters owned by Atlas Industries."

"Just a minute." I could hear muffled voices in the background. After a brief exchange she returned to the phone. "We only own one helicopter. A single pilot, seven passenger Bell 222. It's used for executive transportation," she explained.

"I see. Would you happen to know the registration number? I need to check it against my inventory list."

"Hold on," the secretary said impatiently. Again, I could hear her talking to someone else. "Okay," she said, returning to the phone. "Joe says it's N1058."

14

While I was impersonating an insurance agent, Lou was conducting his own investigation.

As I was to discover later, he did not go downtown "to do some checking." Instead he turned right on Townsend and headed for the north side. Some of the ethnic neighborhoods in Syracuse had been dissolved as whites fled to the suburbs and blacks were displaced from the center of the city by commercial development and gentrification. The north side was an exception. It remained a bastion of white ethnicity, mostly Italian, with small pockets of German and Polish residents. Lou stopped in front of a small, three story building with a family owned grocery store on the ground level. The upper two stories appeared, to the casual observer, to be apartments. In fact, they served as office and headquarters for George Hartman, kingpin of gambling and other illicit activity in Onondaga County.

He explained to me afterward that he didn't want to bring me with him to meet Hartman. He wanted to protect me in case Hartman was involved in the Majorski case. But his decision was influenced even more by his suspicion that Hartman would be reluctant to speak candidly if a third person were present.

Apparently Hartman was indebted to Lou. Several years ago, Augie Lupino, a rival "businessman," made a bid for Hartman's territory. Finding a lukewarm reception to his offer for a friendly buyout, Lupino switched strategies and went for a hostile takeover.

At the time, Lou was working on assignment to an organized crime task force, one of those high profile multi-jurisdictional political initiatives. The task force brought together local, state and federal police agencies to remove crime from the streets of the nation's cities.

The Governor was scheduled to visit Syracuse to announce a large anti-crime campaign. Lou heard through the police informants network that Lupino was planning to move against Hartman on the same day the Governor was scheduled to appear in Syracuse.

Knowing the political embarrassment this would cause and being aware that a lack of concrete evidence made it impossible for him to act officially, Lou opted for a rather unorthodox solution to his dilemma. He went to see Hartman and warned him about Lupino's planned attack. He promised Hartman police protection if he would leave the city for a few days.

To Lou's surprise, the crime boss graciously accepted his offer. Hartman did not tell him to mind his own business; nor did he offer any macho protest about being unafraid of some two-bit punk. Instead he thanked the lieutenant and told him he would return the favor.

Several months later Lou read in the newspaper that Augie Lupino had been found in a car parked in the bushes next to the towpath that ran along the Erie Canal, just east of Buffalo. He had a bullet in his head.

Lupino's killer was never found.

Now, Lou entered the grocery store and looked around. Spotting a heavyset gray haired woman arranging the fruit, he approached her and asked to see Mr. Hartman. The woman did not acknowledge Lou, but walked to the cash register where she reached under the counter.

In a moment, a well-dressed giant emerged from the rear of the store and politely asked Lou if he would care to follow him. The man was close to seven feet tall and weighed more than three hundred pounds. They left the store and re-entered the building through a side entrance. Climbing a non-descript wooden stairway in a poorly lit hallway, they stood before a narrow plywood door that had been coated with a mahogany stain. The giant knocked once, the door was pulled open and they walked into a lavishly furnished room. The lush forest green wall-covering and bright colored prints were a marked contrast to the drab hallway. The three soft Italian leather sofas, set on a rich red oriental rug, formed a comfortable nook. Hartman rose from the sofa and motioned Lou to join him.

As he sat on the adjoining sofa Lou noticed the small thin man with a pasty complexion standing next to the entrance. The man stood absolutely still. If Lou had not seen the door open, he might have wondered if the small man was still among the living.

"Welcome, Lieutenant DeSantis. It's been a long time," Hartman said in a deep, soft voice.

"Three years," Lou replied.

George Hartman was not a run-of-the-mill crime boss. Educated at Choate and Princeton, he spent a year doing graduate study at the London School of Economics and two years working for the Common Market, now known as the European Economic Community, in Brussels, before joining the family business.

Upon his return he worked during the day in the business office of the wine importing company owned by his father and uncle. In the evening, he served an apprenticeship in the "other" business, the one that brought in the lion's share of their revenue and for which they did not file a tax return.

When his father and uncle retired to Florida in the early eighties, George became chief executive officer——of both businesses. Under his administration, the family enterprises became more lucrative and more powerful. While the robust economy during the eighties certainly contributed to this growth, much of the credit belonged to Hartman, who introduced state-of-the art technology and management practices into the family businesses.

In spite of the strong aversion he felt for criminals, in general, and organized crime bosses, in particular, Lou found himself drawn to Hartman. He admired the man's sophistication, his appreciation and knowledge of culture, his precise and logical manner. He saw in this suave crime czar many of the qualities he strove for himself. Lou only wished that Hartman would direct his many skills in a more positive manner.

"I do not ordinarily meet with law enforcement officers in my northside office," Hartman said, opening a fancy box of European cigarettes. He offered one to Lou, who politely declined. "In fact," he continued, "I cannot recall more than two other instances in which such a meeting occurred. Ironically, one of those occasions brought you here to help me."

Lou had an urge to add that he had also been helping himself. He suppressed the urge and simply nodded, instead.

"Now I presume you are here to ask for my assistance. As you may know, Lieutenant, I feel very strongly about personal obligations, and I am certainly indebted to you for the information you provided to me several years ago. If there is some way I can aid you, I will."

The giant, who had gone to a room in the back of the flat, returned now with a silver tray which held two steaming cups of cappucino. Next to the cups were a silver bowl with freshly whipped cream and a smaller matching bowl containing a reddish-brown powder that Lou guessed was cinnamon. As he ladled cream into his cup, Lou pondered how to approach Hartman. He had no doubt that the executive mobster felt indebted to him. On the other hand, Hartman might be involved in this mess. Mannie Bosco had worked for the sports book king until his untimely death, plus he had seen Hartman with Lazard, the sleazy lawyer, at the basketball game.

Lou took a sip of cappucino and put his cup down on the end table. "Do you know Fred Majorski?" he asked, looking closely at Hartman to see how he would react.

"I'm afraid the name is not familiar to me." Hartman showed no sign of recognition. "What gives you reason to suspect that I might be acquainted with Mr. Majorski?"

Lou knew he was in a blind alley and decided to back pedal. "I'll come back to that in a little while, if you don't mind. I know you are acquainted with Paul Kaston."

"Yes," Hartman responded. "Paul and I belong to a number of common business organizations. We've served together on several chamber committees and once co-chaired a small task force charged with re-vitalizing the downtown area."

"Ever been involved in any joint business ventures?"

Hartman paused for several seconds, looking directly into Lou's eyes. "No, we've never worked together," he said softly, with a slight edge to his voice.

"I don't mean to be offensive," Lou said, picking up on the change in Hartman's tone. "It's just that I'm trying to piece together a very confusing puzzle and..."

"Why don't you be more direct then, Lieutenant," Hartman interjected. "It's difficult for me to be helpful if I don't know what you're looking for."

Lou was not sure how to respond. Hartman seemed to be willing to help; his gratitude for Lou's previous assistance appeared to be genuine. But what if the sports book czar was involved in the Majorski affair? Mannie Bosco's murder had proved that the stakes were pretty high. Could Hartman be trusted, or was he just trying to find out what Lou knew? Even worse, if he suspected that he was at risk, would Hartman take some action to protect himself? Lou was not that concerned about himself, but there were others —Marty, Majorski's daughter Janet.

After weighing the alternatives, Lou reached a decision. He would take a chance and be direct with Hartman. At the same time he would keep his eye on Hartman, watching for signs of discomfort. He realized this would be difficult, given Hartman's cool, smooth manner. Taking a deep breath and slowly exhaling, he began. "I have reason to suspect that a man named Josef Sikorski may be connected to Fred Majorski's disappearance. It turns out that Sikorski, as well as several prominent citizens of Onondaga County, including Paul Kaston, are from the same section of Poland as Majorski. When I look a little closer I find that

Kaston was a suspect in a nasty arson case involving an unsavory character named Michael Lindquist. But when the Feds became involved in the case, Paul Kaston's name suddenly vanished and he was never charged."

At that moment the giant re-emerged from the kitchen with more cappucino. Hartman accepted a refill, but Lou declined, fearing that the coffee might distract him from concentrating fully on Hartman. The giant retreated quietly back to the kitchen.

"On top of that," Lou continued, "Mannie Bosco gets blown away while speaking with a man who was with Majorski when he disappeared and the same man is threatened several times and actually attacked by some pretty mean characters."

"I can understand your concern and your bewilderment," Hartman said, listening attentively but impassively.

"One more thing," Lou added. "A lawyer named Lazard keeps turning up in this plot. The same Lazard I saw you speaking with at the Dome the other night."

Lou noticed Hartman glance at the pasty-faced man. His eyes moved so quickly that Lou would have missed it if he had blinked during that instant. But the small man caught his boss's signal and immediately left his post by the door and joined the giant in the kitchen, closing the door behind him.

Hartman leaned back into the sofa, folding his right arm across his stomach. Resting his left elbow on the wrist of his other arm, he cupped his chin in his left hand. For the first time Hartman appeared to be uncertain. As he scrutinized the lieutenant, he tapped his fingers against his cheek. Finally he stopped tapping and leaned forward.

"This will require a leap of faith, Lieutenant DeSantis. I do have some information that may be useful to you. But I am not at liberty to fill in all of the details, nor am I willing to reveal my sources."

Hartman paused, waiting for a reaction. When Lou did not respond, he continued: "Paul Kaston has lived in Syracuse for nearly thirty years. I don't know where he lived before; no one seems to know. When he came to the city he had a fairly hefty bank account. Kaston made some wise investments and purchases. Before long, he developed a very solid base of operations, mostly small, low overhead, high volume cash-and-carry retail stores. From that base he built a conglomerate of extremely successful enterprises. Today, he is a very wealthy man.

"About eight months ago Paul began to act funny. He made a few questionable business deals: sold a couple of small companies for considerably less than they were worth; bought a small chain of shoe stores that hadn't turned a profit since the day they opened. He began to reduce his involvement in community activities. Declined an offer to be chair of the United Way Campaign; stopped coming to Chamber meetings."

"You said he began to act strange eight months ago," DeSantis said. "That was after the arson scandal, after Lindquist's trial."

"That's right. A few of us knew that Paul had loaned Lindquist money in return for a part interest in his real estate holding. I wandered why Paul's involvement never surfaced, but was not particularly surprised. The District Attorney's office is not known for its investigative powers."

"So Kaston's shift in behavior wasn't related to the arson scandal."

"No. The word on the street is that Paul was being pressured by some very wealthy out-of-state investors who had their claws into him."

"The criminal element," Lou said, regretting immediately his choice of words.

Hartman didn't seem to be offended. "I don't know who they were," he said. "But they must have carried a lot of clout. Paul Kaston is pretty secure, financially and personally."

"Any idea where they came from?"

"One of my associates mentioned Pittsburgh, but I don't know that to be a fact."

Lou found Hartman's story interesting, but not particularly startling or revealing. As Lou considered how to move the conversation to a more informative level, Hartman rose from the sofa and walked to the window. Lighting a cigarette, he looked down at the street below as he spoke. "Personally, I think it was more than out-of-state financiers that caused Paul Kaston to be shook up."

"And what might that be?"

"What do you know about Carl Dodge?"

"He's Deputy Mayor of Syracuse; his sister is Emma Kaston, who's married to Paul Kaston; and he was born in the same section of Poland as Kaston and Fred Majorski."

"Very good, Lieutenant. You've done your homework. Carl Dodge came to Syracuse a few years after Kaston. He moved here from Baltimore. Like Kaston, no one knows much about his past. He went to work for General Electric, joined the Democratic Party and became a solid citizen. When the Democrats reorganized in the early eighties, Dodge was rewarded with a bureau chief position in City Hall. From there it was a short jump to the number two position.

"Meanwhile, his sister Emma joined him in Syracuse about a year after he moved here. She was recovering from an ugly divorce and immersed herself totally in philanthropic work. She met Kaston at a charity ball——he was one of the City's most eligible bachelors. There was a brief, lavish courtship and they were married. I attended the wedding. It was very elegant. As far as I know, their marriage has been and continues to be very solid and relatively happy."

"So what's the point?" Lou asked.

"My point is that Carl Dodge has been tied to Paul Kaston's life for a very long time: through his sister's relationship with Kaston for nearly twenty-five years, as a high ranking city official who has more than a casual interest in the economic and political impact Atlas Industries has on Syracuse. And frankly, I'm not convinced Dodge's relationship with Kaston began in Onondaga County."

Lou was surprised by this last remark. "What do you mean?" he asked.

Hartman took a long drag on his cigarette and exhaled. "I have suspected for some time that these two men knew each other before they moved to Syracuse. I don't know where or how, but I think they go back a long way."

The telephone began to ring, but Hartman did not show any interest in answering it. Instead he paused and waited.

After the third ring, the sound stopped. In a minute there was a knock on the door leading to the kitchen. Hartman directed the person who knocked to enter and the small, pasty faced man pushed open the door and walked directly to Hartman. Standing on his toes, he whispered briefly into Hartman's ear and returned to the kitchen, once again closing the door behind him.

Hartman's expression had not changed throughout the entire interchange. Now he allowed himself a small smile. "Please forgive the interruption Lieutenant. I asked one of my associates to do some research on the matter that precipitated your visit. That was him on the telephone."

Lou was beginning to become annoyed with Hartman's circuitous manner. He was convinced that the crime boss was enjoying having a police officer as a captive audience, dependent upon him for assistance. Acknowledging to himself that the potential benefit of this conversation was too important to jeopardize, he decided to play along, at least for a while.

"You were explaining how Dodge may have known Kaston before they moved to Syracuse," Lou said, not wanting to appear too eager about the telephone call.

"The basis for this hypothesis is that Dodge has always had a special influence with Kaston. Now you might be inclined to attribute this influence to the fact that his sister his married to Kaston. But you would be mistaken. Emma Kaston is a fine woman——refined, intelligent, driven by virtuous motives. Her brother, our beloved deputy mayor, is cut from a different cloth. He earned his berth in the Democratic party by performing some unpleasant chores for the leadership. His activities never took him beyond the boundaries of the law——technically——but they certainly would be judged to fall within the lower range of the morality scale. Basically he was the party's hatchet man, negotiating for a larger contribution from someone who wanted a lucrative contract with the city; smearing a little mud on an opposing candidate whose popularity appeared to be rising. That sort of unsavory business."

Lou had known the Deputy Mayor was a tough character, but he had not been aware of his special role within the Democratic Party. He found it ironic that George Hartman, a leading figure in the local underworld, could become so righteous about the behavior of a city official.

"I think Carl Dodge has had his hooks into Paul Kaston for some time," Hartman said. "I can't tell you why or for how much, but I'm fairly confident that Kaston has been providing Dodge with money and favors for reasons unrelated to their relationship by marriage."

Anticipating that the policeman would question the basis for this conclusion, Hartman plunged ahead: "Let me assure you, I am not engaging in idle speculation. You see, I happen to know that Carl Dodge has been habitually engaged in a rather serious vice."

"He drinks?" Lou asked.

"No."

"Sex?"

Hartman shook his head.

"What then?"

A wide grin formed on Hartman's face. Immediately Lou knew the Deputy Mayor's vice. "Does he play with you?" Lou asked.

"No, that would be too risky for a man in his position. He invests with a small outfit in Utica. The proprietor, a casual business acquaintance of mine, 'sold' me this information several years ago when he was experiencing financial difficulties. I did not respect his decision to violate a professional confidence, but I appreciated my colleague's need to generate some additional capital.

"Mr. Dodge is not a particularly wise investor. He often bets more than he can afford and frequently loses. I've suspected for some time that Paul Kaston was supporting his habit. The telephone call I received a few minutes ago confirmed that suspicion. Just in the last year, Kaston has made deposits of more than $40,000 to an account at Utica Federal Savings."

"So, what does that prove?"

"The account is in the name of the man who operates the Utica sports book," Hartman responded. "And I have it on good authority that Paul Kaston has never placed a wager with that firm."

Lou considered this latest information for a moment before speaking. "That ties Kaston and Dodge together in an unorthodox, and probably unhealthy relationship. But what does it have to do with Majorski?"

"You are correct, Lieutenant. It does not describe the lines that form the third corner of the triangle. That is where the leap of faith I mentioned earlier becomes critical." Hartman returned to the sofa, sat down and turned so he was facing Lou. When he spoke, his voice was quieter, more subdued. "As you know, the late Mannie Bosco was in my employ."

Hearing Bosco's name brought Lou to full attention. Now we're getting somewhere, he thought.

"Mr. Bosco performed a number of simple but necessary functions for me," Hartman explained. "About five weeks ago, Paul Kaston called to ask whether he might borrow one of my men to accompany him to a special meeting. I was surprised at his request, especially since Atlas Industries has a whole fleet of trained security personnel. But Kaston had never asked anything of me and I did not think it would be appropriate to question him. So I 'loaned' Mannie to him.

"When Mannie returned, a few days later, he said it had been a strange experience. He said he accompanied Kaston to a large open area out by the railroad yard. They sat in Kaston's big Lincoln for awhile. Then another big car drove up. Nobody got out of the car, according to Mannie."

"Finally, this helicopter dropped down in the middle of the field. A big man got out of the helicopter and walked toward the cars. Kaston got out of his car and asked Mannie to bring his brief case and follow him. Kaston and the big man talked for a few minutes. Not a very friendly conversation, according to Mannie, who said this big man had very evil-looking eyes.

"Just as Kaston told Mannie to hand over the briefcase, this old guy wearing coveralls and a big blue parka started walking toward them. Mannie said he saw the old man before the others noticed, so he began to walk toward him. Before he got to him, the old man took a good look at the big man and suddenly started yelling in some foreign tongue. Mannie, who was not exactly a linguist, thought it was Polish, but he wasn't certain.

"The big man looked puzzled at first, but then he got this angry look on his face, grabbed Kaston by the arm and shook him. By that time the old man had run off toward the railroad yard. Kaston told Mannie to go after him, but the old man had too much of a head start and the yard was totally dark. After a few minutes Mannie gave up and returned to Kaston and the big man, who were engaged in an animated conversation—also in a foreign language."

"What happened after that?" Lou asked, finding himself totally caught up in Hartman's story.

"Kaston gave the big man the brief case," Hartman continued. "The big man had another brief heated discussion with Kaston—still in a foreign tongue—then climbed into the helicopter and flew away. Kaston told Mannie to go to his car, then walked over to the other car, said a few words to someone inside, and returned to his Lincoln. Then they drove back to the city."

"Did Mannie say who was in the other car?"

"He didn't see."

"Too bad. Any idea who the big man in the helicopter was?"

Hartman leaned back and clasped his hands behind his head. Lou was beginning to think that Hartman's pauses and gestures were strictly for effect. He had to admit the sports book boss knew how to create dramatic tension. But he wished Hartman would get on with his story.

Hartman must have sensed Lou's impatience. "I do not know who the big man with the evil eyes was, but I do know several things that might interest you. First, the helicopter fits the description of Kaston's company helicopter. Second, the pilot, whom I spoke with after Mannie's death says he dropped this man at the Rome/Utica airport, about forty miles east of here. The pilot, after a little persuasion, informed me Kaston told him to observe what the big man did after he got out of the helicopter..."

"And?"

"And he followed him——discreetly——to the airport restaurant where the big man ordered a prime rib and a beer and enjoyed a leisurely dinner. After about an hour, the big man paid his bill and left the airport terminal. According to the helicopter pilot, a car pulled up to the curb, he goes in and they drove off."

"Anything else?" Lou asked.

"Yes, the pilot said he was surprised to see the car which picked up the big man was the same one that was parked next to Kaston's Lincoln at the railroad yard. What the pilot didn't know, but Kaston did and now I do also, is the car matches the description of the black Chrysler Imperial registered to the Honorable Carl Dodge, Deputy Mayor of our fair city."

Having finished his intricate report, Hartman pulled out his box of foreign cigarettes and lit one. He looked pleased with himself as he took a long drag on the aromatic cigarette. Lou's mind raced furiously as he considered the many possibilities: Dodge and the big man were pulling a scam on Kaston, extorting even more money than Dodge could by himself. The big man was blackmailing Kaston but also had something on Dodge. The big man was a stooge hired by Dodge to intimidate Kaston, making him even more vulnerable.

Before Lou could pursue any of these scenarios, Hartman rose and extended his right hand. "Now, Lieutenant, I have fulfilled my obligation. I have paid off my marker to you. I wish you great success in your pursuit of the missing Mr. Majorski."

"Hey, wait a minute," Lou pleaded, "I've got some more questions. Have you spoken to Paul Kaston? What about Mannie Bosco, do you know who killed him?..."

Hartman held up his hand. "Enough," he said with the quiet authority of someone accustomed to getting his way. "You are encroaching on subjects that are best not broached by two people in our respective professions. You have my assurance that my mourning for Mannie Bosco will be respectful and civil, in line with the appropriate standards of grieving for an employer who has lost a faithful, hard working employee."

In the midst of his frustration, Lou found himself admiring the way this underworld executive put together a sentence. He was in awe of Hartman's command of language, even though he wasn't sure he understood what the man was saying.

Just as Lou was about to make one last attempt at seeking more information, the giant mysteriously appeared at his side. Realizing he had outstayed his welcome, Lou shook Hartman's hand and followed the giant down the stairs and out of the building.

As he walked to his car, Lou began to wonder whether Hartman had revealed everything he knew. He was fairly confident the crime boss had plans to avenge Bosco's death. Someday he would read in the police report about the untimely death of some thug. No visible motive, no evidence. The crime would probably never be solved.

But was there more? Had Hartman been totally honest? Lou quickened his pace, wanting to escape the nagging questions about Hartman's story. He was not ready to deal with his doubts. He was certain the core of Hartman's story was true and, as he was to explain later, he was anxious to tell me what he had learned.

15

By pressing the side of my face flush against the window, I was able to catch a glimpse of Manelli patrolling the sidewalk at the far end of the building. I had to admit the policeman was clever. From his post by the street corner, Manelli was able to watch the front entrance while keeping an eye on my car, which was parked around the corner.

Being a prisoner in my own apartment was not all bad. While it limited my ability to get more information about Paul Kaston and his connection to Fred Majorski, I had to admit to feeling a degree of comfort knowing Detective Manelli stood in the way of any nasty thugs who might want to take another shot at me.

I was about to convince myself that I could use my forced confinement to do more telephone research when a thick cloud of despondency dropped over me. I tried to focus my attention, but the invisible band pressing against my temples would not allow me.

I walked into the bathroom and splashed my face with cold water, trying to wash away the fog. As I buried my face in the towel, I saw through the haze a blurred, but unmistakable image. The figure in the doorway was calling to me, asking me not to leave. Although the image was fuzzy, I knew it was Sylvia Carling and she was begging me to keep an eye on her husband because she was afraid he was going to do something terrible.

I squeezed my eyes shut and tried to push the scene out of my mind. The harder I tried the more intense it became. I felt as helpless as I had several years earlier when I learned that Jason had been abducted by his father. I cringed as I remembered turning my back on the figure in the doorway and walking away.

I held my head under the faucet and turned on the cold water. The fog began to lift and I knew I couldn't stay cooped up in my apartment. I racked my brain, seeking a plan of escape. Just as an idea sprang to mind, the telephone rang.

My body tensed, anticipating the coarse voice of the man who had been threatening me. Cautiously, I reached for the telephone.

"Hello," I said, tentatively.

"Mr. Fenton," the person on the other end of the receiver responded. It was not the harsh voice of my sleazy phone companion. It was a woman's voice, quiet and high pitched. "This is Gladys Blazek," she said. "Do you remember me?"

"Yes, I remember you," I said with a sigh of relief. "What can I do for you?"

"I thought of something."

"I beg your pardon."

"When you were at my house. You asked me to try to remember anything Fred said. Well, when I was reading this month's *Reader's Digest* I came across an article about Poland. It told about all the changes that are taking place in that country: elections, free enterprise, that sort of thing. The author compared the way Poland is today with how the country was before the Communists took over. He told about the prime minister who led the resistance against Germany from London. That's when I remembered."

Recalling Arthur Paulson's comparison of the two Sikorskis——the heroic prime minister and the vicious extortionist known as the Butcher——I knew that Gladys Blazek was going to tell me that Majorski had mentioned the Butcher's name. I didn't, however, anticipate what she would say next.

"Fred was upset when he talked about this man, Sikorski. We were watching television and the news had just come on and there was a shot of the mayor with a shovelful of dirt. Some sort of groundbreaking ceremonies for one of those giant drug stores. Fred started saying the name——Sikorski——as soon as the picture came on the screen. He was saying the name real softly, like he didn't want me to hear him. It wasn't hard to tell that he was upset, though, very upset."

"Do you recall the name of the drug store?"

"I'm not sure. I think it might have been Healthright or something like that."

"Could it have been Healthfirst?"

"Yes, that was it. Healthfirst Pharmacy."

"Do you recall anything else about the groundbreaking scene?

Something that Mr. Majorski might have been reacting to?"

"No, can't say that I do. He just became upset when the picture came on the screen."

I was certain that Paul Kaston had been there. He didn't fit the image of the Butcher, Sikorski. But what other explanation could there be? "Thank you, Mrs. Blazek, this information may be helpful. If you think of anything else don't hesitate to call." I started to hang up, but the quiet, high pitched voice on the other end of the line caught my attention, once again.

"It's very odd," she said. "Fred once told me his late wife's name was Hannah."

I waited for her to continue, but she did not speak. I tried to wait patiently, but found I couldn't. After nearly thirty seconds, which seemed like thirty minutes, I asked in a voice almost as quiet as hers: "What's odd, Mrs. Blazek?"

"Oh, I'm sorry," she said apologetically. "I guess I was thinking aloud. After I turned off the T.V.—I didn't want him to get more upset—Fred sat there with his face in his hands. He was muttering someone's name, only it wasn't Sikorski. I think it was a woman's name; sounded like Anita. 'Poor Anita, poor Anita' he kept saying. But I'm certain he had told me his wife's name was Hannah."

"Did you ask him about that?"

"No, I couldn't do that, Fred was too upset."

Respecting other people's personal space is overrated. I wished Gladys Blazek had been more intrusive. I reassured the small woman that I would continue to search for Mr. Majorski and told her I would call if I discovered anything.

After replacing the receiver, I walked to the window. Manelli was still standing on the corner, standing guard. Once again I thought about the two thugs who had ambushed me in front of my apartment and the chilling voice of the man who had threatened me over the phone. I thought how safe I was, protected by the large detective standing guard in front of the building. Then I picked up my coat and quietly left the apartment. I walked to the end of the corridor and entered the stairwell. I went down a few steps, peered over the rail, then turned and climbed several flights of stairs to the top landing. There was a metal door to the right of the stairs. I opened the door and stepped out on the roof.

The temperature had dropped a few degrees, but was still above freezing. The gray cloud mass still filled the sky. A light drizzle was falling, little more than a wet mist. I tiptoed to the fire escape at the rear of the building. I peeked over the edge and, seeing no one below, stepped onto the fire escape and climbed quickly down the stairs.

On the ground, I glanced in both directions then ran to a chair link fence that ran along the rear of the apartment. I scaled the fence and dropped down into an alley between two rows of frame houses. Running down the alley I came to the street behind my apartment house. Pausing for a moment, I allowed myself a smile.

Manelli was smart, but not that smart. I pulled a set of keys from my pocket. Then I walked across the street to the gas station where Ollie's green 1970 Volkswagen squareback was parked.

In my apartment, I had considered how to contact Arthur Paulson. I had ruled out calling Buddy Fedorski. Fedorski probably had been warned by Lou to watch for me. I didn't know where the professor lived and was reluctant to give advance notice of my visit by calling. So, I had chosen the only other logical alternative, hoping the old man was a creature of habit.

I felt pretty good as I drove through the grimy neighborhood adjacent to the small tavern with the green and white awning. I had gotten some useful information about the helicopter by drawing on my repertoire of tricks learned from years of studying James Garner on the Rockford Files. And I had outsmarted Manelli, a pretty clever cop. Of course, having to pay for the inspection of Ollie's car plus $38 to have the front end aligned hadn't been part of my game plan. Even that hadn't fazed me much; I was on too much of a roll.

The bile green facade of the tavern looked as appealing as it had on my first visit. Once again, I was struck by how dark it was inside. I stood by the door until I became accustomed to the darkness. Then I walked toward the back of the barroom.

About ten feet from the rear I spotted the large, bald head of the professor. He was sitting in the same booth, facing the back wall.

"Professor," I called out, "mind if I join you for a few minutes?"

"Ah, Mr. Fenton," Paulson responded. "You must be seeking more information. Get yourself a beer and one for me, if you don't mind. I'd be happy to share my humble booth with you."

I bought a couple of Molson Golden Ales at the bar and returned to the booth. The old man looked even more worn and frail than he had in the morning. I had a strong urge to find out how Paulson had gotten the scars on his face, but couldn't bring myself to ask.

I slid into the booth across from Paulson. As I reached over and began to pour the ale into the Professor's glass, the old man grabbed my wrist and took the bottle from my hand. Admiring Paulson's independence, I watched him carefully pour the golden yellow liquid into his glass.

Earlier in the day, I had been impressed by how precisely this blind man had poured his beer. He filled the glass to the rim without spilling a drop. Now I saw how the old man achieved such precision. He poured with his left hand as he held the glass with his other hand. His right hand gripped the tumbler at the top and his index finger rested on the rim, protruding slightly into the glass. By pouring slowly, he prevented a head from forming. When the liquid touched his finger he knew the glass was full.

"What are you looking for, this afternoon?" Paulson asked, taking a sip of his beer.

I described the tenement arson case and how all prosecution activity had stopped when the Feds became involved after the landlord was convicted. I told him of the rumor that Lindquist, the landlord, had a silent partner with a lot of money and that Paul Kaston's name had shown up on the Justice Department's list of suspects.

The old man sat very still as I spoke. When I had completed my account, Paulson stroked the side of his face. "There are several possibilities," he said, "but I am afraid there is only one that is plausible. Which is too bad."

"Why do you say that?"

"I do not know very much about Paul Kaston —he is a very private person. But from what I have heard he is a good citizen and a decent man. He has put back into the community a reasonable share of his company's profits and his wife has always been actively involved in philanthropic causes. I had heard that Kaston was from Poland, but I did not know anything about his background. It just shows that even an old man can be fooled."

"What do you mean?" I asked, anxious for Paulson to get to the point.

"Have you ever heard of Operation Bloodstone?"

"No."

"After the war, World War II, the United States Government became very uncomfortable about the growing power of the Communists. They were particularly concerned about the rise of pro-Communist sentiment in this country. This was before the days of Joe McCarthy, when witch hunting activities were publicly sanctioned."

"You're not suggesting Kaston was a Communist?" I asked.

"No, on the contrary. I think you will understand fully after I explain."

The professor liked to spin a tale. Hold all questions until the end of class.

"In 1948, the National Security Council approved a series of covert war plans, known as NSC10/2. These plans called for a wide-ranging assault on Communism —propaganda, sabotage, demolition —anything that would undermine the Communist movement. The Office of Policy Coordination, within the CIA, was the overseer of NSC10/2. It launched an initiative to recruit leaders of groups that collaborated with the Nazis to enter the United States. Many of these individuals were very intelligent —scholars, leaders of anti-Communist groups. They were brought in under the Displaced Persons Act to perform intelligence and covert operations. Under a socialist or labor cover they would distribute anti-Communist leaflets and publications, deliver radio propaganda broadcasts and worse.

"This program," Paulson explained, "which was active between 1948 and 1950, was known as Operation Bloodstone. It was brilliant in design, if not purpose. The manner in which it was conducted allowed the United States to disclaim responsibility if the operation were to be uncovered."

I was outraged. "You mean these people who aided the Nazis during the war were brought over here and supported by the U.S. government. Didn't anybody know about this?"

"Only a handful of people outside the CIA and National Security Council —and they certainly weren't interested in blowing the whistle."

"But how do you know so much about it?"

"It was uncovered by a congressional investigation of U.S. intelligence operations following the Watergate scandal, almost thirty years later," Paulson replied. "Unofficially, some of us knew this kind of perverse activity was taking place, but we didn't know enough to do anything about it. I wish we had. As much as I despise what the Communists have done to my homeland, it was nothing compared to the Nazis—and those who helped them. In some ways, the intelligent, well educated collaborators ——he ones who were brought over for Operation Blood- stone—were worse than thugs like Sikorski. The collaborators should have known better."

Paulson took another sip of beer. I watched the old man rub the scars on his cheek and wondered what the Professor did with his emotions. He seemed so stoic. "You think Kaston came over through Operation Bloodstone?" I asked.

"Yes, I'm afraid so. But I would rather have more information before I reach a definite conclusion. I will do some research and let you know, as soon as I find out whether Kaston is a swine."

When I didn't say anything, the Professor began to smile. "With age comes patience. I know you are anxious to find out what happened to Fred Majorski. I am, also. But these matters are not simple. If Kaston was a collaborator, he has been able to keep it a secret for more than forty years. It will take some intensive research. But believe me, I will work as quickly as possible."

Might as well add mind reader to the list of Paulson's special abilities. I wished I wasn't so rushed. I would really like to get to know this incredible man. Before I realized what I was doing, I blurted out the question that had been on my mind: "Uh, your face, Mr. Paulson...how did it happen?"

Paulson's hand automatically went to his cheek. His fingers traced the contour of his scars as he spoke: "I am usually a loquacious person; even articulate sometimes, if I may be immodest. But I have considerable difficulty talking about this. Frankly, I do not like to think about it."

"I'm sorry. My curiosity got the best of me. I don't mean to pry."

"Please do not feel bad, Mr. Fenton. Curiosity is natural. We are born with a desire to know about things; especially when they are out of the ordinary. My wounds were inflicted when I was a young man living in Poland. My sight was taken and my face was disfigured by some heinous men who wanted me to reveal the identity of some courageous individuals who were working with the resistance movement. This happened during the Nazi invasion, but the men who did it were not Nazis; they were Polish citizens, slime of the earth who thought they could save themselves by aiding the Germans."

"Was the Butcher or any of his gang involved?"

"No. Same species of swine; different herd."

My curiosity was satisfied. I had no desire to hear more details. I especially did not need to ask whether Paulson had revealed the identities of the men his attackers were pursuing. I was certain I knew the answer to that question.

The front door of the tavern opened. The silhouette of a large man filled the doorway, framed by the daylight that poured into the dark room. Intuitively, I knew the man was coming for me.

At first, I thought it was Manelli. The policeman must have checked my apartment and found it empty. Somehow he knew I had come to this dingy bar. Perhaps Lou had told Manelli I might be here, talking to the Professor.

As the large man walked toward the rear booth, I thought about how to respond. I could leap out of the booth and try to run around the large man. Not likely, I concluded. Maybe I could convince Manelli I was on the verge of solving this case and persuade the large policeman to accompany me to interrogate Paul Kaston. Also not very likely. Before I could come up with a viable plan, the large man, wearing a police uniform, emerged from the shadows and stood next to their booth.

It was not Detective Manelli.

"Hello, Fenton. I can't say it's a pleasure to see you, again. But I am glad I found you here.

For a second, I couldn't place him. Square face, short grey hair. Very large. Then I remembered. It was the ill-mannered policeman who had questioned me in the hospital after I had been clobbered while leaving the Photoflash store. The guy who said he had found me in the bushes.

"Officer Slattery!" I said. "What brings you here?"

"I'm not here for small talk," Slattery said. "Somebody downtown wants to talk with you."

Damn, Lou must have called in. Just my luck that I get Slattery for an escort. Where's Manelli when I need him?

I thanked Arthur Paulson, promised the old man I would keep him informed about my search for Fred Majorski, and told him I would share anything I learned about Paul Kaston or Josef Sikorski. Paulson reached across the table seeking my hand. I took the old man's hand and, once again, was impressed by the strength of his grip. Paulson wished me good luck.

Following Slattery out of the tavern, I noticed that it had become colder as the late afternoon light began to fade. I was slightly surprised when Slattery opened the rear door of the dark brown Chevrolet Caprice, but assumed that the policeman was driving an unmarked police car.

I was more surprised when I slid into the rear seat and found myself sitting next to a heavyset man in a tan corduroy sports coat and brown flannel slacks. The man was holding a .44 magnum and it was pointed at my ribs.

Turning the corner, Lou was glad to see Manelli standing at his post in front of the apartment house. He pulled into a parking space by a fire hydrant, got out of the car and walked over to Manelli.

"Hear anything from Fenton?" Lou asked.

"Nope. Quiet as a church mouse. No suspicious visitors, either."

"Okay, I'm going up to get him. You stay here. I'll be back in a minute."

"Want any help?"

"Nah," Lou said, chuckling. "I'm sure he's pissed at me for providing gratuitous baby sitting. But he's not likely to be dangerous. I'll holler if he becomes too rambunctious."

When he got to my apartment, Lou did holler; but not from fear of his own safety. After knocking several times without receiving a response he picked the lock and let himself into the apartment. Finding it empty, he pulled open the window and stuck his head outside. "Manelli," he yelled as loud as he could. "He's gone. Your goddamn church mouse has fled the sanctuary. Check around the building. I'll look up here."

Lou knew as soon as he had spoken that their search would be futile. He was too angry to think clearly and needed some time to sort out the options, to shorten the list of places where I might have gone. He remembered that I had mentioned earlier wanting to talk to Paulson. Then there was Kaston. I had wanted to confront him after we left Mary Beth Flynn at the *Post Standard*. What about Carl Dodge? Could I have gone to the Deputy Mayor's office?

As Lou mulled over the possibilities he kept getting stuck on the question of transportation. How would I get to these places? My car was parked in front of the apartment building. The only person I had any chance of reaching by public transportation was Dodge, whose office was in City Hall.

Lou knocked on a few doors. No one had seen or heard me. Convinced that I had not sought shelter from a neighbor, Lou climbed the stairs to the roof. He scanned the neighborhood, frantically looking for me. At the northwest corner he paused. Without knowing what he was looking for, he had found it.

The service station. The station where we had dropped Ollie's car that morning.

Racing down the stairs Lou now felt afraid as well as angry. I could be anywhere. And with almost anyone.

"Ollie's car," he shouted to Mannelli as he pushed open the front door of the building and ran out onto the sidewalk. "Fenton has Ollie's car. Get on the radio and tell them to issue a call to look for a 1970 green VW squareback."

Before Manelli could respond, Lou was struck by another realization.

He glanced at his watch. Twenty-five minutes before six. "Shit," he muttered to himself. "I forgot to pick up Ollie at the museum."

16

The large pellets of hail streamed through the pale yellow beams of the Chevrolet's headlights. Dusk had descended on the city and the pinging sound of the hail stones hitting the car, combined with the rapidly darkening sky, created an eerie atmosphere.

The situation inside the car wasn't doing much to make me feel comfortable, either. The heavyset man continued to hold a gun on me, while the man who called himself Slattery drove carefully, staying within the speed limit. He turned onto the eastbound ramp of Route 690 and drove toward the center of the city. We drove through Solvay, the western gateway to Syracuse. The small industrial town used to reek from the toxic waste of the Allied Chemical plant. Even though the plant had been closed for several years, I still wanted to hold my nose when I passed through this ugly village.

When we turned south on Route 81 and did not get off at the downtown exit, I lost the last shred of illusion that my captors were actually policemen.

I tried to figure out who they were. Were they the same two men who had attacked me and then been thwarted by Ollie? Were they the thugs who had abducted Janet Pafko and dropped her in Liverpool? Were they the men Manelli and I had pursued at Janet's house? I had heard Slattery's voice and knew it was not the same as the man who had successfully frightened me on the telephone. But what about the man in the rear seat? He had not yet spoken. I hoped that when I heard his voice it would not be familiar to me.

I was frightened enough as it was.

As we entered Lafayette, the road began to ascend. From this point, Route 81 became one of the most scenic highways in the Northeast. The rolling hills and wide valleys provided a beautiful landscape throughout the year. Lush green in late spring and summer; covered by bright yellow and red foliage in the fall; and blanketed by clean white snow during most of the winter. The view from the road was almost always spectacular.

At the present moment I was not at all concerned with the view.

"Where are you taking me?" I asked.

"You'll find out soon enough," the driver snapped at me. "Keep your lip buttoned. Charlie gets nervous when there's too much chatter."

"Hey Frank, how's the road?" Charlie asked in a surprisingly high pitched voice. "Getting slippery, yet?"

I felt slightly relieved. Charlie was not the same man who had threatened me over the telephone and jumped me outside my apartment last night. Unfortunately the grim situation I found himself in did not allow me to feel too relieved.

"It's getting a little slick," Frank said. "I'd rather be home with a couple of brews and a good round ball game on the tube."

"Yeah, but loyalty comes first, right?" Charlie chuckled. His body shook as he laughed and the muzzle of the gun scraped against my ribs.

Where were these clowns taking me? I didn't think they would drive this far out just to blow me away. Not in this weather. They weren't that stupid. At least, I hoped they weren't.

At that moment, I thought of Ollie. I wondered where she was, hoping she was safe. I wished she were here with me and immediately regretted that I would, even in my fantasies, put her in jeopardy.

Once again I was frightened, very frightened. Standing next to Mannie Bosco when he was shot to death; being threatened by the spine chilling voice of the creep on the telephone; getting jumped by two thugs in front of my apartment. And now this. Crammed in the back seat of a car with a gun in my ribs and an ill tempered police imposter driving through an ice storm to some mysterious destination in the middle of nowhere. These were not everyday occurrences for me. Maybe Mike Hammer or Travis McGee were used to living on the edge of violence, but not me. I was beginning to have a new found appreciation for those dull research interviews I was conducting for my master's thesis.

Even with the intense fear I was experiencing, I was aware of feeling another emotion. If I survived this episode, I would have to face Lou DeSantis. Having to admit that Lou's protective instincts were justified, that I had been mistaken to leave the sanctuary of my apartment —this would be extremely painful for me.

Not as painful as absorbing the full force of a bullet from Charlie's

.44 magnum, but almost.

Until that moment, I had not fully understood my relationship with Lou. Now, confronted with the threat of serious harm from at least two sources—a blunt-nose pistol and a treacherous highway—I saw our relationship very clearly.

Lou was the older brother I never had.

The companionship, the competitiveness, the ambivalent feelings—all of the classical behaviors of sibling rivalry. Lou's overprotectiveness and my equally intense need to rebel.

As the sedan slid along Route 81, I wondered why I had chosen this moment to have such a profound interpersonal insight.

The Chevrolet continued to ascend the winding road, leaving Lafayette and entering Tully, a rural village that had remained relatively untainted by suburban sprawl, despite its proximity to Syracuse. The continual thumping of the windshield wipers provided rhythm as the car clung tentatively to the road. While I had serious questions about Frank's identify as a policeman, I had no doubts about his ability as a driver. The large man gently pressed his right foot on the accelerator, easing up a little on the curves and squeezing the pedal slightly on the straightaway. His large hands delicately adjusted the steering wheel, keeping the automobile on a steady course as it glided along the slick surface.

At the Tully exit, Frank carefully guided the car off the highway and onto a secondary road. He made several turns, almost losing the car's rearend at one glazed intersection, then turned onto a narrow road leading up into the hills.

He managed to keep the car on the road for nearly a half mile before the rear wheels lost traction and began to spin. Not wanting to lose complete control of the car, Frank shifted into reverse and carefully backed the vehicle into a small clearing on the side of the road.

"Okay, Charlie," Frank said as he turned off the engine. "We're takin' a little hike. Make sure our guest is all buttoned up."

Charlie backed out of the car keeping the gun trained on me. With his other hand he motioned me to slide over and get out through his door. I eased myself out of the car, took two steps and slipped on the icy road. My legs flew up and I fell flat on my back.

So much for a quick getaway.

The driver pulled me to my feet and the three of us slowly started walking up the hill. By staying on the earthen shoulder of the road, which was still covered with hard crusted snow, we managed to maintain traction. Unfortunately for me, I was not wearing boots. After a few minutes, my feet were very wet and cold.

"Jesus, Frank," Charlie said pulling up the collar of his sports coat, "least ya' could do is tell me I needed to dress warm."

"Shove it," Frank replied. "How was I to know we're gonna get stuck in an ice storm?"

"Yeah, well next time watch the weather report. I don't appreciate this kind of assignment."

Neither did I. I still didn't have a clue about who Frank and Charlie were or where they were taking me. And even though I had serious doubts about what awaited me at our destination, I was beginning to hope we would get there soon, before my feet froze.

After about a half mile we came to a long driveway on the right side of the road. Frank turned into the driveway and Charlie and I followed; me in front and Charlie just behind, pointing the gun at my back. The crunching sound of our footsteps filled the silent night as we followed the snow packed rut made by a previous car. The snow was deep, shielded by the tall trees that lined the driveway.

I could not see a house. The driveway curved sharply to the left and the dense woods revealed only a small light in the distance. To my dismay, the driveway was very long. Just as the pain in my feet began to turn to numbness, we stepped into a large clearing. On the left were two cars: a dark blue Jeep Wagoneer and a white Lincoln.

Straight ahead was a huge log building that looked more like a lodge than a house. A wide stairway led to the porch that ran the entire length of the building. Frank knocked on the heavy wooden door. Almost immediately the door opened and we stepped into a large entry hall.

"You must be Mr. Fenton," the man who opened the door said, extending his hand. I took this gesture as a good sign. After all, who would shoot you after shaking hands?

I shook his hand.

The man who greeted me was just under six feet tall. He appeared to be in his late forties and was built like a running back. He had a full head of wavy red hair that framed a ruggedly handsome face.

"I apologize for the rude manner of transporting you here," the man said to me. Looking down at my wet shoes, he added, "why don't you take off your shoes and socks. I'm sure we can find a dry pair of socks."

"What about us, Noah?" Charlie said. "Don't we count?"

"Sure, Charlie," Noah said, leading us down a couple of steps into a huge pine paneled living room with a huge plate glass window on the back wall. In spite of the sleet, I could see the lights of the village at the bottom of the hill. I stood at the window, looking out into the night, wondering what was going to happen to me. I heard a door open, then several quick footsteps. Turning around, I was surprised by what I saw.

Standing on the landing above the living room was a tall, silver haired woman dressed in a bulky white cowl neck sweater, long charcoal gray skirt, and black high heel leather boots.

Emma Kaston looked even more striking than I remembered.

17

While Manelli was calling in the alert about Ollie's car, Lou called the museum. The woman who answered the telephone said she hadn't seen Ollie but would look for her. She returned in a moment and told Lou that one of the other workers had seen her leave about an hour ago. She did not say where she was going.

Lou decided to bite the bullet. Not wanting to implicate anyone else, he told Manelli to return to headquarters and wait for his call. Then Lou got into his car and drove downtown.

He was going to pay Deputy Mayor Dodge a visit.

The last bit of light had disappeared. Although the temperature had fallen a few degrees, the rain had not yet turned to sleet or snow. As he drove to City Hall, Lou considered calling Captain Lincoln, his supervisor, to let him know what he was doing. After considering the pros and cons he decided not to call. Knowing Lincoln, he would probably advise Lou to come in to discuss the matter with him; to weigh all the alternative strategies and select the most viable option.

Lou did not have time for logical deliberation. He had a bad feeling about what was happening and was afraid that Marty—and maybe Ollie—might be in jeopardy. There were too many bad signs. And most of them had Carl Dodge's name in bold letters.

Besides, Larry Lincoln was a political animal. He was a good cop but a very conservative supervisor. If Lincoln had any doubts about Dodge's involvement, he would keep Lou away from the Deputy Mayor. On the other hand, if Lou convinced Lincoln that Dodge might be one of the bad guys, the captain would want to run the story all the way up the supervisory chain before taking any action.

Lou, in spite of his own play-it-by-the-book inclination, felt he had to act now.

He pulled the car into a space on the side of City Hall and walked up the steep staircase leading to the front entrance. The building, which resembled a cathedral, sat on the north side of Clinton Square. In the nineteenth century, the waters of the Erie Canal passed beneath this seat of city government, carrying people and cargo across New York state. Now, Erie Boulevard occupied the space where the canal had once been. The view was not nearly as scenic, with the road constantly congested with cars and trucks. As for movement within City Hall, some claimed it was nearly nonexistent.

The guard at the reception desk told Lou that only the Mayor and his assistant were in the building. The Deputy Mayor had left at about 4:00 P.M. He had not said where he was going.

For a split second Lou had an urge to go to the Mayor's office and share his suspicion about Dodge. His police officer sense quickly returned, however, and he decided to pay a visit to Dodge's home, instead.

Inside the car he called to verify Dodge's address. Then he asked to speak to Manelli.

"What's up, Lieutenant?" Manelli asked.

"Nothing much. I was going to ask you the same thing."

"Pretty quiet here. Just one message. The Bull stopped by. Said he had a piece of information that might interest you."

"Yeah?"

"He said he rechecked Fred Majorski's personnel record. The first time he pulled it from the computer he thought there was something funny about it. When he went back to check the record he found that someone had been messing around with the file. I guess he has some way of knowing if anyone has made changes. Something to do with passwords. I don't really understand that computer crap..."

"What did he find?" Lou asked impatiently.

"Bull said there have been some changes made in the basic data form. He wasn't exactly sure what has been changed. Probably date of birth, birthplace —something like that."

"Birthplace?" Lou repeated, trying to make sense of Bull's finding.

"That's not all."

"Huh?"

"Bull said he's able to trace where the change was made from. He said whenever anyone goes in to modify a file they have to put in some kind of access code. It doesn't show up on the file, but it gets recorded in the computer system, somewhere. That way they can keep track of where something is entered, in case there's a problem."

Jesus, Lou thought, Manelli sure is wordy today. He's beginning to sound like me.

"Anyway,"Manelli continued. "It looks like the change was made from City Hall. It had the Deputy Mayor's code on it."

18

"Nice place, you have here," I said to Emma Kaston, trying to buy some time to make sense of the situation. If it had been Paul Kaston I would not have been surprised. I probably could have fit Malcolm Lazard, and even the sport book czar, George Hartman, into the puzzle without too much trouble. I would not have been floored if Carl Dodge had been standing in the entrance to the living room.

But Emma Kaston? Art lover. Champion of charitable causes. One of the most elegant women I had ever seen. There was no way I could fit her into this sordid scenario.

"Thank you, Mr. Fenton," she said. She had a lovely, mellow voice, with just a trace of an accent. "I regret that your first exposure to our cabin has to be under such unfortunate circumstances."

"Me, too," I responded.

"I beg your pardon," Mrs. Kaston said.

"It's nothing. Just a stress reaction. I'm not used to being escorted at gun point through an ice storm."

"Yes, of course. I can appreciate how upsetting this has been for you, Mr. Fenton. I hope after we have had an opportunity to talk that you will understand why I employed such a crude approach. Please have a seat," she said, indicating a large upholstered chair by the fireplace.

I sank into an oversized armchair next to the fireplace. The heat from the blazing fire felt good. Emma Kaston walked slowly across the room and sat on a matching chair, facing me.

"Before we begin, let me introduce these gentlemen," she said, pointing to the three men standing at the end of the room. I was relieved to see that Charlie had put away his gun. "This is Mr. Noah Masterson, Chief of Security Services, for Atlas Industries. I believe that you may remember Mr. Frank Slattery. The last time you saw him he was wearing a police uniform. And this is Mr. Charles Knox. Mr. Knox and Mr. Slattery are also employed by the Security Department at Atlas. As you will see, after we have talked, none of these gentlemen has been acting in their capacity as security officers in this matter."

Masterson smiled and waved awkwardly at me. The other two men did not acknowledge Mrs. Kaston's introduction. In their wet clothes they looked as if they would rather be standing in front of the warm fire.

Mrs. Kaston nodded at Masterson and the three men walked out of the living room. They turned into the hallway leading to the other end of the cabin and disappeared. Emma Kaston looked directly at me, waiting until the men were out of earshot.

"I need your assistance," she said, peering into my eyes. "I have gotten myself into a...how shall I say...a very awkward situation. I am not accustomed to such circumstances. Quite frankly, I am not sure what to do."

I had a difficult time imagining anything awkward about this woman. At the same time, I had seen some apparent disparities between her elegant, graceful demeanor and some of her other behaviors—like sicking those two goons on me to "escort" me at gunpoint to Tully.

Mrs. Kaston seemed to sense my puzzlement. "Let me explain. Several weeks ago I returned home from a board meeting of the Refugee Resettlement Council. When I came through the garage door leading to the kitchen I heard some voices in the living room. My husband, Paul, was having a very heated exchange with Carl Dodge, the Deputy Mayor, who also happens to be my brother. At first, I could not understand what they were saying. But the tone of their voices frightened me and I decided to stay in the kitchen.

"After a little while I was able to follow their discussion. Apparently my husband and my brother had been involved with some unsavory character. At first I could not comprehend the nature of their business. But it was obvious that it was not completely legitimate. It seems this other man was holding something over my husband's head. I believe he was extorting large sums of money from my husband. They also talked about another man, someone who had intruded on a meeting he should not have been at."

I noticed that Mrs. Kaston's lower lip had begun to quiver. I considered saying something, but decided to let her continue.

"My brother was very upset," she said. "He was speaking very harshly to Paul. He said the other man—the extortionist, not the intruder—was extremely angry and was threatening to do something horrible if the intruder was not dealt with."

Suddenly Mrs. Kaston rose from her chair and walked to the window. She gazed out at the night, trying to retain control. "The view is usually so beautiful," she said.

Watching her shoulders rise and fall as she tried to regain control, I was torn between wanting to comfort her and knowing that I had to confront her. I rose quietly from the arm chair, took a couple of steps toward her and stopped.

I asked gently, "Does this have anything to do with Fred Majorski?"

For a second she did not react. Then her body began to tremble, slowly at first, then more violently. I was so struck by her convulsive movement that it took me several seconds to realize the barely audible moans were coming from Emma Kaston.

I stood absolutely still and waited.

Slowly, the trembling subsided and the moaning faded. Mrs. Kaston turned and faced me. Her mascara-streaked face had lost its radiance. She looked old and tired.

"Yes, Mr. Fenton. This has everything to do with Mr. Majorski," she said, sighing deeply. "This is extremely difficult for me. I have not told this to anyone but Noah, and I did not share all of the details with him. Please try to bear with me."

"Take your time. I'm not going anywhere," I said, immediately regretting my lame attempt at humor.

Emma Kaston did not seem to notice my remark. "Mr. Majorski was the intruder my brother and husband were talking about. Intruder is actually not the proper term; unfortunate bystander might be more appropriate. I heard my husband say that Mr. Majorski inadvertently stumbled into a very tense encounter between Paul and the man who has been threatening him. For some reason, the extortionist —I don't know his name, but I'm fairly certain he is from Poland—was very upset that Mr. Majorski had seen him. He must have made some very dire threats because Carl was saying some awful things to Paul."

"Like what?"

"He told Paul he had discovered the identity of the man—Mr. Majorski. He said they had to do something to assure that Mr. Majorski did not talk about what he had seen. He warned Paul that if *they* did not do something, the other man would take some very drastic action. Carl said this man would expose Paul, would destroy his business and ruin his reputation. Carl said it was not only Paul, but also himself that was at risk. He pleaded with Paul to help him, but my husband would have no part of it."

"Carl said he would expose your husband?" I asked. Mrs. Kaston

158

nodded.

I wondered if the extortionist could be the Butcher, Josef Sikorski. Or was it possible that Paul Kaston was, in fact, the Butcher? Could he have changed his name and started a new life in this country? Not likely, but possible.

"What do you know about Operation Bloodstone?" I asked.

Emma Kaston closed her eyes and sighed. "You've done your homework thoroughly, young man," she said. Leaving her position by the window, she returned to the arm chair and sat down. I followed, but did not sit. Instead I leaned against the stone wall of the fireplace, arms across my chest, waiting for her explanation. I looked down at her hands, which were folded in her lap. "I thought I knew everything about my husband," she said. "But after my brother left, I confronted Paul about their argument. At first, he was evasive. But I persisted. Usually I give in when Paul doesn't want to talk, but I guess fear was propelling me.

"Finally Paul told me what this man, the extortionist, was holding over his head. When Paul was a young man, living in Poland, he taught at the University. He had a promising career as a research chemist. This much I have known for many years. What I did not know was Paul also was politically active as a member of the young conservative movement. He told me——and I believe him——he never really supported Hitler and his Nazi followers, but he was a very patriotic young man with strong political views.

"After the war, Poland was devastated. As much as Paul was disturbed by the destruction that had already occurred, he was even more troubled by the prospect of a Communist takeover. With the university in a shambles, Paul felt the outlook at home was very bleak. When he had the opportunity to join Operation Bloodstone, he jumped at it."

I considered what she had just told me. If it was true, I could rule out Paul Kaston as the Butcher. That left the extortionist as the prime candidate.

"This man somehow found out about my husband's past and has been threatening to expose him. Even though Paul's involvement in Operation Bloodstone was relatively innocuous ——he wrote and distributed anti-Communist literature, and infiltrated a socialist group——the knowledge of his past could have a devastating impact on Paul, personally and professionally."

"How has he been able to keep it a secret all of these years?" I asked.

"When Operation Bloodstone was terminated in the early 1950s, the U.S. government arranged for some of the participants to make a fresh start. They resettled them throughout the United States and helped them get new jobs. Something like the Federal Witness Protection

Program. Paul was given a job as a chemist with Allied. He saved most of his salary, invested wisely, and with the help of some wealthy financiers, was able to start his own business. As you probably know, he has had nothing but success since that time."

A regular Horatio Alger story, I thought, not feeling overly sympathetic toward Paul Kaston. Now that I knew what was motivating Kaston, I was anxious to move on to my primary concern. "What happened after you spoke with your husband?"

"I pleaded with him to pay the money, to do whatever it took to get this man to leave us alone."

"And?"

"Paul said it was no use. The man was not only very selfish, but also very cruel."

"What about your brother? Did he have any ideas about what to do?"

Mrs. Kaston shook her head. "My brother is a very weak man. He has gotten as far as he has by preying on other people; taking advantage of those with less power and attaching himself to those with influence ——leeching money and favors from them any way he could. I am ashamed to admit I have known for sometime that Carl has been exploiting Paul and yet I have not done anything about it."

I was about to ask her about Fred Majorski when there was a short series of loud crackling sounds followed by an enormous thump outside the house. Masterson and Knox ran from the other end of the house to the front entrance. With their guns drawn, they carefully opened the door, checked the area in front of the house and quietly slipped through the doorway.

In a few moments, the two men returned, their pistols tucked away. "Nothing to worry about, Ma'am," Masterson said. "A big willow tree toppled from the weight of the snow. Whole thing fell over, even pulled the roots out of the ground." The two men returned to the far side of the cabin.

I studied the silver haired woman sitting across from me. Some of her composure had returned, but she looked frail and vulnerable, not nearly the imposing figure she had been before their conversation. I was struggling to find the best way to ask about the trainman. I was concerned about how she might react and afraid to hear the response she might give.

"Mrs. Kaston, do you know what happened to Fred Majorski?" I finally asked.

"I do," she responded with less affect than I had expected.

My heart began to pound. "Well for God's sake, tell me!" I yelled.

Mrs. Kaston stood up and began to walk toward the other end of the house. At first, I thought she was going to summon the three men to deal with my impudent behavior. Instead, she turned and beckoned me

160

to follow her.

We walked down a long hallway, past several doors. At the end of the hall was a dark wooden door. Mrs. Kaston knocked twice. A latch was turned on the inside and the door was slowly pulled open.

The room appeared to be a bedroom. It was a large room, paneled with cedar and decorated with paintings of country scenes—lakes, forests, mountains. The furniture was made of sturdy maple. A large four poster bed, a tall dresser, a dressing table with a mirror, and several chairs.

Knox stood by the door. Masterson sat on the edge of the bed on the other side of the room. At the end of the room, sitting in an arm chair, was an older man dressed in baggy pants and a faded blue robe. His hair was unkempt and his face was covered with gray stubble.

I stared at the man in the blue robe. He looked familiar but I could not identify him, at first. Then a window opened in the back of my mind and I realized who he was.

The man in the blue robe was Paul Kaston.

19

Syracuse's twenty minute rush hour had ended and Lou was able to make good time driving to Dodge's home on the east side of the city. Fortunately the rain had stopped before the temperature fell below the freezing point. The heat generated from the heavy traffic kept the city streets from freezing.

Carl Dodge lived in a small house in the hills near Drumlins Country Club. It was a modest one story brick house, not nearly as attractive as most of the other houses in the neighborhood. If Dodge was soaking Kaston for big bucks, Lou thought, he certainly wasn't spending any of it on his house.

Lou drove past the house. At the end of the block he made a U-turn and parked on the corner, a half dozen houses down from Dodge's. The sidewalk was covered with a thin glaze of ice and Lou had a difficult time keeping his balance.

Dodge's Chrysler Imperial was parked at the foot of the driveway and several windows in the house were lit. Sliding up the front walk, Lou rehearsed what he planned to say. How do you tell the Deputy Mayor you think he's involved in tampering with government documents, and extortion, not to mention kidnapping and possibly murder?

Dodge greeted Lou with a nervous smile and a weak handshake. He invited him into the kitchen where he was preparing dinner——kielbasa and boiled potatoes. The aroma of the sausage reminded Lou that he had not eaten for several hours. Dodge offered Lou a bottle of ale. Lou politely declined, but accepted a glass of root beer.

"What brings you out on this nasty night, Lieutenant?" Dodge asked, turning the sizzling kielbasa in the skillet.

"I'm doing an investigation and I have reason to believe you may be able to help me."

"Oh? In what way?"

"A man is missing. A railroad man named Fred Majorski." Lou watched for a sign of recognition, but found nothing but a strained smile, which appeared to be permanently fixed on the Deputy Mayor's face. "We have reason to believe that Mr. Majorski did not disappear of his own accord."

"What does this have to do with me?"

"That's what I was going to ask *you*."

Dodge's smile vanished. He turned toward Lou, his right hand clenching the large cooking fork. "Is that an accusation, Lieutenant?" Dodge asked angrily. "I think you're out of line, way out of line. I ought to call the Chief right now."

Lou quickly considered his options. He could back off and hope Dodge would see the wisdom of not making the issue visible. He could call Dodge's bluff. Or he could push the Deputy Mayor to see how he would react.

Backing off would definitely be the safer choice, Lou thought, but not the right one, in this instance.

"Forget the Chief," Lou said. "I think you should call the Mayor. I'm sure he would like to hear your explanation of how large sums of Paul Kaston's money seem to have found a direct line from his account to yours...or how you have become proficient at using the City's computer to alter personnel records. You might even want to share with him how you spend your leisure time. I'm sure he would be interested in having your bookie's phone number."

Dodge's face turned red but he tried to control himself. "Enough, Lieutenant. That's quite enough. I suggest you leave before you make matters worse for yourself. You are already in very serious trouble."

Not nearly as much as you, Lou thought, as he walked to the door. He wished Dodge a good evening and stepped gingerly down the front path. At the car, he turned and looked back at the house. There was no sign of the Deputy Mayor. He opened the car door, got in, and slipped the key into the ignition.

But he did not turn the key.

Instead, he sat back and leaned his head against the head rest. He had acted on impulse and that was unusual for him. But he had no regrets about his actions. His only regret was that Dodge hadn't offered him any kielbasa before their confrontation. The sizzling sausage had smelled very good.

Thinking of the kielbasa made Lou even hungrier. He pushed the image of food out of his mind and prepared to wait.

He did not have to wait very long. In less than fifteen minutes, Dodge emerged from his house, carrying a small valise. Using a side step, he navigated the slippery driveway. Just before he reached his car, Dodge lost his balance, but avoided falling by grabbing hold of the rear end of the Chrysler.

The Deputy Mayor glanced quickly in both directions before opening the driver's door. He tossed the valise into the front seat, and slid into the driver's seat. As soon as the engine started, Dodge put the car in gear and turned right at the end of the driveway.

Good guess, Lou thought, starting the engine of his car. He waited until Dodge reached the corner. Then he pulled out of the parking space and, leaving a comfortable gap between his car and Dodge's, set out to follow the Deputy Mayor.

20

"Surprised, Mr. Fenton?" Emma Kaston asked. "My husband suffers from Alzheimers disease. We have known for some time that he is sick, but the symptoms were not apparent until recently."

"But...but he was on television recently," I said. I was shocked at the sight of the disheveled businessman.

"Yes, I know," Mrs. Kaston responded. "His symptoms come and go. But he has been deteriorating quickly. This week he has been in very bad shape."

The man in the blue robe seemed oblivious to our conversation. His vacant eyes were fixed on the corner of the room where the wall met the ceiling.

"Alzheimers is a terrible disease," Mrs. Kaston said. "Not only has it destroyed Paul's brilliant mind; it also has robbed him of his dignity. After the argument with Carl he began to regress rapidly. I was afraid the extortion threats were accelerating his problems and might provoke him to do something foolish. I also was concerned about Mr. Majorski."

"You thought something might happen to him?" I asked.

"Yes. But I also was concerned that Mr. Majorski might tell someone about the meeting he observed. There might be an investigation and Paul's past identity would be revealed. Under normal circumstances this would have been devastating. With his present condition...I can't imagine what it would have done to him."

Without warning, Paul Kaston lurched forward. Leaving his seat, he moved toward the door. He seemed to be involved in an animated conversation with someone whom the others in the room could not see.

165

"How was I to know?" he yelled, followed by, "leave me alone; just leave me alone."

Before I could react, Masterson leaped from the bed and took hold of the agitated man. Very gently, he led Kaston back to the chair and eased him into the seat. He knelt beside the chair trying to reassure the man in the blue robe that everything was all right.

"You see," Mrs. Kaston said, wringing her hands. "One moment he's quiet, the next he's raving about something no one can understand. I can't bear seeing him this way." Her voice began to crack. She appeared to be losing control, again.

"Have you seen a doctor?" I asked, uncomfortable with the elegant woman's visible pain.

"Several times," she responded. "They say it's a degenerative disease. He will continue to become more disoriented and unpredictable. Eventually it will kill him."

"I'm sorry," I said, still feeling awkward.

"Sometimes I wish he would die. He's lost so much already. His intellect, his self-respect. There's almost nothing left of him. The only thing that remains is his good name in the community. Everyone still sees him as a civic leader, a successful businessman, a good citizen."

With her last words, I finally understood. I had been caught up in Emma Kaston's anguish and grief. Ironically, my empathy had diverted my attention away from the message behind her emotions. Now I saw it clearly.

"Mrs. Kaston, what have you done with Fred Majorski?"

"Don't worry. Mr. Majorski is fine. In fact, I will take you to see him in a moment." Her voice was not as strained as it had been.

"Where is he?" I asked, feeling an odd mixture of relief and agitation. The statement that Majorski was alive had not fully penetrated my senses. It did not yet seem real to me. I had an intense need to see the trainman, to confirm that he was still alive.

"Please be patient," Mrs. Kaston pleaded. "I know you think badly of me. But I need your assistance and I need you to understand so you will help me."

As we spoke, Masterson signaled to Knox who quietly moved behind me, blocking the doorway.

"When I realized my husband would either have to participate in illegal activities to silence Mr. Majorski or risk public exposure of his past, I became frantic. Both options held terrible consequences. I was certain that whatever happened, Paul would be destroyed. In his present condition he is just *so* vulnerable. I know he carries a terrible burden of guilt for having been part of a movement he now knows was destructive and evil. If he felt he had been responsible for harming Mr. Majorski it

166

would have pushed Paul over the edge.

"The alternative seemed equally disastrous. If his past identity were to be revealed, if the community were to find out that the man who ran Atlas Industries had sneaked into this country as a Nazi sympathizer, the public outcry would be enormous. Paul takes great pride in what he has accomplished, in the position of respect he has acquired in the community. For Paul to lose his reputation, his stature . . . it would be devastating."

I was beginning to understand her dilemma. Between a rock and a hard place would be an understatement. "Did you speak to your brother about any of this?" I asked.

"Yes, but he denied anything was happening. He said he and Paul had been arguing about a business deal Paul was involved in the day I overheard them. When I told him I had heard them talking about extortion, he said I must have misunderstood. Even after I told him Paul had admitted someone was blackmailing him, Carl insisted there was nothing to worry about. He knows that Paul has Alzheimers; he said the illness must be making him paranoid."

"What about the extortionist? Were you able to find out anything about him?"

"No. Nothing. I was at my wits end, feeling very desperate. Just when I thought the situation was hopeless, I had this idea. That's when I called Noah."

At the mention of his name, the security chief glanced at Mrs. Kaston. She smiled at him before continuing. "I told Noah my husband was in jeopardy, he was being threatened by a dangerous man. I explained that I could not go to the police without putting Paul at greater risk—which was true. I pleaded with Noah to help Mr. Kaston. Without giving him any details I told him Mr. Majorski was also in trouble, although he might not realize it."

"And you persuaded Noah to kidnap Fred Majorski?" I asked, surprised at the elegant woman's incongruous behavior.

"My actions were in Mr. Majorski's best interests," she said defensively. "I was trying to protect him."

"That may be true, but you were clearly acting outside the law. We can save that debate for later, however. Right now I'm more interested in what you've done with Mr. Majorski."

She tried to catch Masterson's eye, but he continued to attend to Kaston. When Masterson did not respond, she walked past Knox, beckoning me to follow. She stopped at the second door on the right and called Slattery's name. I heard the sound of a bolt being shot back into its case. Then the door opened. Slattery stood in the doorway, his face drawn into its perpetual scowl. Over Slattery's shoulder I could see a body lying on a narrow bed.

Emma Kaston led me into the room. Stretched out on the bed, wearing a gray sweatsuit was Fred Majorski. His eyes were closed and at first, I could not tell if he was alive. I was reassured when I noticed the trainman's chest slowly rising and falling.

"You see," Mrs. Kaston said. "Mr. Majorski is fine. We've given him a sedative to assure that I would have an opportunity to explain the situation to you. He should be regaining consciousness soon. Don't worry, we have taken good care of him."

I was numb. After days of worrying about the trainman, even fearing that he was dead, I was now confronted with the reality of an unconscious, though obviously alive, Fred Majorski. It was more than I could process.

"What the hell have you done?" I blurted out. "What gives you the right to snatch a man from the place he works, carry him off to the middle of nowhere, fill him with drugs, and hold him captive?"

"Calm down, Mr. Fenton. I had no intention of harming Mr. Majorski. Once he wakes up he will tell you, himself, he has been treated very well. I need for you to understand that I had no choice. This man's life was at risk."

"So you say," I responded, not sounding convinced. "How do you even know that Majorski is the so-called intruder?"

"My brother found out. The meeting with the extortionist took place on the edge of the train yard and the man was dressed like a railroad worker. My brother used his position to find out who might have been in the vicinity at that hour. He checked work schedules, personnel records—including ID photos—and made some discreet inquiries. Everything pointed to Mr. Majorski, including the fact he was born in the same part of Poland as we were."

"So, what does that prove? He's part of the Polish connection?"

"There's no need to be sarcastic. It is obvious that my brother and husband knew the extortionist from Poland. Apparently Mr. Majorski knew this evil man, also. And what he knew upset him very much."

"Did Majorski tell you what he knew?"

Mrs. Kaston looked at the man lying on the bed. "I...uh..."

"You haven't spoken to him at all, have you?"

"No. I thought it would be better if I did not become directly involved. Noah has handled everything. He and Mr. Slattery have been taking care of Mr. Majorski."

Hearing Slattery's name triggered an unpleasant memory. "And I suppose you weren't involved with setting me up at the Photoflash store."

Majorski rolled over on his side. "Let's go into the living room," Mrs. Kaston suggested, moving toward the door. I followed reluctantly. She sat in the same chair she had occupied before. I stood next to the fireplace. I could hear water dripping from the roof onto the snow covered ground. A sure sign the temperature outside was rising. Standing by the warm fire I felt fairly hot—in more ways than one.

"I can appreciate how you feel," she said. "What's this rich, old woman doing? Abducting an innocent man; leading you away from the trail, into a false case, a blind alley, to divert you from finding him..."

"Divert is an understatement," I said, remembering the enormous headache I suffered after being smashed in the head outside the Photoflash store. "Say, was that Slattery who whacked me?"

"I am ashamed of what I did. But I hope you can understand how desperate I was..."

"And still are."

"Yes, I suppose so. But I have finally reached a decision and feel some relief now that I know what I must do."

I felt a sudden rush of panic as I fantasized that her relief might come at the expense of Majorski's life...and my own. After all, this was the woman who had arranged for me to be knocked unconscious just for being on the trainman's trail. Now that I actually knew she had taken Majorski, she might be capable of doing *anything*.

Emma Kaston must have noticed my discomfort. "Don't worry. I do not intend to harm you. In fact, I really want you to assist me in carrying out my plan."

"You sure have a strange way of asking for help. I didn't realize kidnapping was habit forming. Have you ever considered using the telephone?"

"No, that would not have worked. You see, I was not certain how you would react when you found out I had abducted Mr. Majorski. I needed to see you face-to-face."

I wanted to feel more sympathetic toward this elegant looking woman, but I couldn't overcome my anger toward her for what she had done to Majorski...and to me. "I hope I won't disappoint you if I don't smile," I said. As I glared at her another frightening memory resurfaced. "I suppose you didn't intend to harm me when you sicked those other creeps on me. The one who threatened me on the telephone, and the two thugs who jumped me in front of my apartment."

"I do not know what you are talking about," she said, looking puzzled. "I have already admitted I arranged for Mr. Slattery to...sidetrack you. But that is the extent of my aggression toward you. If you do not believe me, we can call Mr. Lazard. He can verify what I have told you."

"No thanks. A character reference from Radovan Karadzk might be more credible." I knew that she was telling the truth, but the knowledge that Emma Kaston was not involved in the other two incidents did not comfort me. It meant someone else knew I was connected to Fred Majorski. And whoever had this knowledge certainly did not have friendly intentions toward me.

"Mr. Fenton, what do I have to do to make you understand I had no choice? I *had* to remove Mr. Majorski from the situation he was in. They would have killed him. This man from Poland...he will stop at nothing to get what he wants. I have never seen Paul or my brother so frightened. They would have done anything this man wanted. I...Icannot even bring myself to voice the horrible possibilities my mind has considered."

Under other circumstances I would have found it difficult to believe that the Deputy Mayor and one of the City's most prominent business-men could be drawn into such a terrible scheme. But these were not ordinary circumstances. With the memory of the spine-chilling telephone threats fresh in my mind, I could find no good reason to doubt Mrs. Kaston's frightening scenario.

"Okay," I conceded. "I'm ready to listen. What kind of help do you want from me?"

For the first time that evening, I detected the beginning of a smile on Emma Kaston's face. "What I want," she replied, "is to find a way to return Mr. Majorski and to protect Paul from any further harm. I would like you to help me accomplish both of these objectives."

I sighed. Most of the anger I felt toward Emma Kaston had dissolved. My reaction to her now could best be described as pity. "Let's start with the facts," I said. "Whatever your intentions were, when you took Mr. Majorski you broke the law. I'm fairly certain this act would be classified as kidnapping, which is a Federal offense. As far as protecting your husband —there isn't anyway to assure that. When the story of what happened to Fred Majorski comes out —and it will—your husband's past life, his political history in Poland, his involvement with Operation Bloodstone, will certainly be revealed."

"I was hoping..."

"Hoping won't count for much in this situation," I said, immediately regretting my remark. "Your best option, your *only* option is to call the police and tell them what you've done. If your husband or brother are willing to cooperate they may be able to put the extortionist away. There's no way to protect your brother. His political career will be ruined. If your suspicions are correct, he's likely to go to prison. I hate to say it, but the best hope for your husband is that the Alzheimers will shield his mind from the ugly reality surrounding him.

"As for you...you've got enough money to hire a top-notch law-yer—someone other than Malcolm Lazard. With any luck, the court will take into account the extenuating circumstances, might even show a little mercy."

Mrs. Kaston paused before responding. She appeared to be considering what I had said. "I appreciate your frank observations, Mr. Fenton. However, I am afraid there is a further complication."

"What's that, Mrs. Kaston?"

"This afternoon, before I sent the two men to get you, I was feeling very, very frantic. Paul's behavior was deteriorating rapidly and I did not know what to do. In desperation I called my brother, Carl, and told him Mr. Majorski was here."

Before I could respond, I was startled by the sound of glass breaking.

21

The sound came from the end of the house opposite the bedrooms;
I began to move in the direction of the noise. Before I reached the edge
of the living room, Masterson and Slattery rushed past, guns drawn. I
followed them down the hall into the kitchen.

The window over the sink had a large, jagged hole. Shards of glass
were scattered everywhere: on the counter, in the sink, on the floor. In
the middle of the floor, surrounded by broken pieces of glass, was a rock
the size of a man's fist.

Masterson looked out the window, but couldn't see anything. As he
bent to examine the rock, there was a shriek from the middle of the
house.

All three of us rushed to the living room where we found Emma and
Paul Kaston, Charlie Knox, two strange men and a woman. I had
difficulty processing the scene. My immediate reaction was that I was
looking at one of those "what's wrong with this picture" puzzles. Mrs.
Kaston stood with her back to the fireplace, facing the other five people.
She was leaning toward the others, arms outstretched, frozen in mid air.
Charlie Knox stood next to Paul Kaston, supporting the frail man with
his left arm. In his right hand he held his .44. It was pointed at Paul
Kaston's temple.

One of the new men, a short stocky person wearing a dark brown
parka, was holding an AK-47 aimed at Emma Kaston. The other man
wore a long black wool coat and a mink Cossack hat. He was taller than
the man with the automatic weapon and did not appear to be holding
a gun. He had a large face with a square jaw, wide nostrils and enor-

mous protruding ears. In spite of his oversize features, the most prominent part of his face were his small, beady eyes. They were deep brown, almost black, and were constantly in motion. The dark agate eyes slid from side to side, nervously scanning all of the people in the room. He stood next to the woman, his hand resting on the back of her neck.

The woman had both arms behind her back. It took my mind a few seconds to register the identity of the woman standing next to the man in black.

"Ollie," I shouted in surprise.

"What the hell is going on, Charlie?" Masterson asked angrily.

"Sorry, Boss," Knox responded. "The pay's a little better on this end."

"Asshole," Slattery muttered, glaring at Knox.

The man with the AK-47 shifted his weapon in our direction. "Okay," he said. "Put your guns on the floor—slowly—and push them over to me with your foot."

I froze at the sound of the man's voice. It was the same voice that had sent a chill up my spine when I picked up the telephone two days ago in my apartment.

Slattery looked at Masterson, who nodded. They followed the short man's instructions.

"How about you, handsome?" the short man asked, pointing his gun at me

"I...Idon't have a weapon," I replied, holding my hands up.

"Watch these guys, Knox," the short man said, motioning Masterson and Slattery to move aside as he walked over and frisked me.

Finding no concealed weapon he directed us to line up in front of the fireplace, facing into the room, with our hands clasped behind our necks. Meanwhile he took Emma Kaston by the arm and yanked her toward him, placing her between himself and the three of us standing by the fireplace.

I still was not able to put all of the pieces together. I knew what Carl Dodge looked like and he wasn't here. And neither of the men looked old enough to be the Butcher, Josef Sikorski.

Who were these men and what did they want?

And what was Ollie doing here?

Before I could find the answers to these questions the strange scene became even more bizarre.

Looking up, I saw a gray clad figure emerge from the bedroom hallway. The man was stooped over and shuffling slowly toward the living room. I didn't know how to react. If I alerted the intruders they would easily add this latest arrival to their group of captives. If I didn't say anything, and his presence startled Knox and the other two men, the man in gray was at risk of being shot.

The dilemma was quickly taken out of my hands. The man with the darting eyes saw me lower my gaze. Sensing that something was happening behind him, he spun around.

Fred Majorski was at the edge of the living room, only a few feet away, when the man in black turned toward him. Majorski's eyes widened and he screamed in a hoarse voice, "Aaaggghhh." Coming out of his slouch, the trainman leaped toward the man in black and crashed into his body with surprising force, starting a chain reaction. The man in black fell backward into Emma Kaston. They both toppled to the floor. As he fell, the beady eyed man loosened his grip on Ollie's neck, but not before his momentum caused her to stumble into the arms of the short man with the AK-47.

In spite of the impact, Majorski did not fall. When he saw the man in black lying on the ground he jumped on him, arms flailing wildly.

Masterson took advantage of the momentary disruption. With lightning speed he dove at Knox, jarring the gun from his hand and pushing him away from Paul Kaston. While Masterson went for Knox's gun, Slattery came up behind the heavyset turncoat, grabbed him by the hair, and savagely smashed a large fist into his round face.

During the commotion the short man had managed to retain his grip on the AK-47...and Ollie. Pointing his gun at Masterson and Slattery he shouted, "Hold it right fucking there, assholes. Move a muscle and I'll turn you into a blood spouting fucking geyser."

Up to this point I had not moved. I was mesmerized by the action, frightened by the violence. Now my full attention was focused on Ollie, hands bound behind her back, in the grasp of the gun-toting goon who had frightened me so terribly just by talking to him on the telephone.

Instinctively, I reached over to the rack that held the fireplace tools. I picked up a brass poker and took a step toward the man with the AK-47. The short man turned toward me as I whipped my arm around and released the poker. The metal rod twirled through the air making a full rotation before striking the short man on the left shoulder. He cried out in pain but held on to the gun. Forgetting Ollie for a second he swung the gun toward me.

A second was all that Ollie needed. She bent her knees and pushed off her toes, thrusting her head up. The top of her head struck the short man solidly under the chin, snapping his head back sharply. The gun flew out of his hand and he fell backward, landing on the floor with a thud. He did not move.

Masterson picked up the automatic weapon and looked around. Slattery held Knox in a hammerlock with one hand, his other arm wrapped around the heavyset man's neck. I untied the rope that bound Ollie's wrists. Emma Kaston sat on the floor cradling her husband's head in her arms. And Fred Majorski sat on the chest of the man in black, pinning his arms to the floor, staring into his dark, beady eyes.

"Mrs. Kaston," Masterson said. "I think it's time to call the police.

The beautiful silver haired woman looked lovingly into the vacant eyes of her husband. She stroked his cheek with her fingertip. Then she looked up at the chief of security.

There were tears in her eyes as she nodded weakly.

I did not get back to Syracuse until after midnight. The police had difficulty locating the Kastons' country home. When the officers finally arrived, they insisted on questioning everyone before returning to the city. Emma Kaston refused to say anything until she saw her lawyer. Paul Kaston was not able to say anything. Knox and his two associates were not interested in being cooperative. Masterson and Slattery said they were with Mrs. Kaston, and Fred Majorski was too groggy from the sedative to say anything coherent.

That left me and Ollie to do most of the talking and Ollie didn't know enough to be helpful.

I recounted the story of Fred Majorski's disappearance and gave them a detailed account of the evening's activities leading up to the confrontation at the Kastons' Tully home. I didn't add much to Emma Kaston's story since I still didn't know much about the two men who had kidnapped Ollie and barged into the lodge with the assistance of Charlie Knox.

After forty-five minutes of intense questioning, another pair of policemen arrived in a transport van. One of the officers was Ernie Lewis, who had responded when Mannie Bosco was shot at Suburban Park. To my relief Lewis persuaded the other officers to suspend their questioning until we returned to the city. He also agreed to swap vehicles with one of the officers and drove Ollie, me, and Fred Majorski back to the city.

The outside temperature had risen several degrees since Slattery had eased the large Chevrolet off the slippery road. While there were still patches of ice on the secondary roads, the county trucks had sprayed a layer of salt on the highway surface, melting the ice.

The trainman sat up front with Lewis, while Ollie and I sat in the back. I tried to think of something to say to Ollie but kept coming up blank. She sat quietly, staring out the side window. I didn't need a Ph.D. to know she wasn't happy with me and I couldn't really blame her. Which was too bad, since at that moment I was feeling pretty good about finding Fred Majorski alive, and wished I could share my good feelings with her.

Ernie made several attempts to start a conversation with Majorski, but with no luck. The large man sat stiffly, staring straight ahead. I wondered what the old man saw as he gazed out at the cold, dark night. If someone asked me to wager, I would have put my money on a woman named Anita. I would also place a side bet that Anita was no longer alive; had probably not been for a long time.

"Jesus, Marty," Ernie said, looking into the rear view mirror, "you've been leading one very dangerous life, lately. What's the matter; graduate school too tame for you?"

I chuckled quietly. I didn't have the energy for a hearty laugh. "Right now graduate school looks pretty good. A wicked parametric statistical analysis is about as much of a challenge as I can handle now."

Ernie shifted his eyes so he could see Ollie. "I'm ashamed of you, Marty. A tough guy like you. This little incident should have your adrenalin pumping... Oh well, I guess you won't have any trouble falling asleep tonight. Maybe Ollie and I can go out for a couple of beers while you're getting your beauty rest."

I sneered at the back of Ernie's head as Ollie said, "Not tonight, Ernie. Maybe some other time. You can bring your wife. Marty and I have some unfinished business."

"Uh huh," Ernie said, giving his full attention to the dark highway.

I asked Ernie to drop me at the neighborhood tavern on the west side where I had been picked up by Slattery and Knox. I hoped Ollie's car was still there.

The tavern's outside lights were still on. Leaving Ollie and Majorski at her car, I walked quickly toward the nearby green building. I opened the heavy wooden door and stepped inside. There were a couple of men sitting at the bar. The bartender looked as if he were beginning to close down for the night.

The bartender acknowledged me with a nod. Moving past the bar, toward the rear of the tavern, I waved at him. I felt like a regular. As I approached the last booth, I was struck by a pang of disappointment.

The booth was empty.

Once again, my desire to share the good news had been thwarted.

I had hoped to be able to tell Arthur Paulson that we had found Fred Majorski—alive; to tell him the man called the Butcher had been caught; good had triumphed over evil. I wanted to thank the brave little man, to let him know he could rest a little easier.

All of that would have to wait for another day.

I was glad Ollie had chosen to drive. I wasn't certain I had the energy or concentration to drive safely across town. It had been an incredible day, in many ways. Meeting the Professor, learning about the horrible things that had happened in Poland during the War. Escaping from my own apartment only to be kidnapped by two Atlas security men. Seeing

Emma and then Paul Kaston in a way I never would have imagined. The sudden attack by the two men who could only be described as evil. And Ollie, appearing suddenly in the grasp of the two intruders, then acting so swiftly and powerfully to disarm the man with the frightening voice. She had saved the day...and my life.

The events of the day had drained me. At least I thought so until we approached the small wood frame house in Eastwood. As we pulled in front of Janet Pafko's house, I was overcome by a strong surge of anxiety. My heart beat quickened and my stomach began to churn. I felt queasy. Until that moment, I had happily anticipated the reunion between Fred Majorski and his daughter and grandson. When I had called Janet from Tully, she had been in a sound sleep. It had taken her a minute to absorb the news that her father had been found. When she finally understood he was alive, Janet had let out a spontaneous shriek that caused me to pull the receiver away from my ear.

Her excitement had been contagious. The numbness began to fade and the impact of what had happened finally reached me. I had managed to find Fred Majorski and, other than being sedated, he appeared to be unscathed. Granted, my role in the investigation had been relatively minor. But if it had not been for my persistence we might not have located Majorski before the two thugs got to him. This time I had followed through.

Riding through the quiet streets of the city, I could barely contain my eagerness to see the look on Janet's face when she was reunited with her father.

As we entered Janet Pafko's street my enthusiasm quickly turned to fear. For the first time I realized that delivering Fred Majorski would not only create a reunion with his family; it would also bring together Ollie and Janet Pafko, two women for whom I had very strong feelings. I wasn't certain how they would react to each other. Even more frightening, I didn't know how I would respond.

Walking up the front path with Ollie and the large trainman, my throat tightened. I looked over at Majorski. The big man did not look as stupefied as he had earlier. Still, he showed no sign he was about to be reunited with the two people he cared most about.

I pushed the doorbell and stepped back. In a few seconds the door swung open. Janet Pafko stood in the doorway, dressed in a long flannel nightgown. She held Billy in her arms. The little boy, his arms draped around her neck, looked very sleepy.

As soon as he saw his grandfather, the boy came awake. He let go of his mother's neck, twisted around and leaped toward Majorski.

Just as the boy looked as if he were going to fall to the floor, the large trainman came to life. He reached out his arms with surprising speed, grabbed Billy under the arms and pulled him to his chest.

"Grandpa. You're home, you're home! I missed you, Grandpa."

Majorski looked down at his grandson and smiled. "I missed you, too, Billy."

Janet put her arms around her father and son, and squeezed very hard. She stayed there for a moment, head pressed against Majorski's shoulder, tears running down her cheeks. Then she turned and gave me a big hug. Her display of affection surprised me. Reacting spontaneously I put my arms around Janet and squeezed.

After a few seconds I realized Ollie was standing next to me. Feeling embarrassed, I turned to look at the woman I wanted to marry.

Ollie had a puzzled look on her face.

Wanting to remove myself from this awkward situation, I quietly extracted myself from Janet's embrace.

"Why don't we sit down for a few minutes," I suggested. "Perhaps your father can fill you in on what happened."

As we walked to the living room, I tried to sort out my feelings. I definitely was uncomfortable being with these two women at the same time. Ollie was strong and self sufficient. I felt confident that she liked me, even found me attractive. But she didn't seem to need me, at least in the same way I needed her. I believed that if I were to vanish tomorrow Ollie would be upset, but she would have no trouble getting on with her life.

Janet, on the other hand was so vulnerable. Even in the brief time I had known her, she seemed to have become dependent on me. I only had to look into her green eyes to feel her need for help. Like a magnet, her eyes seemed to draw me toward her. I realized these were extraordinary circumstances, having her father disappear without warning, being abducted from her own home. Still, the intensity of her need was clear.

But, was it really that simple? Were Ollie and Janet really so different? Could I put them into such neat categories: one was independent, the other couldn't cope without help; one was in complete control of her emotions, the other wore her feelings on her sleeve.

The more I thought about it, the more confused I became.

After all, hadn't Ollie become tearful when I had failed to call her after Mannie Bosco had been killed. And, although I couldn't clearly read the expression on her face when Janet hugged me, it was obvious that Ollie's reaction was more than casual and detached.

As for Janet Pafko, she continued to function fairly well, in spite of all the stress. She was doing a good job of caring for Billy. She managed to go to work every day. Her house looked fairly neat and clean.

Maybe she wasn't as helpless as she appeared.

Women were so damned complicated. Given a choice, I would take a good *New York Times* crossword, anytime. In my heart, I knew that was a lie. But at least with puzzles, there was always a solution.

Sitting next to Ollie, I glanced at her face. She looked tired, but there was no trace of her earlier expression of bewilderment. Janet offered us something to drink. Majorski declined. Ollie and I asked for coffee.

Once we were settled, the trainman recounted the events of the past few weeks. He spoke slowly, stopping frequently to collect his thoughts. The effects of the sedative had not worn off completely. He talked about the night he walked into the meeting being held next to the helicopter on the outskirts of the railroad yard. He described what followed, including his kidnapping and internment at the Kastons' lodge in Tully. Finally, he shared the story of what had happened many years ago in Poland and how these events had come to haunt the small group of men who had come together in the hilltop house in Tully earlier that evening.

By the time Majorski had finished, everyone in the room was exhausted. Majorski sat slumped in the easy chair. To my delight, Ollie had curled up on the sofa, her head resting on my shoulder. Billy had fallen asleep in his mother's arms. Janet, who looked as if she were barely awake, carried Billy up to his room before saying goodnight to Ollie and me.

At the front door, Janet thanked us for returning her father. I assured her we were happy to have been able to help, hoping as I uttered the words, that I was indeed speaking for Ollie as well.

As we stepped outside, Janet reached out and touched me gently on the shoulder. Turning toward her, I noticed that the smile on her face was different. She no longer looked frightened and helpless. Instead, she appeared to be confident and relaxed, almost serene.

I was also aware that my own reaction was different. I no longer felt I had to help Janet. I didn't feel protective toward her.

And, most striking of all, I was no longer attracted to her.

It wasn't that I didn't feel anything. I still liked her, even thought she was pretty. But the magnetism that had drawn me to her was gone.

I wondered what Professor Singleton would say about that.

We were silent as we drove to my apartment. Ollie concentrated on driving, her eyes fixed on the area just in front of her car, where the Volkswagen's dim headlights barely illuminated the road. I kept glancing at Ollie, trying to read her expression, but her face revealed nothing. No frown, no grimace, no hostile glare, and nothing even closely resembling a smile. All of her energy seemed to be focused on driving.

Finally, I could no longer contain myself. "Ollie, can I ask you something?"

"Sure," she responded keeping her eyes on the road.

"Uh, is there anything you want to ask me? You know, about what happened back there at Mr. Majorski's house."

"I don't know what you mean, Marty."

I thought I detected a faint smirk.

"Don't make this difficult for me, Ollie."

"I *really* don't know what you're talking about."

"You know, Majorski's daughter, Janet Pafko. When she put her arms around me."

"And you put your arms around her."

"Cut it out. I'm trying to be serious. I want you to understand."

"Okay," she said, finally turning her head toward me. "Help me understand."

I wondered how I could cut my losses. This conversation was definitely not going the way I wanted it to. "It was just...just a gesture of appreciation for what we did to bring her father back."

"What *we* did?" Ollie asked, raising her eyebrows. "How come I didn't get a hug?"

"Jesus, give it a break. I'm trying to tell you: Janet Pafko doesn't mean anything to me." At least now, I thought, my conscience almost clear. "She was happy to see her father. She's grateful for my help. I'm glad I was able to help her."

"That's nice," Ollie said. "That's very nice."

The sharp edge of her sarcasm made me wince. My first instinct was to apologize, to tell her I was sorry for having dragged her into this mess. I wanted her to know I felt bad about the display of affection at Janet Pafko's house, but there was nothing going on between me and her. More than anything I wanted to get out of this awful situation with Ollie. I didn't want to spend all of this energy trying to get her to not be angry with me. I wanted us to be together, to hold each other and shut out the frightening events of the past few days.

As I groped for the right words to turn the situation around, I suddenly became angry——not at Ollie, but at myself. Why was I acting like such a jerk, chasing after Ollie trying to sooth her feelings and convince her she should want to be with me. What a wimp! No wonder she wasn't willing to make a commitment. I certainly wouldn't want a long-term relationship with such a spineless creature.

With a burst of energy, I turned to her and said, "Let's get something straight. There's nothing going on between Janet Pafko and me. While I was looking for her father I got to know her pretty well. I was concerned about her and took an interest in her well being. I found her to be a nice person. I may even have become more personally involved than I should have, but now that her father is back, it's over. There's nothing between us."

Ollie started to say something, but I didn't give her a chance to respond. "What's more important," I said, "is what's going on with you and me. I've finally realized what a fool I've been. Always pursuing you; pushing you to make a commitment. I can't believe how blind I've been. You're the first woman to accept me for who I am; no more, no less. You don't like me for what I can do for you. You don't *need* me to do for you. And I haven't known what to do with that. I couldn't believe that you might like me. Yet, to my surprise, you did. It was too good to be true and I was afraid of losing you. I felt if I didn't have some commitment, some kind of guarantee from you, then something awful would happen. You would wake up some morning, realize you didn't need me, and walk away. I was looking for a warranty, not a relationship."

Ollie waited to see if I was going to say anything else. When I showed no indication of continuing, she pulled over to the curb, turned to me and said, "Is that supposed to make me feel better? You give me this nice little speech about how you've finally realized what was going on between us. You analyze why you've been so insecure, confess to becoming personally involved with Janet Pafko, and throw in a little self pity. And you expect that to make everything okay?"

That wasn't quite what I had expected her to say. "But, I..."

"Well, you're wrong, Marty. That doesn't make anything better. Your nice little words aren't worth squat, especially when they're stacked up against your actions. You don't care enough to call me when you're beaten up or after you come within inches of taking a bullet in the chest. You run off to comfort some woman you've never met rather than stay and work out our problems. And you snub your nose at Lou's efforts to protect you and deliberately put yourself at risk. You're a real shit."

I felt as if I had been sucker punched. I had dropped my guard and Ollie had let me have it. As I struggled to regain my composure, I glanced over at Ollie, wary of what she might do next. She was staring out the window, and seemed oblivious of my presence. To my surprise, she did not look angry. When I looked at her eyes I saw an even more disturbing emotion —fear.

"Ollie, are you okay? Is something wrong?"

She didn't say anything, but began to tremble. Her body started to shake and her lip quivered. I reached over to put my arm around her, but she held up her hands and shook her head. I withdrew my arm and sank back in the passenger seat, not knowing what to do. Two minutes ago she had been lambasting me for being a fool. Now she sat in a catatonic stupor, looking as if she would fall apart if I touched her.

After a very long moment she whispered something that I couldn't understand. "What did you say?" I asked quietly.

"My father."

"What about your father, Ollie?" As soon as I said it, a terrible thought filled my mind. "My God. Did your father do something to you? Did he hurt you? Is that what you were trying to tell me outside the museum the other day?"

With tears sliding down her face, she shook her head slowly. "No, he didn't hurt me——at least not physically. He never even touched me."

Now I was totally bewildered. I was accustomed to Ollie being strong, being in charge. Seeing her sitting there, trembling and looking helpless didn't fit. The whole scene didn't make sense to me.

The headlights of a car coming toward us blinded me momentarily. In that instant I realized we might sit in the car all night if I left things to Ollie. "Do you think you can drive?" I asked softly.

This time she nodded.

We drove slowly to my apartment. Fortunately there was a parking spot in front of the building, the first good omen in some time. I offered my arm, she took it and we walked up to my flat.

After I had fixed each of us each a cup of hot tea and draped the quilt my grandmother had made over Ollie's shoulders, we sat on the lumpy sofa in the living room and she told me why she avoided getting too close to men.

Ollie had previously told me a few things about her family. She had grown up in a wealthy suburb of Hartford, Connecticut. Her father was an insurance executive and her mother worked as a buyer for a large department store. Both parents were interested in the arts and liked to travel. From the time she was a young girl Ollie had been exposed to theaters, concert halls, and museums.

What Ollie hadn't told me until that night, was how her father had betrayed her mother and her.

When Ollie was six, her father became involved with an attractive young woman who frequently performed in the local repertory theater. Her father, who was a member of the theater's board, met the young actor at a reception following a benefit performance. They carried on an affair until Ollie's mother accidentally discovered a receipt to a New Haven hotel for a day which he was supposedly at a business meeting in Tulsa. When she confronted him, Ollie's father admitted he was having an affair and announced he was leaving his family to live with his mistress.

Ollie's mother started drinking heavily and Ollie, who had been daddy's little girl was devastated. After six months, her father grew tired of the younger woman's histrionics and returned to his family, tail between his legs. Her mother accepted him back, claiming it was for

Ollie's sake, and warned him to keep his eyes and hands to himself.

They all tried hard to put aside her father's infidelity and rebuild their family. Apparently they did fairly well for a few years——until Ollie and her mother returned early from a weekend in New York City and found her father and a buxom blonde soprano frantically trying to get dressed.

This time Ollie's father showed no interest in going off with his paramour. Unfortunately for him, Ollie's mother had no interest in letting him remain. That evening he moved to a hotel and the following week found an apartment in a high-rise in Hartford. He never spent another night in their home.

Ollie saw him once a week and spent the customary holidays and two weeks in the summer with him, but her feelings for him were not the same. She could not forgive him and never regained the trust he had twice betrayed.

When Ollie finished telling her story, I took her in my arms and held her. We did not speak, but this time the silence was comfortable.

After a few minutes, Ollie leaned back and looked at me. Her eyes were red, but they were no longer filled with fear. "I'm tired, Marty."

"Do you want me to drive you home?"

"No, I'd like to stay here if you don't mind."

That sounded good to me, especially since I didn't relish going outside into the cold, again. While Ollie used the bathroom I put clean sheets on my bed. So much had happened that night. I was having difficulty processing all of it.

The ride to Tully; being confronted with Paul Kaston and then Fred Majorski; the skirmish with Knox and the two intruders. As if that wasn't enough, I also had come to grips with my feelings for Janet Pafko; been raked over the coals by Ollie; and finally, had watched in amazement as the woman I loved shed her armor and revealed the painful memories of her childhood that she had kept inside herself for so many years. I didn't know what it all meant and I wasn't sure where it would lead us, but I did know that the events of that evening had definitely changed our relationship.

I was getting an extra pillow from the closet when Ollie returned from the bathroom, wearing nothing but one of my blue oxford shirts. Seeing her shapely, muscular legs, I felt a stirring in my groin. I moved toward Ollie, but stopped as she climbed into bed and pulled up the comforter. In the harsh light of the bedside lamp's naked bulb she looked pale and tired. She had an aura of vulnerability that I had not previously noticed.

As much as I wanted to be with Ollie, I knew the time was not right. Too much had happened that night. She did not look like she had the energy to make love and even if she was ready, I was not. There would be other times——*better* times——for us to be together.

I tried to curb my glands as I approached the bed. I knelt by her side and leaned over. "I love you, Ollie," I said softly.

"I know you do, Marty." She reached up and kissed me gently on the lips.

I turned off the light and went into the living room. It surprised me that I didn't feel tired. Whether it was the aftershock of the evening's events or my roiling hormones, I was too worked up to go to sleep. I picked up the latest issue of *Popular Puzzles* and began to unscramble the letter of a cryptogram.

Less than three minutes later I put down the puzzle, unfinished. I paced between the kitchen and living room, trying to figure out what to do with my excess energy. After a few rotations, an idea came to me. I tiptoed into the bedroom and stood over Ollie, watching her sleep. She looked so peaceful, not at all like she had during her last waking hours. It was as if sleep had chased away the demons that had been hounding her.

I picked up my briefcase and returned to the living room. Sitting at the bridge table, I pulled out my thesis material and laid it on the table.

Two and a half hours later, as the first light of dawn appeared in the living room window, I put down my pen and arranged my note cards in a neat stack. Then I slid a paper clip onto the completed first chapter of my thesis.

22

The sunlight streaming through the window made the DeSantis' breakfast dining room table look like a cover from *Food and Wine* magazine. Angie was pure Italian when it came to culinary matters —-except for weekend brunch.

The ritual was always the same. First, she stopped at Snowflake Bakery. After chatting with the other customers in line—there was always a line on weekends —she placed her usual order: a large Jewish rye with seeds, half dozen salt sticks, walnut coffee cake chock full of cinnamon and nuts, half pound of rugelah and assorted danish. Next she stopped at the bagel store before picking up Nova Scotia lox, whitefish, creamed herring and cream cheese at the deli.

Finally, she returned home where she prepared a huge omelet filled with ham, cheddar cheese, and whatever respectable leftovers were left in the refrigerator.

Not great on cholesterol, but definitely scrumptious.

The four of us were doing a good job devouring Angie's feast. There was not much conversation while we ate. I had managed to catch a few hours of sleep before Lou called to invite Ollie and me to brunch. I accepted without hesitating, knowing from experience what kind of spread Angie prepared. I also was curious to find out what the police had learned. I let Ollie sleep for another hour before going into my bedroom. She smiled at me when I woke her. By the time Ollie and I had showered, dressed, and driven to Angie and Lou's house I was famished. I wiped a fleck of cream cheese from my lip and leaned back in the chair as Angie topped off my cup from a freshly brewed pot of coffee.

"How did the bad guys get you?" Lou asked Ollie as he munched on a salt stick lathered with butter. "I thought you were some sort of tough lady."

Ollie blushed. "I guess I'm more gullible than I thought. This guy came into the museum about 3:30—the short guy with the big gun. He was dressed in a police uniform and said you had sent him. He told me you wanted him to bring me over to the Public Safety Building to look at pictures of some guys who might have jumped Marty the other night. I didn't even question him. He had the uniform. He knew about the attack. How was I to know?"

"Was he one of the guys you subdued the other night?" Lou asked. "I hear you were kind of intimate with them."

Ollie's face became even redder. "It was very dark and I wasn't really focusing on their faces."

"Jesus, Lou," I interjected. "Sounds like you've got an epidemic crime wave. Better take all those officers off the drug detail. You've got some kind of serious uniform snatching problem here. First Slattery, then the goon with the big gun. How's a citizen going to know the good guys from the bad guys?"

"That's going to be a tough one," Lou responded. "Especially for a citizen who has the good judgment and resourcefulness to escape from the security of legitimate police protection and plunge directly into the wailing arms of a pair of hired guns posing as policemen."

"What's that say about me?" Ollie asked, raising her eyebrows.

"No offense, Ollie," Lou said. "I feel bad that I forgot to check on you. If I had, you wouldn't have gotten caught up in this mess."

"And I wouldn't have this awful headache," Ollie said rubbing her head.

"And I might not be here to enjoy Angie's delicious omelet," I added. "Maybe I should be grateful that you're such an airhead, Lou."

Angie smiled. Things were returning to normal. "Don't be so hard on Lou. He did manage to figure out that Carl Dodge was dirty. And he made certain he didn't get away."

"That wasn't hard," Lou said with a chuckle. "The honorable Deputy Mayor took off from his house and headed straight for the airport. Of course, it might have helped if he had called ahead to find out that all flights had been canceled on account of the weather. Either way, he wasn't going anywhere."

"What did he say when you confronted him?" Angie asked.

"Something about having to represent the Mayor at some conference. Which became more difficult to justify when we found a passport, $30,000 in cash and a couple of out-of-state bank passbooks under another name, in his valise."

"Maybe he was starting a foreign aid program for the city," I said, reaching for a cheese danish.

"I think Deputy Mayor Dodge had his own ideas about revenue sharing," Lou responded. "After I left his house I waited in the car. I was certain he would make a move. I didn't know if he would contact his co-conspirator —whoever that was—by phone or in person, but I figured he was shook up enough so he might not be thinking too clearly."

"Why did Dodge change Mr. Majorski's personnel record?" Ollie asked.

"Majorski came from the same town as Dodge," I replied. "The Deputy Mayor was afraid someone might make a connection between the two of them —especially after Majorski disappeared."

"Unfortunately, Mr. Dodge is not too swift in the geography department," Lou said.

"What do you mean?" Ollie asked.

Lou looked over at Angie as he explained. "Bialogard—the town Dodge substituted as Majorski's birth place—is in the northwest corner of Poland. I remembered from my course on modern European history that the western portion of Poland was originally part of Germany. It became part of Poland after World War II when the German borders were realigned. Mr. Majorski was born in 1927. Therefore, he couldn't have been born in Poland, if his birth place was Bialogard."

Angie smiled at her husband, who looked very smug at the moment.

"I'm glad to hear that your fifteen years of night school really produced some useful learning," I said.

"Feel free to call on me for knowledge or wisdom, anytime," Lou said, reaching for a bagel.

While Lou and I were trading quips Ollie was thinking about the Deputy Mayor. "Dodge might have been one of the people who called the house where they were keeping me," she said.

"Yeah," Lou said. "After he realized there was no way out, Dodge started to sing like a tenor. He told me how he was forced to go along with the extortion scheme, how Sikorski threatened to expose Kaston and make his own life miserable."

"Sikorski," Angie said. "Isn't that the man you called the Butcher?"

"No, not the Butcher," Lou responded shaking his head. "The son of the Butcher."

"Huh?" Angie said.

"The extortionist is Josef Sikorski—Jr," I explained.

"And every bit as charming as his father," Lou added. "Junior lives in Gdan′sk, the largest shipping port in Poland. According to Dodge, Josef Senior kept a list of people who emigrated to the United States; people who might not want their former political affiliations revealed. Those who joined Operation Bloodstone enjoyed a favored status on his list.

Occasionally he 'sold' information from his list to people who were coming over here. With a little ingenuity, the new immigrants could pick up pocket change by suggesting to the people on Sikorski's list what might happen if their past histories were to become public knowledge."

"Is that how Dodge became 'connected' to Paul Kaston?" Ollie asked.

Lou nodded.

"You mean he knew Kaston before his sister became involved with him?"

This time I responded. "Mrs. Kaston suspected that Dodge had an unhealthy relationship with her husband. In the last few weeks Kaston admitted to her that he had known Dodge in Poland. Dodge was a young punk who used to take advantage of the Jews who lived in the ghetto. Nothing big time like Sikorski, but pretty sleazy nevertheless.

"A few years after Kaston arrived in this country, Dodge contacted him. Dodge had come over with his sister, who is almost ten years younger. They had relatives in Baltimore. Dodge left his sister in Baltimore while he set out with Sikorski's list to seek his fortune. He found Kaston in Camden, New Jersey.

"Keeping Camden safe from Communism," Lou said.

"Yeah," I continued. "At that time Kaston didn't have any money, but Dodge managed to get his hooks into him for a few dollars a month..."

"A good long term investment for Dodge, I'd say," Angie quipped.

"Definitely," I said. "Dodge kept his hand in Kaston's pocket as he climbed the financial ladder. Picked up a nice piece of change over the years."

"Even after Kaston married his sister?" Angie exclaimed with disgust.

"Carl Dodge is not a very nice man," Lou said. "Plus he had a nasty gambling habit that made it difficult for him to live on the salary of a public servant."

"How do you know that?" I asked, surprised.

"Just good police work," Lou replied, obviously pleased with himself.

Ollie tossed a piece of rugelah at Lou. He caught the small piece of pastry in one hand and popped it into his mouth. "Okay, Mr. Genius," she said, "how does Sikorski come into the picture?"

"Sikorski—Senior, that is—apparently believed that the true value of his list would be realized in the future, when he found a way to deal directly with its membership. He was convinced that someday he would find a way to leave Poland and come to this country."

"Not a bad political forecaster," Ollie said.

"Unfortunately, he didn't get an opportunity to execute his plan," Lou said. "However, he did manage to pass the list on to his son, with detailed instructions on how to use it. When the Communist regime in Eastern Europe crumbled and trade lines to the West were reopened, the young Sikorski seized the opportunity. He took some of his family's hard earned money and started a small business. He figured there would be a good market in this country for the machinery being produced in Poland. So he became a trade representative for heavy equipment manufacturers interested in doing business with the U.S. of A."

"A great cover for traveling," Angie said.

"Exactly,"Lou said. "His father had kept tabs on Carl Dodge. Junior had no difficulty locating the Deputy Mayor. From there he moved on to an even more lucrative target — Paul Kaston."

"But how was he able to gain such power over them in this country?" Ollie asked.

"Like all predators, he knew their vulnerable spots. He understood how to play on their fears. For Dodge it was the threat of losing access to Kaston's money. The steady flow of cash not only allowed him to enjoy some nice perks, it also supported his more than modest gambling habit. Dodge also had good reason to believe he was at risk of losing more than money if he messed around with Sikorski. For Kaston, the fear was simpler. He was deathly afraid of losing his reputation as an exemplary businessman and citizen. He was a pillar of the community. Status was extremely important to him. And if Sikorski's own sinister presence wasn't enough to inspire fear, the Butcher's son had enough money and contacts to hire some seamy characters to help him overcome any cultural obstacles he might encounter."

"Sounds like a pretty scary fellow," Angie said.

"You might say so," Ollie said, remembering with disgust the feel of his clammy hand on the back of her neck.

I stretched my arms and arched my back. I was beginning to feel the effects of last night's ordeal. The four cups of coffee I had drank with breakfast were also catching up with me.

I excused myself and went into the small bathroom off the kitchen. Standing over the toilet I noticed how the deep purple lines in the striped wall paper were exactly the same color as the toilet cover. It was a detail I had not noticed before today. I never ceased to be amazed by Angie's talents. I found myself wondering how Ollie might decorate our home if we were to merge our households, but I quickly redirected my thoughts. I didn't want to think about that subject.

I flushed the toilet and turned on the faucets of the sink. Looking into the mirror, I was struck by how grubby I looked: dark pouches under my eyes, two days of growth covering my face. I had not slept well during the few hours I was on the living room sofa. Images from the previous evening kept intruding on my sleep. Emma Kaston's soiled elegance; Paul Kaston's vacant stare; Sikorski's darting eyes. And the contorted face of Fred Majorski as he leaped on the man who was responsible for this mess.

I lathered my hands with soap and held my hands under the warm water.

A helluva night, I thought, remembering the look on the short man's face when he realized Ollie's head was on a collision course with the underside of his jaw. Now, away from the action and adrenalin, I was aware of how close I had come to dying. And how my persistence had put Ollie in jeopardy.

Wiping my hands on a towel, I thought about my former job as an air traffic controller. If it had not been for Ronald Reagan I might still be sitting in a tower looking at little blips moving across a radar screen.

The stress in the tower was just as intense, but the working conditions were definitely safer.

I finished drying my hands and returned to the dining room. Lou was explaining to Angie why Majorski had reacted as he did when he saw Sikorski in the Kaston's living room. "He actually thought the man who was holding Ollie was the elder Sikorski, whom he had known in Poland, in the 1940s."

"It's really ironic," I added. "Sikorski was his father's son in so many ways. No only did he take up his father's profession as a cruel extortionist, but according to Fred Majorski, Josef Junior also bears an uncanny physical resemblance to the elder Sikorski. After Majorski came out of his drug induced stupor he explained to us what happened. He had been working late one night several weeks ago when he stumbled into a strange gathering. Several men were standing near a helicopter. Majorski approached to find out what they were doing. He aimed his flashlight at the men and was astounded to find caught in the beam of his light, the face of a man he had not seen in more than forty years—Josef Sikorski, also known as the Butcher.

"Majorski said that seeing this horrible man from his past terrified him so much that he instinctively turned and ran. He told me he can't recall where he was going. The shock of seeing the Butcher scared him so much he just kept running. The next thing he remembered he was standing at an intersection on the edge of the train yard, feeling completely winded. Before he could move, a car drove up, slowed, and sped past him. It was a big black Chrysler. Majorski managed to get a look at the driver before he floored the accelerator. He recognized Carl Dodge from the evening news on T.V."

"Did Majorski tell anyone what he had seen?" Angie asked.

"No," I said. "For the next few days he was in a state of constant fear. He was terrified that Sikorski would find him, perhaps even kill him. He was convinced that if he told *anyone* what he had seen, the Deputy Mayor would find out and inform Sikorski."

"What a nightmare," Angie said.

"Even worse," I said, "when Kaston's security people called him at the train yard the morning I met with him, he was certain they were Sikorski's men. They told him they were holding his daughter. If he did not meet them they would harm her. He met them and they took him to Kaston's country home. It was not until after the bizarre episode last night in Tully that Majorski realized he was not being held by Sikorski."

"The whole story is bizarre," Lou said. "According to Emma Kaston, Sikorski didn't have the foggiest idea who Majorski was the night he intruded on their little meeting. Her husband told her that Dodge was the one who identified the trainman. He was afraid Majorski might talk, so he did some research on who was at the train yard that night."

"There was only one Polish speaking worker who fit the description," I added.

"What was the connection between Majorski and Sikorski?" Angie asked.

"Aside from the fact that they sound like a double play combination for the Pittsburgh Pirates," I said, "they lived in the same neighborhood in Bialystok. Majorski is a few years younger than the Butcher. Even though he wasn't Jewish, Majorski had a number of friends in the ghetto. One special friend——a young woman named Anita Glassfeld had the misfortune of falling into the Butcher's grasp. He promised to find safe passage for her and her sick mother. After taking the few valuables she had, the Butcher brutally raped and beat her. Anita died in the alley where Sikorski had taken her.

"Majorski was devastated. He had tried to warn the young woman, but she was too desperate to listen. Majorski went after the Butcher, but Sikorski was much stronger. He beat Majorski badly, sent him to the hospital. Shortly afterward, Majorski's family sent him to England.

Angie shuddered. "That's disgusting. How can people be so cruel." Lou reached over and took her hand.

Ollie wrinkled her brow. "I'm still confused," she said. "I know that Emma Kaston had the Atlas security people take Mr. Majorski. But what about the men who took Janet Pafko from her home and dropped her in Liverpool? Were they the same men who cruised by her house the day you were standing out front? And how about the two guys who jumped you after the reception at the museum?"

"Can't tell the players without a scorecard," Lou quipped, reaching for another piece of rugelah.

Apparently Dodge and Sikorski thought Majorski had gone into hiding," I said. "They sent their diplomatic entourage to Janet's house on a fact finding mission. They concluded that Janet either didn't know where her father was or it would take more than friendly dialogue to loosen her tongue."

"That's when they turned to plan B," Lou said, sticking a finger in his mouth to dislodge a piece of raisin that was stuck between his teeth.

"Yeah," I said, taking a sip of coffee. "When they realized I was involved they brought in the heavy artillery. The guy who scared the shit out of me on the phone —the same charming fellow who wielded the AK-47—was a diplomat on loan from Utica. A regular piece worker, pardon the pun. He brought a friend who also enjoyed intense negotiation. They picked up Knox later. He was recommended by Carl Dodge who certainly has credentials in the field of loyalty."

Lou hesitated for a second, then reached for another piece of walnut coffee cake. "Marty was a very popular guy. Between Emma Kaston's efforts to divert him from looking for Majorski and the Dodge/Sikorski campaign to keep him from prying into their lucrative efforts to collect money from Paul Kaston, Marty did not want for attention."

Angie pushed her chair away from the table and stood. "I've had about all of this gruesome story I can take. Do you want anything else before I clear the table?"

Ollie shook her head. I held up my hands to let her know I had eaten enough. Lou hesitated a second before he said, "Leave the danish. I might have room for one more."

While Angie cleared the table the others continued to talk. "What's going to happen to all those people?" Ollie asked.

"Carl Dodge will probably relocate to less spacious quarters at one of the State's correctional facilities," Lou said. "There may be a jurisdictional battle with the Feds because of his political office, but either way he won't be placing bets with the local bookies for a long time. The thugs —Knox, the guy with the AK 47—will definitely be spending time at Auburn."

"How about Sikorski?" Ollie asked.

"That's a different story altogether," Lou said. "As a Polish citizen, traveling on a visa, he will try to argue that the United States has no business prosecuting him. Given the circumstances and a good lawyer he may succeed in bargaining for a return to Poland with a revoked visa. Paul Kaston's current mental state doesn't make him a very good witness and Carl Dodge is such a big fish, that the Feds may be willing to make a deal with Sikorski if he gives them enough incriminating information about the Deputy Mayor's role in all of this."

"Not my idea of justice," Ollie said. "Speaking of which, what ever happened to Sikorski's father, the original Butcher?"

Lou looked at me with a wry grin, then turned to Ollie. "Maybe there is a little bit of justice in this world. Dodge told me the Butcher died a few years ago, as the result of an accident. He choked on a large piece of steak."

They were silent for a moment, letting the irony of Sikorski's death sink in. I played with my spoon and thought of all the violence I had experienced. As I reviewed the events of the past few days, I realized there was still a loose end. "Lou, what about Mannie Bosco?" I asked.

"Good question," Lou said. "My initial reaction was that Bosco's death had been arranged by Dodge or Sikorski. Mannie had been at the train yard meeting with Sikorski, Dodge and Kaston. He had been there when Majorski stumbled into the strange gathering at the edge of the railroad yard, and he had seen the trainman react to the younger Sikorski, who resembled his father, the Butcher. Bosco was obviously a liability.

"I was surprised, though, by what seemed to be a genuine expression of bewilderment when I questioned Dodge and Sikorski about what had happened to Mannie Bosco. Dodge admitted that Bosco had accompanied Kaston when they went to the train yard. He denied knowing anything else..." Lou stopped abruptly, raising his eyebrows as if he had seen the proverbial lightbulb. "The guy you saw at the disco, Marty; the one who ran out after Bosco was shot; what did he look like?"

"I didn't get a good look at him. He was a small, wiry guy. The only other thing I remembered is that as he ran along the balcony, I caught a glimpse of the side of his face. He was too far away to see his features, but I was struck by his skin. It was very pale."

"I don't think we're going to solve Mannie's murder," Lou said, mumbling something about George Hartman.

"What do you mean?" I asked.

"Nothing. I'm just talking to myself. When I dropped you at your apartment ——at least I thought you were at your apartment ——I paid a visit to George Hartman."

"Do you think he had anything to do with Bosco's murder?" I asked, bristling at the idea that the crime boss might be responsible for Bosco's death ——not to mention my own near fatality.

"Possibly, but I'm not certain. The fact is we'll probably never know."

"I feel bad for Emma Kaston," Ollie said. "Even though she kidnaped Mr. Majorski it seemed that her intentions were decent. She wanted to protect her husband ——and Fred Majorski."

"I doubt the court will see it that way," Lou said. "Kidnapping is a pretty heavy duty offense. The judge may show some mercy, but I'll be surprised if she doesn't do some time."

Remembering how the once proud and elegant woman had expressed her agony and frustration to me last night, I felt sad. I wished she would have come to me *before* she snatched Fred Majorski from the train yard. "Whatever happens," I said, "I don't think Mrs. Kaston is going to have a very happy future."

"Strange, isn't it?" Lou said. "The only one who probably won't be significantly affected by this is Paul Kaston, the person at the center of this whole messy affair. He seems to be oblivious to everything that's happening."

"I'm not so certain about that," Ollie said. "I think he knows what's happening. He just can't do anything about it."

"Even with his political past," Lou said, "he strikes me as sort of a tragic figure, in the Greek sense of the word."

"Angie would be proud of you, Lou," I said. "That night school is doing wonders for your cultural enrichment."

"Funny man," Lou said, trying to kick me under the table.

I pushed my chair away from the table, out of reach of Lou's foot. "Well, at least there's one bright spot in this sordid situation," I said.

"What's that?" Ollie asked.

I grinned. "Fred Majorski gets to go back to his daughter and grandson, Billy, and to his quiet friend, Gladys Blazek."

At that moment the telephone in the kitchen rang. After a brief conversation, Angie called out, "Phone for you, Marty."

I walked into the kitchen and took the telephone from Angie. "Hello, Fenton here." There was no response, only the sound of someone breathing. I tightened my grip on the handset. The tension in my hand flowed to the rest of my body and I began to perspire. My head told me I was no longer in danger. My gut gave me a different message.

"Who is this?" I said, my voice filled with anger and fear.

At last the person on the other end of the line responded. "Mr. Fenton, I've been concerned about you," the caller said, breathing heavily.

I sighed with relief. It was Ms. O from the We-Care Answering Service. "Ms. O, what have I done to deserve the pleasure of your telephone call?"

Mr. Fenton, you're so sweet," she said, panting into my ear. "We haven't heard from you in more than a day and we were worried about you."

Today her voice was more like Kathleen Turner than Marilyn Monroe.

"I'm fine, Ms. O. I appreciate your concern for me," I said, immediately regretting the positive feedback I had given her. She would undoubtedly seize the opportunity to initiate verbal foreplay. "Do you have some messages for me?" I said before she could respond.

"I most certainly do. I've tried to call you several times. When I didn't get a response I looked at our emergency file and found this number."

"What are the messages?" I asked impatiently.

"Well, let's see," Ms. O said, drawing out each word. "Your landlord called to say they would be shutting off the water, Monday, to repair the water lines. That's too bad. Let me know if you need someplace to take a shower..."

"Anything else?"

"yes, your mother, Mrs. Fenton, called. She's such a darling. She would like you to call her as soon as possible. And a Mrs. Blazek called. She wanted to thank you for your help. She said she'll call you later. Have you been performing heroic deeds again, Mr. Fenton?"

"Is that all, Ms. O?"

"No, there was one more call. Lieutenant DeSantis called yesterday. He's such a nice man. Conscientious too, though I wish he would loosen up a little. Tension isn't good for you. Anyway, Lieutenant DeSantis said to give you a message." She paused waiting for me to say something.

"What was the message?" I said, giving into her game.

"He said you should be very careful. He told me to tell you to call him before you do anything."

A little late, I thought. I thanked Ms. O before she could breathe into my ear again. I hung up the phone and turned to Angie, who was loading the dishwasher. Trying to contain my exasperation, I asked her the question that had been forming in my mind.

"Angie, how much does an answering machine cost?"